SIDETRACK KEY

SIDETRACK
KEY

Jessica Argyle

MACLAWRAN
Key West

Published by Maclawran
maclawran.com

ISBN: 9798370588419

FIRST EDITION

Book design by Sean MacGuire
Cover painting by Jessica Argyle
Edited by Alyssa Matesic and Brendon Goodmurphy

Printed in the USA

For Sean, who believes in me almost as much as I believe in him… for the outrageous fortune of sharing our life together for all these years.

If you want a happy ending, that depends, of course, on where you stop your story...

— Orson Welles

PART
I

JUNE 1, 1936

Ferries to Key West

Via the Over-Sea Highway

FROM MIAMI
89 Miles to Ferry at Matecumbe
45 Miles from Matecumbe to No Name Key
40 Miles from No Name Key to Key West

Ferries leave Matecumbe (Southbound) 11 10:30 A. M. Daily
Ferries leave No Name Key (Northbound) 8 A. M. Daily

For Reservations in Miami Call Key West Information
Booth, Tel. 3-1393; 303 N. E. 1st Street . . . in Key West,
Call Tel. 460.

RESTAURANT SERVICE ON FERRIES

CAR RATES

Cars under 14 feet	$2.00
Cars 14 to 15 feet	3.00
Cars 15 to 16 feet	3.50
Cars 16 feet and over	4.00

(Including Driver Only)

PASSENGER RATES

Passengers	$ .50
Children under 12 years	Free

FREIGHT RATES

Trucks, ½ Ton (Loaded or Empty)	$3.00

Deduct 50c for unloaded trucks listed below:

Trucks, 1 Ton	4.50
Trucks, 1½ Ton	5.50
Trucks, 2 Ton	6.50
Trucks, 2½ Ton	8.00
Trucks, 3 Ton	9.00
Trucks, 3½ Ton	11.00

Trailers have same rates as regular motor trucks.

Motorcycles (including Driver)	1.00
Each Extra Passenger	.50

RATES AND SCHEDULES SUBJECT TO CHANGE

The Miami Star Diner was so silent, Elle almost longed for the "Pin Money" brigade to liven the place up. They had picketed on Christmas Eve outside the motel restaurant, one of the few places open after dark. The sight of Elle laughing with a customer must've been too much for the matriarch and she barged through the door, stood in the center of the dining room and accused Elle of "taking bread from the mouths of families. Go ahead, ask her," she said, pointing at Elle, "Ask her if she dropped the name of her husband so she could work."

Elle considered inviting them in for a cup of coffee and a rest, killing them with kindness, but she couldn't stomach it.

Jack, the owner, came from back and said, "Elle Woodman lost her husband to the storm. Show a little respect." And though she was grateful, she didn't need anyone to fight her battles.

Later Elle heard an elderly man say, "Dollars to donuts, he's alive and on government payroll, building the highway through the Keys. Double salary and no children to feed, not one."

When anyone asked about Billy, Elle would say her husband disappeared in the great Labor Day hurricane as if he simply floated away then neatly dissolved into a watery horizon alongside four or five hundred other worthies. Tragic, she might add. Old soldiers here to build a road alongside the same tracks that refused to send a train to save them until after the storm closed in. By then, it was common knowledge that the government resented acknowledging their service. Superstitious souls imagined Flagler's ghost exacting revenge on the men for building a road to upstage his vision.

But Billy was dead all right and not by the hurricane that washed hundreds of vets out to sea. That would shock the old windbag, Elle thought. If she knew what really happened to Billy and how happy Elle was to drop his last name.

Washing up, Jack said, "I have something to tell you. But first," he dried his hands and pulled an envelope from his apron. "Merry Christmas," he said. "Go ahead, open it."

"You know I won't do that," Elle said. And he knew, because she had worked for him for over a year, beginning with her job as a cook at No Name Key Lodge. Elle was discreet where money was concerned. She slid the envelope into a breast pocket under her apron.

"I've sold No Name Key lodge," he said.

"What? For this?"

"It was a straightforward choice. They offered me more than No Name was worth. Much more. And it's going to take years for the Keys to recover now that the railway is destroyed and years more before the highway is finished."

A booming voice from the dining room interrupted them. "Is anyone actually working here?"

Elle reached for the tray of rice pudding. "I'll take these out before they get a skin."

"No, I'll do it. Start those." He nodded toward stacks of dirty dishes, most without a smear of food left behind. "Stay in the kitchen, please."

"For God's sake—not on Christmas day." Elle heard him say from the dining room. "These people paid good money and deserve to enjoy their Christmas dinner in peace."

This would never happen in the Florida Keys, where meals were close to a spiritual experience. But her time was up here. The diner was in a rough area of Miami, and Jack counted on a busy Christmas season to justify her pay.

Scattered tables with single men hunched over their plates, a nervous couple with a baby and toddler in tow who couldn't have been over seventeen years old and a few coming in for a piece of pie who couldn't spare the cost of a meal. A matted white dog hung around the dumpster outside Elle's kitchen, hoping for scraps.

The elderly couple and mute boy who stayed in the single room by the stairwell mouthed along to Bing Crosby's "Silent Night" until they could no longer remember the words.

After the dining room emptied, and Elle finished drying the last mug and placing it on the shelf, the owner reappeared. Elle felt for the envelope safely stashed in her pocket.

"Look," he said, a thin smile on his face. "The new owners of No Name Key Lodge agreed to keep you on. They asked not to tell who they are, but you've met them before." He waved away her thank you and continued, "I had to choose. Either here in Miami or keep the old lodge, but I couldn't swing both and I gotta say, it was a straightforward choice. And if I were you, I'd stay on No Name long enough to sell that old cistern of yours if you can. It's the second access to the wharf and the only reason it's worth a nickel. Who knows, they might just want it."

Then what? she thought. "I thought the Keys were the future, what you always told me."

"That was before the storm. And there'll be another one. Just a matter of time."

Well, you just lost your job is some Christmas present, she thought. "How long do I have?"

"I can pay you until New Year's." His usual, direct stare had flattened, blurred at the edges, the sorrow as much for her as his own embarrassment at being unable to survive the Depression intact. "Like the lodge, I have to choose between you and family, but I can't pay both."

"You don't owe me an explanation. I planned to go back to No Name anyhow." She missed the water, the solitude, the acceptance she felt. In the Keys, women worked next to men next to families from all over, most measured solely by the work produced because of the scarcity of talent. The hard part was gaining a foothold in the treacherous terrain. Unlike Miami, the Florida Keys couldn't afford to resent skilled labor, no matter your gender or the color of your skin or where you came from.

Over the next few days, she kept as much distance as serving allowed from the trickle of customers in the hotel dining room. It was bad enough when they were angry, but the depression this season brought on was worse. Men who weren't home with a loving family, who didn't have a tinseled tree or a house to put it in. During off hours, she mostly stayed in the room with the dripping faucet that looked out on the bruised Florida sun, the only thing that mattered, the warmth that allowed her to move around, to plan. But she would stay the week out. Money was money.

2

The ferry was late, and Elle sat on the dock recalling the first time she had been at this exact spot, little more than a year ago, though it seemed a decade since escaping Billy.

Although 1936 was only a couple of days old, it already held challenges. It took Jack less than a half hour to drive her here, and when she exited the car, the terrain was spongier than she remembered. The storm had been hard on this place. The ferry wharf was missing planks and seemed to list to one side. Elle remembered the blindingly white ferry come in, almost two years before. Back then, the "Key Wester" was a blur of cheerful partygoers, men in straw boater hats, women in fluttering skirts, bright scarves blowing in the breeze like parrots in flight. She remembered laughter and glasses clinking, as if they were all off on some grand tour and not the narrow waterway through the Florida Keys. And although she wasn't included in the festivities, Monty, the ferryboat captain, offered her a glass of champagne. *Any excuse for a party*, he'd said and winked at her. Later she accepted a fancy sandwich with the crusts cut off and somehow, that slight gesture contained the promise of a world that was not so tight-fisted. He spoke while she gazed at the waterway that joined the sky in an unbroken blur of blue imagining a tear in the fabric big enough to step through.

As the day's heat bore through her clothing, a bright blue coupe approached the narrow landing. A curly blonde head craned through the open window. "Hey, miss," the girl yelled. "Is this the ferry landing or what?"

The couple in the car looked to be about her age, although she felt a decade older. "Doesn't look like it's coming," the girl yelled.

After they drove off, Elle noticed a freestanding pole and realized it used to have a sign attached. She spotted the board face down on the wharf. When she turned it over, she read, Ferry Landing Closed Until Further Notice. But there had to be some transportation to the Keys after the Labor Day hurricane wrecked Flagler's railroad. The highway connecting the mainland to the Keys was still under construction, so where was the new ferry landing? Her boss had given her a lift here and Elle wondered how she would return to the hotel. Then suddenly, the bright blue coupe reappeared.

"You want a lift to the real ferry landing?" the thin man yelled from the driver's seat. And Elle remembered the chance she had taken a year before and how well that had turned out. When she hesitated, he threw his hands up and said, "it's no skin off my nose," and turned the steering wheel to head out.

Elle yelled after him, "Yes, I'll come. Thank you."

"Now we're all in the same boat," he said. The blonde girl replied, "Oh Harry, what a dumb joke." She turned to Elle and said, "Please excuse him, miss, he means well." And something about this young, happy-go-lucky couple reassured Elle. She smiled at the two of them, shrugged her shoulders and said, "Sure, whatever you say."

He jumped out and sprang the door open. "In back," he said. He looked slightly peeved and that told Elle it was his girl who insisted they return for Elle. This was proof enough they were harmless, for Elle's long history told her that people were rarely who they appeared to be. She tossed her suitcase in back and jumped in. Something about the Florida Keys made everything in the world seem possible.

"Matecumbe, here we come," he said

She remembered the old ferry landing at Matecumbe. "You sure it's still there?"

"I guess we'll find out," he said.

"Harry, slow down," the blonde said. She had told Elle her name, but it had already flown out of Elle's head. The road flattened as they drove through Key Largo, the trees sparse, scrub pine and pelicans flying overhead in lazy random plane formations. Elle could smell the swamplands, the musky odor of life brewing, and the trees dancing in the midday's haze.

The second piece of luck was seeing Monty, slouched casually at the helm of the "Key Wester." His cap hugged his forehead, Babe Ruth style, and his half smile widened into a grin when he saw Elle.

"What happened to you?" she said, taking in the raised scar on his face from cheekbone to jawline.

"Gator bite," he said, "but man was he tasty. Ever try gator steak?"

"C'mon I'm serious."

"Me too. It was delicious."

She actually didn't care what had happened, just wanted to hear the fantastical tale he would spin. He was here. She was easy in his company and eager to return to No Name Key. The couple never emerged from their car in the sparsely populated ferry, probably making out and relieved to be alone again.

"Yes ma'am," Monty said to another passenger. "The wind picked up a twenty-pound boulder like it was a pebble and smashed him in the head. They say he made it until morning." The last time Elle heard this story, the boulder weighed ten pounds, she thought. "That used to be Indian Key," Monty said, pointing to a leveled bit of land, small and shrunken in the sun.

Many of the tiny Keys seemed diminished in size after losing their lush vegetation. Now she saw how narrow the strips of land really were, like a man stripped of the suit that hides his scrawny shape. The ragged and naked Keys made Elle feel protective, wanting to shield them from the gaze of the judgmental passengers. The closer she came to No Name Key, the more she relaxed, until finally they arrived at the swampy shoreline, pushed further out by the storm.

"Look Monty," she pointed to a flash of white from a small Key deer feasting on mangrove roots.

"You're not hoping for your old job back, are you? Don't think there'll be much more call for a cook than when you left a few months back."

"I was promised," she said.

"Too bad you don't have something of your own. Workers building the highway ask about you. Seems your cooking is some kinda legend in these parts."

"Do you know who the new owners are?"

"You're not gonna like it, Elle."

In that instant, she knew. "No. Not the Rowlands." The homecoming drained of its joy. Only the mangy, one-eyed cat, staring as if he didn't believe it was really her, brought back her hope. "You took better care of him than I did," Elle said.

"Some of us keep our word," he said.

"Well, the old man promised the new owners would keep me on."

"Then ask Brushy, not Blanche."

She gave him a look that said, of course I will. How stupid do you think I am?

3

Stunted trees and a tangle of vines formed a wonky fence around Elle's converted cistern. Inside her yard, odd configurations of herbs and vegetables struggled. Tomato seedlings punched little white fists through grainy soil, their abandoned seed carapaces like flightless wings.

Elle opened the gate, and a thunderclap came from somewhere. Then the telltale hiss of a vulture echoed on dark water, pushing the smell of putrefying flesh. Somewhere out in the mangroves, a turkey vulture was raising its young, and the heavy thud of this large hopping bird made its way through the swampland as Elle moved into open terrain.

The fishing boats reserved for guests of No Name Key Lodge were all absent, replaced by Blanche and Brushy Rowlands' luxury Indiawood cruiser, The Big Wheel. In the five days she'd been back from Miami, she hadn't seen Brushy anywhere and suspected that Blanche was here alone. So she decided to wait, hoping to avoid a confrontation. But it gave Elle an uneasy feeling that she and Blanche might be the sole inhabitants on this side of the small island.

The dark flatlands seemed to have expanded, palm trees tilting north, clean shaved on one side, marking the wind direction of the 1935 Labor Day hurricane.

Little had grown back, not a sweet flowering bush in sight and the dark shoreline pushed farther out, intensifying the loneliness on No Name Key. Elle's favorite time to walk along the shoreline had always been at sunset, after the workmen took their dinner and the kitchen was clean and orderly. She remembered this as Blanche's usual naptime, shoring up energy for the long night of drinking ahead.

A light flickered as Elle passed by the lodge, so she stepped up her pace to get by unseen. Exposed in the open field, Elle raced toward the dim side path that veered to the water, level by level, on slabs of eroded coral. Once out of sight, she would step behind the wall of the ancient strangler fig onto the tangled lace of mangrove roots. She knew each careful step and loved nothing more than tiptoeing on this bridge between universes. Neither land nor air nor water, but a middle place like nowhere else in the world but No Name Key.

Almost past the center of the generous lodge veranda, a bright pain hit her eyes. Someone was aiming a flashlight at her.

"Elle. Get the hell over here." Blanche danced the flashlight down Elle's body, marking a trail of light to the veranda. Blinded, Elle stumbled over the thick raised root of a gumbo limbo tree and turned away.

"I'm busy." Damn. No way she could ask about her old job now. And where was Brushy, anyway?

The hurricane lamp flame turned up, illuminating the ridiculous plantation style columns and ornate brocaded swing. Blanche waved the flashlight like an ageing majorette. Finally, she lay it down and picked up her glass, twirling the ice cubes. Music like a child's broken xylophone.

"Forget something in the crab traps?" Blanche lingered over each word, as if the sound of her voice was more important than the answer. The pale blue swing barely moved when she rose. When Elle didn't answer, Blanche stretched a leg, pointed her toes and straightened the seam of her silk stocking. "Well?"

"What business is it of yours?"

"I said, did you forget something in the crab traps? A hand? A foot?" Blanche jutted her neck out like a pigeon, enunciating each word. "Billy's head?"

Slow-moving air mingled with the meaty odor of composting earth with Blanche's perfume. Elle fanned her face and turned away.

Blanche jerked her head and pointed her glass toward Elle's secret crab trap hideaway. "I know what you did to him."

Could she have seen? Heard? But Elle had been alone on the island waiting for the storm to pass. Her eye caught the screen door just then, partly open. Was someone listening? A trap? Another in the clouds, behind the trees, one under the scarred jawbone of coral?

"You're crazy. Everyone knows the storm took him out..." she stopped mid-sentence. "And I know what you did *with* Billy."

Blanche's white face jutted out at her. "He never had a chance. He a war hero and stuck with a chippy like you."

"War hero? Is that what he told you? Oh my God." Elle said. "You were in love with him." This struck Elle as hilarious. "All the choice in the world and you go for... Billy?"

"I was... I was his friend."

Elle wanted to tell her how happy she was the bastard was dead. Instead, she turned away, leaving Blanche speechless. Elle would have to train herself to silence. No more seeking like-minded company. No casual talk that could turn after a confidence given. Her air of sadness would be mistaken for having lost a husband in the war, then the hurricane. She hadn't counted on Billy being as powerful in death as he had been in life and wondered how many more women had been tricked? The sadness in the way some women move, the careful quiet when their man's careless talk blotted them out. Blanche must have believed she saw clear through to the secret soul of Billy. Elle remembered the way he could bring her tears to the surface and how she once thought that meant something. But she was different now. She had bulked up, grown thick and muscled. She could drive each and everyone of them off the bank and into the drink if she'd a mind to. I think I scare her, was Elle's last thought as she made her way to the water.

4

Since her return from Miami, something in her cistern caused the roof of her mouth to pucker. Elle awoke from a fitful half sleep. Something was tickling her leg. When she threw off her sheet, a freakishly large scorpion hit the floor, scuttled across the rough concrete and disappeared through a crack in the wall. Under the yellow glow of her kerosene lamp, black mold furred the joinery of floor to wall, exploiting anything that wasn't sealed tight. First thing in the morning, she'd paddle to the old Conch's shop on Grassy Key for whitewash and bleach.

After No Name lodge installed modern plumbing, the cistern was sold to the hermit who owned much of the island. He used it occasionally for storage, selling fruit and vegetables from his small grove to businesses, mostly in Key West. But after a few crop failures, he sold it to Elle for fifty dollars. Behind a treed-in fence, the cistern remained out of sight and closed. It weathered many storms that lay siege to the Florida Keys, and Elle enjoyed owning something no one could take from her.

A year ago, the hermit helped her construct a Tiki thatched roof and set up a sink to pump fresh water from an outside barrel. Braided palm fronds made perfect carpeting and the old lodge owners were kind, letting her know when one or another cabin owner wanted to be rid of outdated or damaged furniture. A long, scratched table became a honey-colored teak counter after a few rounds of sanding and oiling.

Soon she had too many chairs and tables, an unlikely collection of hurricane lamps and more curtains than she would ever use, considering the cistern had no windows. But the prize was a purple ormolu armchair that would have been perfect in a Barnum and Bailey advertisement. The first time she spotted it, a few lodge construction workers were posing this way and that, making lewd suggestions, emulating various sex acts. "Look at me. I'm the queen of the glades," a drunk carpenter said, rubbing imaginary breasts. They abandoned it that evening, too tired or drunk to saw it apart and toss it into the trash heap. While the island slept, Elle spotted the curlicued silhouette glowing purple in the full moon, facing out to sea as if longing to return to some banished queendom. She dragged it behind her gate, almost embarrassed by how taken she was with the gaudy chair. After cleaning the brocade upholstery and oiling the wood, it thrilled her to discover it was the most comfortable chair she ever sat on, with room enough to cross her legs, lean back and devour a detective magazine from the lodge. She angled it back to the door, turning it away from the troubles of the world.

As her cistern took on a sense of comfort and privacy, she decided it had become a cottage. One day, she would seal it properly, add plumbing and extra rooms, but most of all, she would have windows. Huge floor to ceiling windows and smaller ones in new rooms that you could open and close, with shutters against the storms. She kept those plans in a small journal alongside an outdated catalog from Sears Roebuck, also retrieved from the trash when the 1936 edition arrived at the lodge.

Although her job as lodge cook came with a room, every improvement to the cottage strengthened her desire to stay there and loosened Billy's hold on her. When she told him she wouldn't leave the island, he moved in on her with the same inexorable will as a hurricane. In the end, both Billy and the hurricane disappeared, leaving her tough and intact. And now, when she thought she had a permanent home, mold gnawed at the foundation. All around her, men were desperately seeking ways to survive and support a family, and she was the least important person on anyone's list but her own.

She arranged a cot in her small sheltered yard, hoping to catch a couple hours of sleep while it was still dark before preparing lunches for the highway workers, Monty's brilliant idea.

"If you tasted the food at the camp, you'd know why they'll pay whatever you ask, Elle." He winked at her. The plan worked well enough, but her income would shrink at the same rate the highway grew when it was too far to follow the workers. Elle pushed these dark thoughts away, concentrating on the day ahead, when noise from the wharf drew her attention. Maybe it was Brushy and she could ask him if he knew of anything. He had always been fair to her.

Elle pulled a loose pair of overalls over her nightshirt, threaded her way past her vine-smothered fence, and headed to the wharf.

"You can't dock there. Barely enough room for the ferry," Elle yelled to the well-muscled ruffian manning the complicated ropes. Cat beat her to the Rowlandses' yacht and jumped onboard.

"I mean it," Elle said, pointing to the showy brass and India wood luxury cruiser with a dismissive wave.

"I take my orders from her," the ruffian said, gazing reverentially at the woman walking toward them.

Blanche Rowlands wore dazzling white sailor pants, moonlight cutting a sharp shadow that accentuated the center press. Her matching blouse had fluttery sleeves trimmed in navy. In the middle of the damp and sweaty tropics, she wore clothing requiring constant upkeep lest anyone forget her status.

"Elle Woodman," she said, "What are you doing up?" She folded her arms in an exaggerated gesture. At the sound of Blanche's voice, Cat leaped from the boat, sprinted down the wharf and out of sight.

"You heard me," Elle said. "This is the ferry landing and you know it."

The rig man nodded, an empty gape on his mug as he lassoed rope from elbow to wrist in a figure eight.

"I'm running this place now," Blanche Rowlands said, gesturing to the sprawling lodge behind them. "New menus, and fishing testimonials in papers all the way to New York city. People are already mailing in, asking to be put on the waiting list, because we are already full up for the season." She stopped to take Elle in and said, "I thought I made it clear you are not welcome on the property."

Elle felt a strap fall from the bib of her overalls, making her aware of how unkempt she looked. She flattened her red haystack hair for something to do with her hands.

"But there is something you could do for me if you're interested," Blanche said in a kindly voice.

Elle responded too quickly, "What?"

"Stay the hell away from the lodge unless I call for you. And keep your gate tightly closed. I wouldn't want guests to think there's a flop house nearby."

For over a year, Elle had prepared the menu at the lodge, rotated supplies so nothing went to waste, and made deals with farmers from the mainland for seasonal fruits and vegetables.

Blanche focused on an officious man who exited the boat before her. Elle hazily recognized him but couldn't remember where, and briefly wondered if Blanche had traded Brushy in for someone younger.

Behind him, a woman tried to push a large trunk onto the wharf from the Big Wheel. She looked tiny, but it might have been Elle's vantage point or the size of the enormous steamer trunk, the kind that announced an extended stay. He turned toward the woman on the boat, his movements abrupt and menacing.

The tiny woman jumped as he pushed the trunk back onto the yacht and hissed something in her face. Elle turned away, embarrassed for the woman.

He's creepy, she thought, watching him lope back to Blanche's side with an ingratiating smile, like a rabid raccoon uncertain if he was predator or prey.

When the small woman stepped onto the wharf, she seemed in a state of confusion and made no move to join them.

He advanced toward Elle and held his hand out to be shaken. "My name is Nathan Foreman," he said, but Blanche pushed it down and shooed him away. "Oh please," she said. "It doesn't matter."

It took a moment to recognize them. They had been at the last lodge party before the hurricane. A patronizing smile replaced his look of confusion, and he turned away from Elle. His wife hurried to catch up, her long skirt rustling. They must be from somewhere cold,

Elle thought, or maybe another century. No one dresses like that. Although it was January, the temperature was in the 70's, too warm for long sleeves and skirts.

"Here," Blanche said, handing Elle an advertisement torn from the New York Times.

Make 1936 your best holiday year ever.
Vacation at No Name Key Lodge for year-round fun.
Exotic fare to rival the best New York establishments.
Largest dance pavilion south of Virginia.
Finest sports fishing in the whole wide world.
*Tournaments * Orchestras * Sightseeing*
Telephones available upon request.
Twice-daily ferries.

"You're wrong about the ferries," Elle yelled at Blanche, who was already retreating.

Part of the charm of No Name Lodge was the impossibility of access by land, designed for the new leisure class who could easily afford the $3.50 ferry fee and escape the cold winter months in this rich man's playground, holing up in the private trailers flanking the lodge. No Name Key Lodge was a reliable ferry stop, a jewel on the waterway from the mainland to Key West, with the finest sports fishing in the world, or so the newspaper ads and full-color brochures said.

Blanche's advertisement suggested a grander vision for this secret paradise. Her own Shangri-La in what she called "the American Caribbean." The storm that killed thousands was a useful dramatic tale. The Miami Herald called it "The Great Labor Day Hurricane of 1935. 700 dead and counting."

Perhaps Blanche was right. Throughout the 130-mile chain of islands known as the Florida Keys, opportunities from the disaster were already feeding the wild visions of men down on their luck and fleeing to the warmth of Florida. The empty stretches of land fueled dreams of industry rising on the depleted shoreline. Flagler had built the Casa Marina in Key West and Blanche imagined No Name Key as the next frontier, part of a chain of islands she wanted to rename.

"You have keys to most of the cabins. And I want them back." Blanche said to Elle, holding out her hand. Of the twenty-four cottages flanking the lodge, half were seasonally rented, the rest privately owned, and all serviced in varying degrees by No Name Key Lodge.

Foreman wore an ironic, half-smile as if burdened by the weight of repressing his brilliant observations, but his wife seemed absent, staring at the lodge with fixed desperation. *She's miserable,* Elle thought, taking in the woman's blank face as if any response would be a mistake.

"You can stay in the cook's room this evening, Nathan." Blanche said.

Nathan and Ruby Foreman would be the first to live in the room where Billy met his end. Her cottage might have mold problems, but at least it wasn't haunted.

Rains fell almost continually since the Labor Day storm, and although the pathway had turned to muck, the Foreman's navigated it easily. A baby bird warbled in the treetops, then stopped mid chirp, as if spooked.

Blanche called out, "Joe, where are you?"

Everyone turned to take in the muscled ruffian behind them on the Big Wheel. He dropped his neat pile of rope and smiled stupidly, as if he and Blanche were alone on the wharf. He moved so quickly and silently for such a large man that he startled Elle. He had a scrapper's flattened nose and breathed with an annoying whistle.

Blanche fake-stumbled on the short pathway to the lodge, and right on cue, Joe rushed over and scooped her up. In front of everyone, he cradled her to his chest, and she clung on like the swooning twit in that King Kong moving picture. The smile on Foreman's face stiffened, but Blanche would set the rules as she liked.

"I'll get my belongings out of the bedroom," Elle said. "Then it's all yours."

"Hey! Who gives the orders around here?" Blanche snapped. Joe gave her a knowing look. "Oh, sure," Blanche said, giving him the eye. "But be quick about it. Joe and I have to check the cottages anyhow."

"For damage," he said, and no one had the stomach to look at either of them.

"We won't be long," Blanche said, lapsing into a small giggle.

"Hey, what's that supposed to mean?" the lug retorted, in a phony, peeved voice.

Good. They will eat, she will get laid, and I will have my valuables back. Didn't take either of us long to get over Billy, Elle thought, without a trace of sadness or regret.

5

They passed the locked office before reaching the small blue bedroom reserved for the live-in cook.

"She can't be serious?" Nathan said. And Elle was grateful someone was with her. This was the first time she stood at the door to the blue room where Billy met his fate.

But Nathan had already headed into the kitchen. "When was this built? It looks old," he said. And although Elle knew it was no longer hers to protect, she deeply felt the offense to her clean and ordered kitchen.

"I can barely pass through the door into the pantry," he said, exaggerating his size, holding his elbows out. A good, rose-patterned China cup teetered on a wall hook before Elle settled it back into place.

This place had saved her, and she knew how much she would miss the old routine, the familiarity of her cooking pots and the crowds of people wanting to be won over by her recipes and good-natured, hard work.

When times were slow, she experimented, combining unusual flavors and concoctions that the owners' sixteen-year-old niece, Sheila, wrote up for her in her fancy script. Sometimes she took credit for the recipe, sometimes she called it a classic, as if it had been around forever. Little went to waste in her kitchen, cans on rotation, flour and eggs always used before they got stale.

Sheila would hum and draw any chance she got. After she left, Elle discovered pencil images of the dancing guests, musicians, and Monty stealing a kiss from a singer. Elle took the drawings to her cottage, telling herself she would return them to Sheila when she next saw her. As Elle moved into the large room, she remembered a party when Sheila gathered up abandoned drinks, poured them into a pitcher, and downed the entire mess when she thought no one was looking. Sheila loved sampling Elle's treats, having developed an early taste for alcohol and sweets.

Pleasures were scarce for the workers and Elle enjoyed saving treats for them, out of sight on the highest shelves. At party time, she hid supper and dessert for the musicians who often played nonstop at the whim of a soused guest who refused to go to bed. Elle smiled, already nostalgic for her old job.

"Come back here to see your room," Elle said in an unnaturally loud voice. She headed back to her old bedroom and opened the door. Immediately, a metallic smell accosted her. Once you smell copious amounts of human blood, you never forget the odor. Her stomach heaved, her shoulders tightened.

Nathan stood at the door and seemed to take no notice of it, but she was grateful to have anyone with her in the room.

She focussed on retrieving a pair of handmade candlesticks from her father, a tin of buttons and a box of red canvas left behind in the wardrobe. The drawer was stiff and screeched horribly, only giving partway. She willed her shoulders to relax and sat back on the bed to collect her breath. The room was tiny, with barely enough space to sit at the foot of the bed with the drawer open. Then she remembered the bloody mattress and her shoulders stiffened. No, she had nothing to worry about. Monty had helped her replace it with one left in a cabin. After he had departed with the ferry full of terrified guests, she burned the mattress cover and stuffing in the barrel and dumped the springs in water to join the rest of the floating hurricane debris. Her shoulders ached with the release of fear. When she tugged at the drawer for the second time, it let out a scream like Billy after swallowing the potion she prepared for him. Nathan smirked from the doorway, snapped his cigarette lighter, repeatedly striking the flint to get a spark, giving his lips a sneer as he pulled air through his cigarette.

"God knows what went on in here," he said, holding a delicate tea saucer for an ashtray.

It's only a room, Elle said to herself, but when the thought brought no comfort, she said it again, at a loss. The two of them perched by the door, watching her in a way that made Elle feel as if she was the ghost, and not Billy.

Then she saw it: a tooth at the foot of the cupboard. Good grief, she thought, is that possible? Is someone playing tricks on me? She had cleaned the place carefully, Monty keeping her company while she scrubbed. Monty's googly eyes were a small price to pay for his presence, so frightened of Billy's lurking spirit in the room. But a tooth? Sure, the blows to his head with the heavy pitcher could have loosened one; she didn't remember checking his mouth to see if any were missing. Surely, Elle thought, I would have already found it with my broom.

The couple followed the line of her vision. "What's that?" Ruby shrieked, and all three leaped at the tooth.

Nathan grabbed it and danced around the room. "This what you're looking for?" He was about to open his fist when Blanche Rowlands yelled from somewhere close by.

"What the dilly-o? I can't leave you alone for a minute," and then she saw the cigarette smoldering on the fresh bed linen and a broken saucer on the floor.

"That's revolting," Blanche said, staring hard at Elle.

Nathan shook his head at Elle in disgust.

"What's that you got?"

He nodded toward Elle. "She says it's hers," and opened his fist.

Elle gasped. They all stared at it until Blanche let out a mean laugh, more a snort and said, "It's a button, a toggle button." She stared at Elle. "What did you think it was? A tooth? Big enough to belong to a wolfman if it was."

Elle remembered the set of horn buttons with leather loops she snipped from the wool duffle coat she had been foolish enough to bring from Boston.

Blanche Rowlands stared hard at Elle, narrowing her eyes, drawing it out, like she knew what happened.

But it didn't matter what she knew; it only mattered what she could prove, which was exactly nothing.

"Clean up this disgusting mess," Blanche said to Elle "Maybe we'll show a decent profit once you're not running the kitchen."

Elle understood she was being blamed for the broken saucer, the burned bed linen. The three of them turned to leave, and Ruby looked at Elle sympathetically, which was almost worse.

No Name Key Lodge was no longer her lookout.

The ferry horn blew, and Blanche patted her hair in the wardrobe mirror. "The workers. Come to build my new dance pavilion."

Elle gathered up the candlesticks, a glass cat figurine and a small photo of her mother in a green enamel frame, face down where she had left it. This was the single picture she had of her mother as a young girl, all stiff and starched but with a telltale grin and wild eye despite the clothing restraints.

Blanche moved toward the kitchen while Elle slipped away, down the hallway and outside into the dwindling light.

"And don't come back until I call for you."

***

Billy liked roads... liked driving Elle away from the splintered family that couldn't bear her presence. He told them he was one of the select few hired to work at the Ford River Rouge plant in Dearborn, Michigan, a man of the future, but he could've saved his breath. Even if it were true, it didn't matter. Her family couldn't have cared less, so long as they no longer had to provide her a bed.

Billy could fix just about anything. But when he hooked up with Jerry Herda in a radio repair business, he earned his first jail sentence. Jerry trusted him easily enough to make him a partner in those early days. They set the business up with all manner of tube testers and schematics that Jerry didn't understand, but could afford. "It's one or the other," Billy always said. "Money or know-how, and that's where I come in." When he got out of jail, Billy married Elle in the lobby of a roadside motel after finding a desk clerk who moonlighted as a Justice of the Peace.

'He's been a lady's man for years,' is what his friends told her. Or 'there he goes again,' when Billy and Elle moved into his friend's place, Billy between jobs. No one believed he truly loved her, that she would be the one

thing he would hang onto and hang on hard. "I'd date you if I could," Billy's friend said behind Billy's back, casting carnal smirks her way, as if she was there for the asking. As if she had a choice of whether to be with Billy or anyone else. When Elle demanded they leave, Billy slapped her hard for the first time. He was the force that fuses the flower, as impossible to change as the heat in the tropics.

Elle would tell people how they came here on Roosevelt's American New Deal a as part of a Works Progress Administration (WPA) never mentioning that everyone else turned him away. She was surprised at the natural affection she felt toward Florida. That is until Billy realized how much she loved it here. She told him she could work, that others besides him would value her skills, but he shook his head and looked down whenever she got going.

"But where else can we go?" She asked when the WPA told her she wasn't allowed in the work camp, married or not. So, she lied and told Billy she had a job caring for an uncle's child back in Boston. She knew Billy wanted her hobbled in a room in an isolated neighborhood, exhausted from chores and other people's children until he could come up with another con, another dream.

When Elle slipped out of the work camp that morning, a loud, bright ferryboat moving south activated her fate, moving in the opposite direction she planned, where no one would expect her to go. When she boarded the Key Wester, she was cautious, checking the passengers, sidling up to Monty the ferryboat captain, asking if any of the old soldiers were on board who might tell Billy they saw her.

Missus, they called her when she found the job as a cook at No Name Lodge. Fear had lined her face, roughed her up, her labored movements mannish and unapproachable. In some strange way, she grew to feel that Billy's malevolent spirit was actually helping her.

Within a few months she made herself indispensable, doing the work of three. Best way to garner favor from the owner was to please the guests, so Elle dragged out the old cookbooks from the library, adding this and that and planting herbs to coax exotic flavors from the stingy soil.

"Make the lime pie," guests would say, and marvel at a sprig of this or that in their drinks. And so the owner let her order the meat and the ice, then asked her to design the fare. Within two seasons, mealtimes were as much of a driving force as the fishing fever, and guests almost forgot about the heat. Elle made a big deal about breakfasts, saving the tips left discretely for her. Monty was in cahoots, spreading word of her cooking so she would let him stay in an empty cabin, laughing into her fist at the women who snuck into his room when their husbands retired for the night. Elle remembered a big blonde, her bias-cut ivory silk trailing like a flash in the night, disappearing behind his door.

And Elle became used to the adulation for her kitchen. In the middle of a great depression, she was having the time of her life, with two places to live, staying in her room behind the lodge kitchen while she ordered a sink and a stove for the little cistern at water's edge, she bought from the hermit.

She found peace in the herons honking, vultures hissing, the geckos skittering and the deadly hot summer where business slowed enough for her to gather her wits and plot her course. She had turned it into a home. Until the summer of 1935, in the cradle of her triumph, when Billy found her at No Name Key in the bartered cistern she turned into a home.

6

$\mathcal{E}$ lle tied a towel around her waist and softly shut the vine-choked gate to her cottage. She had lately taken to early morning swims before the sun rose and guests at the lodge would be up. At times she was a silent witness to mismatched couples sneaking out of cabins. Once, a meteor shower illuminated the massive wingspan of a turkey vulture returning to her secret nesting grounds. But she had never seen the light on in the kitchen. Never, not once, since Blanche Rowlands banished her from the lodge did she see any sign of care in the kitchen.

The water was cool for January in the Florida Keys and early enough that no one was around, and she would have this piece of the day to herself. She moved past her skiff, bobbing on its tether to the empty expanse of water alongside the wharf, reserved for the ferry.

She tossed her nightshirt alongside a linen towel in her skiff and dove in, circling then swimming under the pier. She raised her head to breathe the gap of air between wharf and water, her vision adjusting to the deeper darkness.

Sturdy iron rings marked spots where she had threaded ropes to tie the last two crab traps with Billy's remains. It had been a quick solution to get them out of sight until she could take them out to sea. She remembered the panicked vibrations from stampeding guests, desperate to board the last ferry out before the storm closed in. After everyone left, she returned, but they moved beyond her reach, swaying in the water like surreal bird cages and Elle couldn't muster the courage to untie the ropes and pull them out so she waited and by the time the hurricane passed, they had disappeared.

She shook her head to slough off the vision. Billy's body would be unrecognizable now, taken out by waves from the storm and the poor job she had done to secure the traps. Certainly, no one would be ghoulish enough to keep it. Elle flipped onto her back and floated safely in the warm darkness. Feeling her heart rate diminish, she opened her legs and arms and imagined the secret folds and crevices of her body flush with healing water, carrying away the sweat and dirt of the previous day. An intense silence surrounded and lulled her into near oblivion. Perhaps she would finally sleep and lose herself in the unheard luxury of a deep nap until the middle of the day.

Remaining on her back, she floated toward the dawning light and heard a loud gasp as she emerged. Brushy Rowland's head bobbed up and down, craning to see who was emerging from under the wharf. She must have looked like a dead body. She half-waved at him, pushing at the air to make him disappear. "What?" she yelled, resentful at the intrusion.

"Thank God, Elle," he yelled, his mouth open. "It's you."

Brushy Rowlands. The man who allowed his wife to fire her. He must've arrived on an evening ferry with the group of builders. Elle made out the unnatural black of his hair as he squinted into the sun. "Can't I get any privacy?" she said. Brushy was thinner than she remembered, but Elle resented paying any attention to the Rowlandses. She felt her anger rise, her heart rate increase, remembering how he never stood up to his wife. The last time she saw him was before the Labor Day hurricane. Although he'd always been kind to her, he was a weak man, unable to stand up to his wife.

A smatter of ibis gathered on the wharf, dipping their curved needle-nose beaks into a shallow pool of rainwater from yesterday's sudden storm. Why was he smiling? Didn't he expect her to be angry at losing her job? Elle pointed to the yellow marker.

"I own this side,"she said, pointing to the pathway at the edge of the wharf. "Everything on the right side. So, you can just head back the other way."

Of course, she owned the property the cistern was on, but could only negotiate legal access to the wharf, something she insisted on when she bought it from the hermit. Did Brushy Rowlands think it meant nothing? Stepping on the property marker infuriated Elle. Blanche had done the same three days earlier.

Brushy looked back toward the lodge. "I'm sorry," he said, his voice low. "Can we go somewhere to talk?"

"Isn't that what we're doing?" Let him ask again, dammit. She held onto the underside of the dock, poised to launch herself under and away.

"Blanche doesn't know I'm here. Please."

The entire morning suddenly had a stale warmth to it. The sun bobbed, struggling to rise. Brushy approached life like a game-the way he moved people around where they were most needed or offered the most amusement. People like the Rowlands want to remain in a life and death position of importance to everyone around them, and Elle was sick of them. She detested his tidy seersucker jacket, which was about to be stained by a rivulet of black hair dye bleeding into his collar.

"Where's your towel? I'll get it….," he said. He trailed off as Elle muscled her way onto her small skiff, bobbing close to the wharf's edge. She wrapped a nubby length of sand-colored linen around her waist and headed for her property, not indicating that he was welcome.

He didn't speak until they entered the gate to her yard. "I'll pay you double. Just work the few weeks Abbott is here with his group."

"Abbott?"

"Engineer from Miami. Blanche hired him to turn the library into a dance pavilion, complete with a widow's walk.

"Oh, sure. I'm dying to have four bosses now instead of one," she said. Elle thought of her lost authority over the menu and kitchen help. "Triple pay and I take no orders from the chef or no deal. I got an offer from Miami," she lied. Elle thought about the sandwiches she sold to the men building the road, an income she could fall back on when the lodge job ended. "And I do what I like on my time off."

"Of course," he said, trying to disguise the look of pity on his face.

Who was he to pity her when he had wealth and choice, yet married a woman who cheated on him any chance she got?

"And I have a little advice for you. Do something about that hair dye. It's ruined your jacket."

A brief look of shock passed through his features before Blanche's shrill voice cut through the trees and through the gate, arresting his response. "Brushy, where the hell are you?" Gone was Blanche's flirtatious lilt from last season.

He raised a finger to his lips, "Shh-h," and they waited until the lodge door slammed shut.

"I need time to consider your offer of three times the pay. I got plans and…"

"Please," he said. Then, "Thank you," although she hadn't yet agreed. He walked through her tiny yard, then stopped under the gigantic Poinciana tree, its feathered horizontal branches shading the flat coral boulder she used as a stool. Although her small property was only a few hundred yards from the lodge, the gentle grade decline and thick brush hid it from view. Brushy unclipped his sunglasses, made a small waving gesture, and said simply, "thank you." He looked desperate.

7

Within a week, she had settled into her old work rhythm at the lodge. Though it was unlikely she would keep her job after the party, she wouldn't miss stepping past her old bedroom every day and half-expecting Billy's bloody ghost limping down the hallway, looking for her. She never returned to the lodge after dark and almost welcomed the new cooks, Ree and Frank Dinkson.

Blanche and Elle avoided each other, leaving Elle to wonder what Brushy told her. But that day, Blanche said something Elle didn't understand. Elle was grating carrots for her gelatin ring, when a puff of smoke hit her eyes and she looked up to see Blanche in the kitchen doorway, flicking ashes manically. "Keep your friends close," is what she said. It always seemed to Elle that Blanche was auditioning for a part in a B film, making some dramatic comment, followed by a grand exit. Elle rarely answered, understanding that her response was completely unnecessary.

In the middle of her first week back, Elle returned home and spotted a rolled sandwich open and empty on the floor, a trail of ants working together to cart off bits of bread and fish. So much effort for so little. She stopped to watch the small crumbs appear to float on air and didn't have the heart to kill them. Instead, she swept them outside the open door, picked up the remains of the sandwich and placed it in her outside garbage bin. Cat probably made off with the Mahi filling, leaving the remains. Good on him, she thought. Every creature for themselves. He purred in his sleep, waking after she wrapped the sandwiches in butcher paper, packed them in a duffle and gathered her bike to walk the quarter mile to the pathway out.

Maybe it was time to pull up stakes. She rehashed her conversation with Brushy; an offer in Miami. Good lord, she had actually told him that. The thought brought her a sudden jolt of pleasure and a laugh began in her stomach and made it out of her lips before she knew it. A family with three young children in bathing suits crossed the narrow pathway to avoid her.

A couple of lodge workers nodded at Elle, and that made her happy. They respected her for one thing or another, and it didn't much matter what it was. The road was uneven, and Cat bounded close by her heels, then moved up ahead into the wild pathless tangle as unchanged as she imagined it centuries before.

"Should call you Dog, not Cat," she said. He was feeling playful and often followed her through the woods. He does what he likes, she thought with admiration. In the middle of a romp, he stiffened and turned his head rapidly, spooking Elle. Across a small circle of bush, Joe was standing and when she moved her head to look his way, he turned his back to her, affirming her sense of being watched. Something told her not to react as if it were the most common thing in the world to see someone hiding behind a tree. Maybe he enjoyed walking in the woods, or maybe he lost something. Was Blanche with him? Somehow Elle knew she wasn't. She waved as if unafraid and when he turned, his face was hollow and his hair looked electrified, tips burned white by the sun.

Elle spoke to herself as she did when she was fearful. In a low voice, she said, "Just going out by the roadway, taking a shortcut is all." When she looked back, he was gone and Cat was nowhere in sight. Her head felt heavy, as if it were sewn onto her neck. No way she would turn to look again. She felt the flip knife under her waistband, then something brushed her leg and she jumped.

"Cat! Oh, damn you."

By the time she arrived in Big Pine, counting change carefully was all that mattered, and she wrote up sums on a pad of paper she carried in a drawstring bag underneath the knife. She attached a pencil in a looped elastic band to make a tidy bundle.

Turned out, the men didn't care that the rolls were warm. Within twenty minutes, they were gone, and she imagined how much she would have if she kept this up. As the Florida sun blossomed into purple and rose, she heard the jangle of coins, and fear suddenly bristled through her. She bent to pick up moss, placing it into the lilac moneybag to muffle the sound of coins clinking. Elle had fished the bag from the trash a year ago, amazed that something so exquisite had been tossed out like it was worthless. The original champagne glass it once housed was long gone by the time Elle spotted the bright gold embroidery on delicate lilac silk.

Cat jumped at imaginary sights in the shadows as they moved through the brush back to the lodge. The place took on an unfamiliar cast. Damn Blanche, she had put her time off. Elle made her way to the footpath, veering left, recognizing the sprawling Gumbo Limbo tree and enormous strangler fig. Before coming into view of the lodge, she made out the sound of breathing nearby. Was something following her? She stopped and listened. Again, she heard a low pant and muffled step.

"Anyone there?" she said to the brush, straightening to her full six-foot height. The knife was where it should be for easy access. Footsteps moved away. There might be more than one. Still, she resisted the impulse to chase them down. Their obvious desire to hide made her bold, turning them into prey. If they were out to do harm, they would have come after her by now. Desperate men who might have lost their jobs because of drunkenness, which was the usual cause for immediate dismissal in the camps. Maybe they thought her an easy target. She had almost three dollars in her bag, half a week's pay for government workers building the road, and certainly worth robbing.

"C'mon out and I'll blow this whistle so loud, all camp will know who ya are…. better be ready to kill me because that's what it'll take. C'mon. Do your dirty worst. I dare ya!" She was so angry at having to scrap it out for the right to breathe air in and let it out that she almost welcomed an opportunity to do damage.

Maybe someone could come with her next time, but the thought increased her anger. Were men always to provide the antidote to the very misery they caused? She remembered the ridiculous suggestion Brushy gave her the other day to wear a skirt when she made out to sell her rolls. It struck her as comical. Imagine trying to run or fight in *that*, she thought. Maybe I could suffocate them with it - use the great skirt as a tent – or a rope to strangle them with. An image of her dragging two men into the open in a twisted rope of small print calico made her laugh so loud that Cat felt bold enough to claw at her leg, letting her know he needed to be fed. One more reason to wear pants, she thought, and waded through the rubbery underbrush, no longer nervous.

Images of Billy and Blanche Rowlands choked her, emerging whenever she felt fearful. If only she hadn't had to kill him here in the place she loved. But maybe that was a good thing.

Maybe No Name loved her enough to push him out and keep her tethered to the island. No Name was as ragged and abandoned as she was, and No Name found her beautiful. She was certain of it. Maybe the land had been jealous of Billy. Like her mother once said about her father, "He's not much, but he's mine."

8

The ferry docked by the time Elle tethered her skiff and pulled up her bucket of mangrove snappers.

"Out early?" Monty yelled from the ferry, an annoying smile plastered on his face, playing to the crowd of lodge workers onboard.

"Some of us got real jobs," she said.

"Well lucky you, Miss." She recognized the voice. Rimer was a master carpenter known for his detailed carvings and marquetry skills. He was covered in wood shavings and chips, his face powdered in a fine sawdust. "You might want to put in a word for Art and me, ma'am, if you see fit." He wiped a hand on his hickory overalls and held it out to shake.

"You're looking at a woman whose only pull is getting fish outta water," Elle said. "In fact, best not mention my name at all." Elle nodded toward the lodge. "I thought you already worked there?"

Rimer removed his hat, a deferential gesture that seemed to embody the hurt and shame of desperate men looking for work. "Well, we did," he said.

"We quit," Art said, closing in Rimer's shadow. Elle recognized his loose and awkward form. She remembered him sitting in a backhoe cab, a foot sticking out the side.

Rimer turned toward his friend and raised his eyebrows to caution him.

"The Lodge has changed since new ownership," Elle said, letting them know she was on their side.

The mood at No Name lodge was harsh; workers exhausted by conditions they assumed would be an improvement on the highway project. The hum of machinery sounded day and night, only coming to a rest at the dinner hour before beginning again for another few hours. Barely a week into dismantling the library, two workers quit and Elle realized she was speaking to them.

"Can't you get your old job back building the highway?"

"Hah," Art said.

"Well, who won't give you back the job?" Monty chimed in, always eager for detail.

Although the question was aimed at Art, Rimer answered, "Nathan Foreman, Mr. Works Progress Administration himself. He's the WPA big boss on Pigeon Key. 'Once out, forever out,' were his exact words. You'd think the money came from his own pocket and not the government."

"Laughed right in our face," Art said, looking down.

Later that day, Elle heard Art shout orders over the clamor of the backhoe. Blanche must've taken them back, as was her practice to rehire men that quit at a lower wage to set an example. Word travels fast on the coconut telegraph and fewer men would give up WPA work on the highway project once they realize they won't be rehired if it doesn't work out, so Blanche was forced to pay more to entice new hires. This two-tiered system created a tense, resentful atmosphere. Even in a Depression, skilled men were valued, and Blanche was desperate to finish the dance pavilion on time.

"She never got over being snubbed by Pauline." Monty said. Pauline Hemingway hosted magnificent parties at her Key West mansion and acted like Blanche didn't exist. Blanche had somehow gotten her hands on Pauline's guest list and sent them all invitations.

When Elle went out back to find a box of linen napkins, Brushy and Blanche were in a heated argument about a fifty-dollar bonus to a talented hydraulics man.

"Are you crazy?" Brushy said.

"I had no choice," Blanche yelled and Brushy smashed a coffee mug in the office, not caring who was around to hear it.

After the office door slammed hard, Elle picked up the box of napkins and headed to the front to avoid them. Halfway there, she heard a resounding slap, and the defeated figure of Brushy emerged, hand raised to his cheek. Joe stood in the background, smiling behind the porch column.

"He was in a total state,"Ree Dinkson said later. "Like that guy in the movies." She imitated some actor, saying, *"Dammit Blanche, you're bankrupting me.* You can hear everything. I don't even need to hold a glass up against the wall."

The closer to the party, the more doors slammed, sharp whispers, then long strangled silences.

Over the next weeks, arguments broke out whenever Abbot and his engineers were out of earshot. Part of the Abbot entourage was a kid named Buster who carted around a tripod and satchel of odd lenses and other camera equipment to 'document the process,' as Abbott put it, which Brushy tolerated for publicity. The cumbersome camera apparatus was annoying to Elle, who discovered it stashed in the lodge pantry one morning. "It's into the drink next time I find it," she warned the kid.

Thursday's, Blanche handed her a pay packet with five one-dollar bills and on Friday, Brushy palmed an additional ten-dollar bill into her apron for that same week's work. Elle labored from sunup to 11:00 AM cooking breakfast and lunch at the lodge, then back to make dinner at 4. In between, she bicycled the three miles to the road crew with a basket of sandwiches to sell. She spent evenings in her own tiny kitchen making the rolls she was becoming known for, stashing them in her collection of zinc iceboxes to keep them fresh. At night she dreamed of ways to increase profit and the house she would buy: the walls, the roof, the grove of fruit trees. One night she imagined herself the owner of No Name Lodge and after that, any other dream just made her sad.

Seemed like everyone had some sort of money scheme and Elle was certain she didn't know the half of it. So she shouldered Blanche's insults, slights and ridiculous demands, all the while gathering equipment, iceboxes, making a smoking chest and testing recipes on the workingmen. But no matter how she tried to interest Ree, the woman had no talent for kitchen work and could barely serve the plates and clean up afterward.

"Better learn something while you have a roof over your head," Elle told her and Ree took it to heart, playing mechanic for the men. Some days, Elle spotted her, covered in grease, elbow deep in a LaSalle engine, the only time she looked truly content. But the husband was as useless as Billy had been - a tossup who was the bigger loafer.

By mid-January, yelling between Blanche and Brushy was replaced by a clipped tone laced with bitterness and contempt. Elle always took the long way to the supply yard, but they were already at it.

"Doesn't he have anything better to do than lurk around my wife?" Brushy said.

Elle imagined he was speaking about Joe, who rarely left Blanche's side.

"C'mon sweetie," Blanche replied. "He's helping us both do jobs we no longer have the strength to complete."

Elle inhaled a little too loudly and Blanche came out, "There's your lurker. Don't think I don't know what's going on between you two."

9

The Sunday barbeque was always well attended, men stuffing their faces with the hand grilled ground meat like those White Castle advertisements in magazines. She made enough to turn a blind eye to men that took some with them in many ingenious ways. Sheets of waxed paper lay on the picnic tables, begging for a juicy meat sandwich or two with the fixings plopped inside and carried away.

Men who didn't take the ferry to Key West to squander their wages spent late Saturday and Sunday eating and sleeping and staring out on the horizon from the wharf. Elle heard smatterings of conversation about the men lost in the Labor Day hurricane. Most knew somebody taken by the storm.

Elle continued out back to pick up a store of charcoal and wheelbarrow it out on the front grounds for the "cookout." Hamburgers were all the rage and seemed to make the men less homesick, so the Sunday "cookout" was becoming a tradition. The smell of charred meat had a calming effect on the men and they became more social, which lent a festive air to the activity.

And Elle enjoyed nothing more than ordering the worthless Joe Palooka around. *Joe, get that grill up, would you? Joe, wrap these spuds in tin foil and be a dear toss them into the coals - quick so they have time to cook.*

Grab me some sausage weenies when you have a chance, Joe. Be a dear... It made her laugh, certain he was too stupid to suspect she was laughing at him.

Whenever Joe left on an errand, the men spoke more freely, understanding that Elle was one of them.

"This guy right here," Rimer aimed his elbow sideways at Art. "Blew our chances of working the highway project, and now we make less than half the pay." Rimer spoke in a casual, joking tone.

"But that makes no sense. You're both more than hole diggers," Elle said. "Surely you get more pay for your carpentry skills?"

"You think it's easy to dig a hole here? He's the real artist. Maybe that's why they named him Art in the first place."

"So, when he does something that costs you the next job, what then?" It irritated her for reasons she couldn't articulate.

"Sometimes looking out for a friend is more important than getting ahead." This sounded like something phony Mrs. Dean, the pastor's wife, would say, but Elle suspected he meant it.

"You don't agree? Each man for himself, is that it?"

"Each what?" She said, drawing a chuckle from Art. "This togetherness routine might be a novelty act for you, but it's the mainstay of a woman's whole life. We go where our partner leads. Even into a burning building." Elle's voice was laced with bitterness.

"Partner?" As quickly as it appeared, the shock on his face was replaced with his usual crooked half- smile. "Well, missy, I guess it's not true of all women."

"Damn straight," she said, and the men laughed, relieved this talk had come to a natural end.

Rimer avoided her after a sour awkwardness emerged between them that Elle regretted.

Before everyone scattered, Abbot showed up with a small group of men that must've arrived on the 6:00 ferry, when the cookout was going full tilt. Nathan followed close by, circling the cookout like a guard dog.

"Gather round and show me what you've done this past week," Abbott demanded. A collective wave of resentment pushed through the food-sleepy crowd. Rimer stared straight ahead, his expression dead.

"Here," Abbott yelled, heading toward the scaffolded area. "What the devil is this?" He pointed to a shallow hole dug near the library. "Who did this?"

Art looked away and Rimer answered for him. "Regulation size of eighteen inches deep and it's still wet."

"It's not deep enough and you know it," Abbott said.

"We're doing it by hand, sir. Teeth on the backhoe break in this so-called soil and it takes weeks to get equipment replaced. Orders are to have it done and dusted in less than a week." He was right. Coral and capstone were too much, even for what industrial machinery they got a hold of. Everyone grumbled about the rush job.

"Everything's on back order," Nathan said to Abbott. He bent down to inspect the large barrels used to mix cement. "Concrete mixer trucks are always delayed, so we got the same formula as Flagler used and are doing it ourselves. Right, boys?" He smiled at the group, but no one smiled back. "We can do this with a little good will and elbow grease. Been in far worse jams. Right, boys?" This was the second time these over-forty-year-old men were called boys and Elle felt rather than saw Rimer flinch.

Within an hour of dismantling the cookout area, work started up again and continued as the moon rose.

This new group of 'specialists' demanded to be put up in the cabins, 'only two to a shack,' displacing the twice hired men now forced to erect tents in worse shape than the ones they left on Pigeon Key. They quit work at 6pm sharp, expecting a good meal and plenty of booze, their slurry banter taunting the vets still working.

Blanche's diet was largely liquid, and it was showing. She looked bloated much of the time and whenever she tried to quit drinking, Brushy snuck a little gin into her morning juice because Blanche was mean without the sedative effect of booze.

Buster, the camera boy, was getting his money's worth, taking pictures of odd things. Blanche was all in, once posing in a red and black lace mask, pursing red painted lips in a hideous parody of a kiss. Elle assumed she planned to use the photographs in her party invitations.

But then something changed, and Brushy seemed calmer, allowing Buster on the yacht to take pictures of them done up as if ready for a sail, despite how badly the yacht needed repair. Elle felt sorry for Brushy taking part in this charade. She delivered iced drinks to the group as they posed on the Big Wheel for a publicity shot. Joe was showing off his hold over Blanche and Blanche showing off her power over Brushy, all three posing for an idyllic picture–then Joe put his arm around Blanche and Brushy pretended not to see what was happening. He must want to appear like the powerful industrialist, with his beautiful bride and the hired help, all in shirtsleeves and enjoying sunshine when it was winter everywhere else in the country.

"That ought to show those jealous Northerners," Brushy said, blinking off the blinding effects of the camera flash.

But then Blanche actually kissed Joe and the clueless Buster took a few more for good measure, saying "You never know which ones will turn out." He claimed to be adept at "cutting out figures, so no worries if someone doesn't like their face on any particular day." And Elle wondered if she imagined the small smile on Brushy's face.

10

own the pathway, water twinkled behind the freshly painted ferry, but few cars were onboard.

Nathan Foreman stood on the dock. A young girl sat on a barrel in front of him, almost like a shield that he was wielding. To his left was a woman, wearing a dark scarf over her head, despite the midday heat. Elle finally recognized his wife, Ruby, who seemed to take her in at the same moment.

Monty pulled a crate of potatoes from under a tarp and Elle reached for it, turning away so as not to stare.

"My wife," Nathan said before anyone asked, "is unwell after falling against the counter."

"What counter?" Ruby had never been inside the lodge kitchen that Elle knew.

"No, not here. Our house on Pigeon Key," he answered, then smiled as Blanche strutted down the wharf, wearing red tap shoes, her favorite way of announcing her presence.

"Elle," Blanche said, "Don't stand there gawking. Get this to the lodge."

Elle ignored Blanche and extended her hand to Ruby. "If there's anything I can get you, I'll be only too happy…"

"Marvelous," Blanche said. "When we need a man's patched overalls, we'll know exactly who to ask." Nathan Foreman let out breath, stifling a laugh.

"I haven't forgotten the beef," Monty said, interrupting the conflict, as was his usual style. When they turned away, he rolled his eyes upward, lifted eyebrows and shoved the cart off the ferry. "You're going to lose that job, Elle," he said when they were out of earshot.

"I've met her before, Monty. What's wrong with her? She never looks right."

"I have no idea," he said. "Except that's their daughter. I forget her name." He seemed to want to go on, but stopped himself. "I mind my business, Elle."

"Yah, sure you do."

Ruby and her daughter moved down the wharf, an explosion of sun blurring their features. Elle waved them over on impulse. Ruby looked behind to see Nathan and Blanche in deep conversation. Her head jutted back at Elle, then she pulled at her daughter's arm, who moved behind her mother with the resistance of a wooden pull toy.

"Do you need my help with something?" Ruby asked.

"No, just nice to see another woman here."

Ruby turned toward the lodge as if looking for someone.

"No, Blanche doesn't count," Elle said. Ruby laughed and her open expression and olive eyes reminded Elle of an old friend from schooldays.

Monty shook his head, "pay little attention to this one. She's trouble." He said, and it annoyed Elle though she knew he was joking.

"What's your name?" Elle asked, bending down to the girl who looked seven or eight years old.

"My name is Betty Foreman." Spoken so formally, Elle almost expected her to follow with rank and serial number.

"Well, Betty," Monty said. Coming up from behind. "Which one do you want?" He pointed to a box of mangoes, papayas and alligator pears. They had forgotten he was there.

"I want an apple," she said, before her mother could correct her.

"Who doesn't?" Elle raised her eyebrows at Betty, nodding in agreement, but Betty looked away.

"You've had her sapodilla pie," Ruby said. "Remember how much you like it."

"Did *she* really make *that*?" Betty asked, her mouth open like a caricature.

"Sure I did and if you like, I can show you how," Elle said. Something about the earnest little girl made Elle feel protective. "But you can't tell anyone my secret ingredients."

"You're talking to me like I'm stupid."

"Betty!" Ruby said.

Before she could chastise the girl, Elle cut in. "Well, you'd be stupid not to learn how to bake the best pie in the South."

A door slammed at the lodge. Ruby jumped, and Betty turned, her expression blank as if trained not to react. "I don't think it's a good idea to be too friendly," Ruby said.

"Hey, Betty," Monty yelled, and tossed a mango at her, which she caught. "Think of it as a tropical apple."

She stared up at him, her expression intense and accusatory. "This is a mango." Her eyes narrowed.

"Thank you," Ruby said, shuffling her daughter toward the lodge. "Ummm, we'll see you later."

"How long are you here? Elle asked.

"Who knows?" Ruby answered. Betty's face was unreadable. She stared at the ground, her lips pursed as they parted company.

Later, on the path back to her cistern, Elle spotted the mango hidden under a palm frond.

11

That afternoon, the lodge was so choked with guests and workmen no one noticed smoke rising from the fire pit where Elle boiled beans. As they simmered, she fried panfuls of batter for the roadside sandwich wraps she sold to men who couldn't stomach one more government lunch.

She set the padlock on the fence, turned up the volume on the radio and spent the afternoon frying, smoking, steaming and rolling food, feeding the cat and the chickens. Charlie the rooster flew through the window and circled her until she tossed the remains of the mango outside for him to finish.

"Elle," from beyond the gate. The voice was familiar, with an anxious undernote, like a curse.

She recognized Art, the backhoe driver. His friend, Rimer, leaned into him, a foot raised slightly.

"Can you walk?" she yelled at Rimer.

Before Rimer answered, Art scooped up his friend, and carried him like a sack of reluctant brides over Elle's threshold, closing the gate behind him with a flick of his long, loose foot. "I'm sorry. There's nowhere else…"

"That's ok," she said. "What happened?"

"Some fool covered a hole with leaves, and I fell in," Rimer said.

Art looked down, ashamed, shifted Rimer's weight to one side and opened the door to Elle's house with his free hand, as if Rimer was lighter than a leaf in the shovel of his backhoe.

Art deposited Rimer on the purple brocade chair. "I'll cover for him while you fix 'im up." And then he was gone.

Rimer looked up at her apologetically. "Once he gets an idea…." He struggled to rise, obviously in pain. "Stupid to have slipped… can't believe I did that."

"How bad is it?"

"Just a sprain," he said, shrugging his shoulders. His eyes traveled to Elle's boots on the brown reed mat flanking the wall. Elle felt strangely embarrassed by the rough boots, the enormous size of her feet. Why was he staring at them?

"They're mine," she said, although he hadn't asked. He smiled but said nothing. "Put your leg up," Elle was more irritated with herself than him. Why did Art bring him to her, and why did she accept? She was a cook, not everyone's mother. She thought about the turtle with a cracked shell, the lame baby chick and a baby vulture she wrapped in a kerosene-soaked sheet and the grim satisfaction she felt watching the fleas hop off his body.

"Lean back," Elle said.

He removed his glasses and placed them on the cross section of fossilized mahogany root Elle used for a side table. Cat circled them, sniffing, and then hissed at Rimer.

"I know what she's like. Any excuse to let you go or pay you less. Don't worry, we'll get you fixed up and back out there in no time."

Rimer looked around, taking in the cistern. Elle liked how he regarded everyone with interest. At the cookouts, he'd goad the men to tell stories, where they were from, especially the crazy stuff, happy to squeeze a laugh or two from the crowd.

"Looks like I'll be the first to confirm the tales the men hear about you. Always wondered what was behind the green wall."

"Tell them you met the great Florida skunk ape," she said, expecting he wouldn't know the local legend.

"Skunk ape came all the way from the Tamiami Trail lured by your sapodilly pie," Rimer answered.

"So, you've heard of him?" Unless you were from this part of Florida, few knew the legend of the Florida skunk ape.

"Florida Bigfoot. Mascot of the Glades. He'd fit right into our little camp. Read and whittle, whittle and read. That's about all I do. Be sure to thank him for the use of his table." He traced a fingertip around the fossilized growth lines of the table beside him. "Early Paleolithic," he said, smiling. Then quickly, "It's quiet in your little cistern, peaceful and private."

"Cottage," she said, and he nodded.

He had noted the quality of sound absorption she was most grateful for. His praise seemed genuine.

"Take off your shoe," Elle said, and brought over a basin of water. "Here," she handed him a linen square. He rolled his pant leg over his knee and immersed his foot. The knee had swollen.

"I'm going to move your leg around," she said, bending to dry his foot. His look was one of such resignation that Elle thought it unnecessary to reassure him. He leaned back, palms behind him, and Elle held his leg at the knee joint and moved it in circles. "You're lucky," she said when he didn't flinch. "Just a sprain."

She ripped a piece of linen expertly, turning a square into a long piece of bandage. He gazed at the woven reed rug under his feet. "Is that how you made those?"

How did he know she had made them? "No, they're from tough old plants here on No Name. This is imported."

"Ahh. Part of the clever décor."

"Yes, I got it to go with the early—what did you call it? Paleo something? My fancy indoor seating."

His sudden laugh surprised her, causing a gentle warmth that wrapped around the two of them.

"Thank you," he said. "I owe you."

She leaned over him. "If you say so, but it wasn't my idea to let you in."

"I know. That's why I owe you. Because you did it anyway."

"You owe your friend, is more like it. Doesn't look like Art takes no for an answer."

"That would make me and Art just about even," he said, but Elle thought she would find it a lot easier to refuse Art. He bent over to put his sock back on. His forearms were thick, hair bleached to platinum over a deep chestnut tan.

"Long story," he said. "Aren't they always?"

"I've got time," she said, now genuinely curious. What was he doing with these people, she wondered, and wanted to ask him where he went to school or who his parents were or was he married?

"I'd better go… before they count heads."

"And pennies."

"And that."

As if reading her mind, and in perfect synch, he said. "I'll take a page out of your book and get that Joe guy to step n' fetch for me."

"Wait," she said, handing him a walking stick she had used for an injury Billy caused her. She avoided touching his hand, afraid of an electrical current. He walked carefully to the gate, smiled at her with his surprising movie star teeth, put his finger to his lips. "Shhhh," he said, and was gone.

Later, when Elle headed to the lodge for breakfast prep, she passed Rimer on the porch, gouging some impossible design into a heavy piece of wood. At least he could sit where he worked. Intuitively, she avoided his eyes, angered that she lived in circumstances where a simple friendship put them both at risk. Everything reminded her of the subordinate position they all were in, the sway the Rowlandses had over them all. On a small veranda table by the kitchen, she came upon Brushy's abandoned pipe and tobacco pouch and impulsively pocketed them both, imagining him needing something he wanted but couldn't have. But someone would be blamed, so she returned it. The common dilemma, getting away with something, usually meant losing something greater.

That morning she flipped eggs, chopped up potatoes and cut the ham, used up the good tomatoes, giving the men extra food, not caring what it would cost her if Blanche found out. The petty retaliations of a menial, she thought.

Throughout the morning she pushed down bitterness, feeling herself an intruder in the kitchen that once was hers. The kitchen she needed but didn't want. After directing Ree to dry the dishes, Elle was relieved to be back at her house to finish the last details of the lunches to sell on the road. She eyed caramels made not so long ago when the joy and hope were still alive in her. How quickly her mood changed these days

12

A thin puddle oozed out from under the crates, hammered together for shelving, and the ripe odor of mold forced its way into her nostrils. Her throat felt furred and the vague smell of vomit percolated — a telltale sign that mold was well-established. If she aired out the place when the sun was highest, night critters would hustle inside, which was likely how she was almost bitten by a scorpion the last time.

Grateful for release, she packed the sandwiches in twin duffels and walked her bike to the road. Cat sensed she was foul and trailed behind her before jumping into the basket and hanging on. His good eye closed, ears flattened as she pounded the pedals, rushing through the brush and onto the wooden bridge. A blur of ibis above her, a spellbound heron, people fishing below. The farther she rode, the more she sloughed off the bitterness she felt, focusing on her natural love of profit. Calculating what she might add to her stash cheered her up enough to wave at a worker who seemed to recognize her. At the roadside, she exchanged the stench of mold for one of tar, set up her sling stand, covering the faded canvas with a long mat of braided banana fiber and stacked the rolls into pyramids flanked by bowls of caramels, free with a sandwich purchase.

A man closest to the road spied her. "She's here," he yelled, and a few followed, then more. Under the table, Cat swiped at the feet of anyone not to his liking. He seemed to know who would toss him a piece of fish and who would rather step on his tail, given the option.

Looking at the faces of the men, her thoughts drifted to Rimer and his odd friendship with Art. The way they depended on each other in a hostile world, and she wondered at the cost of these unions. They were an odd match, the man with the matinee idol face and his friend, a shadowy Slim Pickens.

Evenings, Elle calculated her fortune by adding the extra sixty-dollars from work at the lodge and the promised ten-dollar party bonus. But no matter how she added and scrimped, she couldn't make it work. The highway would take her customers away as surely as it now brought them to her, and the next storm would blow away whatever remained of her house. So far, she hadn't heard a word against women working in the Keys, but knew as soon as she hit the mainland, they would target her for stealing bread from a workingman's table. The Florida Keys seemed a tolerant place, all races welcomed for what they could bring. Even women worked here. Miami was out - streets strewn with garbage, men sleeping in bushes with nothing but swampland in their future.

When thoughts crowded her, she dove off the wharf, enjoying the watery oblivion, swimming with soaped clothing in the secret space that looked forbidding to outsiders but was as inviting as a spa bathtub to Elle, with a view unequaled in the entire world. Tangled root and Spanish moss framed the horizon, moon or sunrise, always accompanied by a bruised and violent sky. The murky appearance of the water helped keep strangers and tourists away.

In the narcotic buoyancy, Elle re-forged her affectionate bond with the little island and wild plans seeped back, always something to do with her cooking talents, her sole indisputable skill. Cat waited on the wharf, shadowing her on land as she swam and floated, moving from wharf to mangrove root to path. A little striped chick followed him, and Elle could've sworn she saw the two of them curled up together, waiting for her to slip out, nightdress plastered to her body.

After her swim, Elle pushed onto her skiff to towel off. Out of sight, on the other side of the wharf, Blanche's voice rose, then Nathan's unmistakable low twang. Men. Everywhere. She was sick of the sight and the sound and the smell of them.

Blanche's intimate tone told her this was a private conversation. Absent were her two signature tones: flattering breathiness or shrill command. That was Blanche–at your throat or at your feet. Elle's small skiff was tied out of sight behind a giant coral boulder and she was about to make her presence known, when Rimer's name came up. Curious, she made herself into a ball and lay down in the skiff, head below Blanche's sightline. If discovered, she would feign sleep. It wouldn't be the first time she slept in the open.

They were talking figures. How much per head. Two bucks for George Smith, *he actually enjoys cutting through rock.* Blanche said, *No one's worth more than a buck and a half.* Were they actually placing a bounty on the men's heads, men already paid by the Government?

"Threaten the backhoe guy. Rimer won't leave his side. We can't afford to lose either of them."

"I wouldn't worry about it. They're in tough straits. Besides, they don't have a clue."

"Have you seen the flying herons he carved? I can't believe we got him so cheap." Blanche squealed with glee. "I owe you," she said, the flirtatious lilt returning. Nathan laughed, then a long silence. Were they kissing?

Blanche sighed theatrically, then Nathan said, "Don't forget to write the booze in as beef. I'll get you five cases by Monday."

"Beef… booze. It's all just so confusing." Blanche's little girl voice nauseated Elle.

The two of them chuckled

"But it has to be in by next week…." Blanche said.

"Count on it, sweet cakes. One thing, I can only spare Jason for a week. He needs to be back on Pigeon Key before the boss is back."

"But I thought you were the boss?" She said, followed by a fake giggle.

Finally, Elle understood how Blanche got the most qualified men from the highway project. Nathan pocketed half what their labor was worth from Blanche and the men continued to be paid in full by the government.

From behind, Joe wheezed through his nose. How long had he been there? She tugged at the rope loudly, as if struggling to launch the skiff.

Blanche looked out, "Who's there?"

"What?" Elle said, as if she had been sleeping.

"You little snoop," Nathan turned towards her. "What the hell do you think You're doing."

"She's been here listening," from Joe, who came up from behind.

Blanche looked out, surprised to see Joe in the distance.

"What the devil are you doing here?" Blanche asked.

"Never know when I might come in handy. Right?" In his nervous laugh. Elle sensed trouble between them.

Elle grabbed her oars and pushed off from the wharf. As she left, she heard Blanche speak loud enough for her to hear.

"Just her, Brushy's slave," Blanche said, loud enough for Elle to hear.

"Better than Nathan's whore." But she said it to herself. The day would come when she would experience the exquisite pleasure of refusing Blanche Rowlands.

"Joe, come over. I want you to meet Nathan Foreman. He runs Pigeon Key, supervising the entire highway operation."

Elle set off loudly paddling, looking backward at Blanche at the apex of a triangle, a rapturous expression on her face. She watched too many movies, Elle thought. A tiny chick watched her from the wharf, confused and distraught, flapping his stumpy wings with so much panic that Elle almost returned for him. But he was already bouncing his way back home.

13

Three weeks before the party, Nathan Foreman escorted four men to take over the gigantic hydraulic ceiling fan operation to cool off the dance and dining room. Next were wall to wall carpets, a luxury Elle doubted anyone else had ever heard of.

Blanche treated Elle like a ghost, never acknowledging her presence. She would wait until someone else was in the room to avoid direct contact.

"Think of it. If anyone drops a glass, it won't break," Blanche said to Ree, holding the kitchen door open for Elle to hear them. But all Elle imagined were wine stains and ground-in gravies. At least with the old carpets, I could bring them outdoors to be doused. No, Elle thought, I won't regret losing this job.

Dinkson was off on a toot, but Elle doubted Blanche noticed.

From the kitchen window, Elle spotted Ruby lifting her long skirt to avoid tripping over a bloated root or construction debris. She dressed like she was from the previous century. Like my old aunt, Elle thought, though Ruby was close to her own age and definitely not over thirty. Something about her gait made Elle curious. This was more than avoiding roots - she was struggling, Behind her Nathan pushing her to move quicker.

Buster was selling her sandwiches on the road, because Ree was useless in the kitchen. She destroyed the casseroles Elle instructed her to make for dinner, so Elle was forced to oversee everything.

After the lunch dishes were dried and put away, Ree entered the kitchen.

"The Foreman guy asked for lunch. I think they're making some sort of costume. You should see the lace and the silk. Emerald green."

Ree was a mess. No manners at all. She blew her hair from her face with a sideways gesture that Elle found annoying.

"I'll make them something special and bring it in myself. A little surprise."

"Mrs. Rowlands said I should go, and no one else," Ree said.

"Gin? She wants her gin? Right."

Ree shrugged. Elle nodded, sliced a ham and some handmade cheese and cranked the flame, frying the two together on slices of white bread until the cheese oozed out the sides. "Tell them it's a croque monsieur."

"A crock-a what?"

"Just forget it." Elle took out a jelly ring of canned peaches from the icebox, then changed her mind and put it back. She arranged the sandwiches and a small side of celery and carrots, placed everything on a tray with sweet tea and filled a cut crystal bowl with ice chips and tongs.

"Be quick. You know how she feels about melted ice being a sign of slovenliness. Do you have far to go?" What didn't they want her to see?

"No, it's in a cabin."

"A far cabin?"

"Number 17. So, the ice should be okay if I go now."

"Tie your hair up for chrissakes. Stop blowin' it."

A few minutes later, Elle cut a third of the ring of jellied peaches on Blanche's favorite pink glass tray with three matching plates decorated with a raised pattern of dancing nymphs.

At Cabin 17, she knocked gently, then pushed it open. "My mistake," Elle said. "I forgot to give this to Ree."

Blanche snatched the stack of plates with such force that one smashed to the floor. Whatever they were doing must've been important because Blanche barred her passage into the room, obviously trying to hide Ruby from view. Ruby was in her underwear, partly draped in an unfurled bolt of emerald silk. Elle noticed bruises on Ruby's arms and legs. Far too many to be from falling. How many accidents could one woman have? Elle locked eyes with Ruby before Blanche slammed the door.

"You look like you saw a ghost," Ree said when Elle returned.

14

The sky turned by the time the dishes were done and Elle returned home to wait for Buster to get back from selling her lunches. The wind blew stronger, appearing out of nowhere, something she had gotten used to. By the time she made it to her chair, she felt the stiffness in her shoulders and busied herself by tidying the counter.

When Buster finally returned, the sky was thick and blackening.

"I'm sorry. The tire was flat, and I had to choose between the wagon and the sling table." Buster stared at the ground, thick eyelashes fluttering.

Elle had made the sling table herself. Genius hinges that folded down to nothing, holding the heavy pleated canvas in place, opening to a sturdy portable long table with a center rib for stability.

"You made the right choice," she said, wondering why he couldn't have stashed it in the wagon and brought them both back. Then she remembered his terror of storms since the Labor Day hurricane. He'd been with the soldiers when the train didn't arrive and never spoke of what he had seen or how he escaped. He remained silent when the men related stories of heroic deeds or near misses in the hurricane. The ones who lost the most often spoke the least.

"It's safe. I'll get it as soon as this passes." He looked up to the sky with a mock scared face. "I left it in a ditch right where the paving ends."

Elle imagined the table rolling in the storm, broken, parts blowing away. She paid Buster off quickly, and when he left, she looked up. The sky didn't look so dangerous, and the sunset was more than an hour away.

She walked her bicycle to the pathway, not bothering to stop when Art shouted something at her retreating form. She waved without hearing what he said.

Rain gusted sporadically, but if she rushed, she had a good chance of making it there and back before it picked up speed. The stronger the wind, the faster she moved, gusts battering her between sheets of rain, and she wondered if the table had already blown away. Still, she pressed on before the wind got worse. Crossing the furrowed pathway to the highway, Elle narrowly avoided a thick palm rib shooting through the air like a machete. She noticed a few bright gray roof shingles littering the pathway, but no houses were in the vicinity and they hadn't taken on the amorphous gray brown of the aged objects in the tropics.

As she crossed the wooden bridge, a powerful gust practically lifted her bike off the ground, throwing a shock of terror through her. Were tornadoes forming? Wind blew from all directions so she took advantage when she could, practically flying in the gusts now coming her way, enjoying the sense of release and the thrill of fear between thunder, wind and lightning strikes close by.

At the end of the paved road, the path turned to muck, and another aggressive gale sucked her bike a few inches off the ground, the gusts more frequent. She crossed the road slated for paving because she didn't remember asking which side he had stashed the table.

A woven mat lay in the middle of the road, but when she bent to retrieve it, it circled up and away, out of reach. She could barely walk against the wall of wind. Lightning struck less than five seconds after thunder, which told her how close it was and how stupid she was to attempt to rescue a pile of metal and timber. A blueprint formed in her mind of just how simple it would be to make another table and she almost turned back, but now the wind was steadily against her and she would be the tallest object on the bridge. Her best bet was to hurry down the hill on the other side of the road and seek cover in the heavily treed distance. Once across, Elle made out stacks of timber too orderly to have been uprooted by the storm. With a sickening realization, the sky turned the same telltale shade of green that preceded the Labor Day hurricane.

Something strange was behind the pile of trees, a large boxy building. Fighting against the muscle of wind, a large cluster of red palm fruits barely missed her shoulder. The winds picked up, threatening to turn anything not tacked down into projectiles. Between gusts, she made progress. Hands clamped on her bicycle, she finally arrived at the building. The front door had an ominous padlock on a heavy chain, so Elle went around to the back. A splayed lock lay on the cement stoop. When she entered, the wide, empty expanse resembled a warehouse. Something moved and Elle feared a door or window had let something in, but this was more like a footstep.

"Elle. What the hell?" Rimer sounded relieved. "You're soaking wet," he said. His voice bounced around the vast room. Elle leaned her bicycle against a wall. Glass panes and lumber leaned against one wall, a large stack of clay roof tiles against the other.

"What is this place?" Elle asked. "And what are you doing here? You don't work on the road."

"Let me guess," he said. "Is this what you're looking for?" He pointed to the sling table by the door.

It took a moment before Elle realized Rimer had found it. Did he actually go in search of it? But she didn't want to ask, afraid it was true and afraid it wasn't true at the same time.

"I know how much you need this and before you ask, yes, I overheard Buster and came to find it."

"Oh, you didn't have to..." her voice trailed off as he moved toward her.

"I wanted to, Elle." He seemed to struggle to continue and then, as if reaching some conclusion, went on, his voice steady and assured. "Precious little I can do for you, a man in my position and you already making your own way, after what happened."

"And what would that be?" she asked.

"Losing your husband, I mean," he said. "It's hard enough to..." Elle looked away, and he stopped talking, probably thinking it was too painful to talk about Billy when Elle really didn't want to hear or say his name ever again.

"Thank you, but really it was stupid to look for it in this storm," He raised his eyebrows, and said, "uh huh," but that came out all wrong because when talk of Billy threatened, she always stumbled over her words in haste to stop the talk. Everyone knew something about how mean Billy was. And if they didn't, she didn't want to tell them. She wanted to pretend she had hardly known him before he disappeared. There was usually a silence when his name was mentioned, everyone thinking it must evoke anguish for Elle before moving to their own traumatic memories of the storm that killed brothers, families, friends, and fellow soldiers.

The large unfinished room created eerie reverberations when they spoke. The wind screeched intermittently, causing him to raise his voice and move closer. "Looks like you'll have to put up with my company for a while longer," he said, and handed her a clean cloth from his pocket.

Elle noticed his long-tapered fingers and the swell of his forearms. She towelled her wet hair, then her arms, and between her breasts, conscious of him watching.

As if sensing her thoughts, he turned away.

"Can I ask you something? Are you related to Art?"

Rimer had a habit of making a soft half-laugh before answering, as if he found the world quietly amusing. "No, we met in the war. He saved my life in Italy and I ran into him by chance a few years back. We met at the march to Washington to demand the bonus they promised us for our service. The Government owes us each $500, and we needed it badly. Anyhow, Art and I got rooms together, to save money."

"Did you ever get the money?" Elle asked.

"Hah. What do you think?"

The two of them carried themselves so differently. Art's face was a never-ending kaleidoscope of barely suppressed emotion and Rimer, ironic and unreadable.

"I know it wasn't your idea to work at No Name and leave the highway project. That's why I thought he might be family."

He smiled and lifted his eyebrows, probably acknowledging that she would be justified in thinking him a fool for sticking his neck out for his friend.

There was nowhere comfortable to sit in the empty concrete room, so Rimer grabbed a couple of quilted tarps used to transport glass and folded them into quarters. "Might as well relax. Don't think we'll be leaving anytime soon." He smiled a gorgeous, white-toothed grin that seemed to come from the center of his being, making him appear certain and peaceful and generous all at once.

"Is Art here?"

Again, his breathy laugh, "I get some time off," he said and because he found her question amusing, so did she and settled into the quilted seat and the sense of being somewhere out of time that he always somehow summoned.

They crouched on their haunches, then sat back and she remembered this is what desire felt like. It had been so long, this nervousness coupled with intrigue and hyper-interest in his every word and movement. She hadn't been alone with a man in ages. Instinctively, she felt for her knife and the impulse confused her. Rimer was safe. He was a good man. She had no reason to think otherwise, but the knife gave her a feeling of substance.

"I have one too," he said, having caught her motion.

"You would be faster than me," she said.

He held a palm out to her, and she placed her hand in it. Warmth and tension surged through her arm as he bent over to kiss her. "I've wanted you to do that for a long time," she said, leaning in. She held the back of his neck, giving herself up to the soft luxury, hearing a low moan and realizing it came from her. Or was it his sound? Her monthlies were over a few days ago, and she knew she was planning to see this through. Why not? Both of them looked to the windows, each catching the other, understanding they shared the same impulse and fear.

He leaned closer into her, his hand at the small of her back reminding her she was a woman. Then he straightened and took out a tobacco pouch, leaving Elle to open her eyes. Yes, he was a gentleman.

"We don't have to be hasty," he said. "Where are you from?"

But Elle was not interested in conversation. He was a very good-looking man despite the clothes he wore. His classic features and especially his smile and single dimple would shine through a clown suit, Elle thought.

"Where are you from?" he repeated. "I mean, where did you grow up?"

"The moon," she answered, pulling him toward her. The hell with waiting.

"Funny girl," he said, breaking the spell of longing.

Elle straightened up, but she wasn't ashamed, just disappointed, then she settled in. She had never been overly fond of conversation, but it seemed to be what he wanted.

"Boston."

"Like you said, the moon," he laughed, and Elle almost reached for him. It seemed the natural end of the discussion. But he moved a bit farther away and reaching for an embrace became too awkward to contemplate.

"I want more than this," he said, shaking his head and pointing to the folded blankets.

Elle wanted to say she thought it was an excellent start, but was tired of the lighthearted teasing.

"Tell me about Billy," he said. "Is he really dead and gone? Officially?"

"Storm took him," Elle said.

"So, you're free?"

"Of a man," she responded, thinking about her bondage to the Rowlandses. "And you?"

"What do you mean?" he looked at her sharply, flustered, the first time she had seen him that way. "I'm not bound to a man. I'm looking to have a family. A wife. I'm tired of being alone."

"Is that what this is? You're just tired of being alone."

"Well, aren't you? Two people have a better chance. Like a small company. We could have children." His smile disappeared. He looked confused. Elle realized he had been thinking about this for a long time.

"I know nothing about you," she said.

"Well, what would you like to know? He asked.

"Tell me about the march on Washington. I heard they shot at the men, burned the tents they camped in…"

He began. Looking relieved, he settled in closer to her on the quilted tarps. "Well, we never saw the cash. Maybe they're hoping we'll be dead by the time it's due in 1945, but some of us found a way to survive. In my case, building the overseas highway…."

Yah, with Art by your side, Elle thought, finally understanding why there was no urgency to his kiss. And although she should be flattered by the deference he paid her, she had never wanted children. A sickening flash of the old longing she felt for Billy intruded, completely obliterating her desire for Rimer. Lust seemed more complicated and meaningful than she wanted, his reaction so different from the way he presented himself and the wry joker she had found so appealing. She wanted something between Billy's lustful brutality and Rimer's dry partnership and was relieved to sit back and listen as he spoke about the march and a different sort of betrayal.

"When we were forced to leave our tents, a parade formed on the pathway and we thought it was in our honor and clapped and cheered. Then we saw our own military attack us, with bayonets, infantry marching behind the cavalry-armored tanks even," Rimer stopped, his anger drained.

"Tell the story," Elle said. "I want to hear it." He spoke until the storm wearied and the room was silent.

Maybe she could do this, and she wanted to tell him yes. He would be wonderful company, and probably a doting father. They could join forces and negotiate a life together. It could work, they wouldn't be the first. Finally, renewed, the storm passed, and it was time to return to No Name.

"You go first," Elle said. "You have more to lose than me."

15

This new group of engineers laughed, drank a lot, and slept until mid-morning, trusting the workers to carry out plans as instructed, and the pavilion skeleton formed at warp speed. Tensions on No Name slackened. The atmosphere changed, the bugs bit less, and only Elle's workload remained the same. Buster came in handy, helping more than she expected. He was pleasant, someone she would have liked as a nephew, a thick-lashed, blithe faced boy who bore no one any ill-will, an attitude Elle found both enchanting and annoying, depending on her mood.

They carted debris off daily and dumped into the swampland around No Name. Workers cat-walked around the scaffolding; the weird Italianate dome rose ever higher, finally dwarfing the main building.

On the wharf, Elle caught Rimer, Buster and Ree chuckling after hours. "Well, it's only the truth. Looks like a giant mushroom," Buster said.

"Or a rocket ship," Ree said, joining in.

"I know what it really looks like, but wouldn't say it around a lady like yourself." Rimer winked at Elle, and she laughed out loud, her mind melding with his.

Once Elle saw the pavilion through Rimer's eyes, she couldn't deny the resemblance to an oversized penis.

Elle liked how Rimer was always quick with a comment that synched perfectly with whatever discussion, and delivered with overstated politeness, finding a second, deeper undercurrent of meaning and calling it out. In the company of women, he came alive. Although he was tall, he didn't stoop when he entered a room, unlike the gangly Art with skin perennially red and peeling. Although the two of them appeared similar when Elle first met them, Rimer glowed in the heat, while Art peeled. Rimer pronounced him, "too fair for Florida," and somehow the comment stuck in the worst way. The same sun that boiled color from Art's eyeballs and burned his skin, tanned Rimer's face and forearms a rich caramel. He looked the image of a soldier from the Civil War, something deeper always threatening to break surface.

Since the storm, Elle hadn't sought him out. A more fatalistic vision had replaced the sense of urgency, as if Rimer had suggested something criminal. She watched him intently, but always from a distance, searching for some clue just beyond reach.

Elle found it impossible to sleep during nights that seemed like brief pauses between duties. She banished Cat from the cot and moved outside, which provided a few nights of relief, until the moon bore a hole through her eyelids.

A few days after the storm, Buster stopped by. "Don't know how he did it," he said. "They actually gave Rimer a raise." Elle knew Blanche never paid more once she got you in her clutches. "He said to give you this. I think it's a heron." The small carving had legs narrower than toothpicks, an impossibly sculpted head and perfect feathery tracings, but to Elle it looked like a stork; she could almost see the blanket with a baby in its beak.

Rimer was tired of wandering. He was sending a message.

The odor in Elle's cottage was worse today, like moldering vomit. After Buster left, she investigated a damp area behind the kitchen cabinets and scraped a discolored cement block and wondered if the walls were crumbling and in danger of toppling. The best she could do is sell it to the Rowlandses, though the idea sickened her.

She almost headed out to see Rimer, preparing a speech in her head, a way to tell him, yes, she would go. But not yet. She had time. Instead, Elle took out her flip knife and kneeled beside a discolored cinder block, tapping with the handle, searching for flaws in the joinery. A moldy patch crumbled slightly under her blade and she hoped it was a shallow weakness she could cut out and repair.

She settled on her haunches and sawed away methodically, imagining a life with Rimer and the children he wanted. At least two, he said. Maybe she would enjoy motherhood. A pile of concrete dust formed. Children could wait. She knew how to prevent pregnancy. A rope of vine peeked halfway through the grout all the way through, tentacled between cracks in the cement, but she couldn't quite reach it, so she stabbed harder and felt something dislodge. When she moved outside to locate it, she realized the stalk had snaked into the thatched roof, exploiting and enlarging weakness in the structure. That's what caused the eerie whistling above her whenever the wind picked up. One more storm would take it out.

She thought of her life now as a careful tread along a narrow pathway to a watery descent. So long as she looked straight ahead, she might escape a slip that would only reveal its treachery when it was too late. She knew enough of darkness not to glance sideways, to see the faces that wished her to fall. Because someone had fooled her once, it didn't mean she would be fooled again.

16

A two-man saw was brought in to cut vegetation around the lodge and stumps removed by hand to form a wide pathway to the wharf. When Elle asked what was going on, Buster said Blanche wanted the land to be "... more orderly, is how she put it."

Black iron poles topped with giant caps of red, pink and white swirled glass flanked the newly formed pathway from the wharf to the lodge. Blanche called them her Venetian streetlamps. "Aren't they magnificent?" she asked everyone. The large wraparound porch was laid with slippery pink marble tiles that destroyed the welcoming, workaday feel of the lodge.

Mountains of glass arrived, protected in wooden pallets, and a hive of glaziers followed to do the work. The sound inside the lodge became deafening as the glass went up. A solid week of yelling orders left Elle with ringing ears. One evening, a sudden flash blinded her. Blanche was curled around an elaborate lamp post, head tossed, black eyes shrouded, and Buster yelling, "Yes! Yes, that."

Blanche planned to line the pathway with the blood red carpet and light the lamps as the party guests arrived. "Can't you just see it?" Elle heard her say to a frightened-looking passenger disembarking from the ferry. But all Elle wanted to see was Rimer. Erotic dreams had assailed her and left her sad and depleted. Once she spotted Rimer in indigo shadow under a shard of moon, sluicing into water off the dock, but when she moved to join him, she caught sight of Art dangling his feet off the wharf, watching.

Three weeks before the party, when Blanche's formal notes of acceptance trickled back, she was so excited that she tossed an invitation to Elle. A line drawing of Blanche swooning, her black gloved hand holding a cat's eye mask, the lamp and unfurled red carpet in the background like a setting sun. Lacy black photo corners held the invitation in place, black text shadowed in red. Just missing the background of scrub brush, Elle wanted to say, annoyed at how exquisite they were.

My Venetian Valentine
Private Masquerade at No Name Key Lodge
Costume party
Billy & the Wailers
Olandis direct from Italy
16-piece orchestra – dance pavilion reveal
See the stars from widow's walk atop the Venetian dance pavilion
Midnight rumble surprise
Dance contest
Best Costume award
Grand prize top-secret drawing

Back in the kitchen, Elle shut the door against chaos in the lodge. She pressed, folded and stacked linen, sorted a mountain of plates, numbered and dated cans of meat and vegetables. She polished the stove enamel and swept the floor, not exiting the kitchen until scrubbing it end-to-end. The only decoration she allowed was a timer in the shape of a chicken, a pegleg windup clock, as practical as it was decorative, a gift from previous owners, and a drawing Sheila made for her of a hodgepodge of animals and objects swirling around center vortex that only allowed a single flower to enter. The girl was a genius, Elle thought, although Sheila's fondness for booze prevented Elle from having her in the kitchen full time.

The Dinkson's were useless, one with her head under a car hood, the other sleeping off a bender, leaving Elle to wonder what they had on Blanche. Buster brought some relief, his wide-eyed trust in the world a balm against chaos. Sometimes, she would test him. "There she goes again," Elle would say about a ridiculous outfit Blanche was wearing. "Black, in this heat?" And he would say something about how most women look good in black, which was true but beside the point. So, when she was in a low mood, she said nothing at all, refusing to be cajoled into his depressingly cheerful universe. Rimer sometimes eyed her hungrily with something in his stare that resembled lust, but was just a little off. But she did not trust her instincts. The only man she'd ever known was Billy. And Jim, she thought, the boat captain who took her to Matecumbe when pretended to look for Billy's body. Was she wrong about Rimer? Was he just elusive?

She caught sight of Brushy here and there, mostly speaking to men on the job, but his heart wasn't in his work. That was plain to Elle. He had lost the look of deliberation she remembered, the way he once confidently inserted his opinion, asked or not. Now he observed thoughtfully, rarely commenting. Something had changed from when he was a shadow on his own property. Why hadn't he called a halt to the entire project? Did he have something else in mind? One morning Elle passed a man docking a canoe and was surprised it was Brushy, who finally stopped dying his hair. He worked the paddle with the deliberate motion of someone more fit than she remembered him to be.

She almost followed him, but Monty arrived with a large box of canned goods and a side of beef for the party, so Elle headed to the dock to help. "All that money down the drain," she said.

"You know Pauline Hemingway ordered a Venetian chandelier. I brought it in on the ferry."

"Ah," said Elle. That explained Blanche's party theme. She must've caught wind of the chandelier and thought it would tempt, or at least annoy Pauline. To encourage ferocious competition, Blanche spread rumors that a car would be the grand prize for best costume.

"The idea of the car happened on the fly, after the Hemingway's said no to her invitation. That's when she got Julius Stone."

"How do you know he's coming?" Elle asked.

"I heard them on the boat. They wanted me to hear, hoping I'll tell everyone," Monty said.

"Well, it worked. Workers asking if he's really coming even though none had even heard of him before this," Elle said.

Stone, always up for a splash, wouldn't promise not to attend Hemingway's party, but Elle doubted they had invited him. Papa, as Hemingway was affectionately known, hated government men and had written an important article exposing the Government for letting the old soldiers drown in the Labor Day storm.

That evening Elle was called in to make a special dinner for the engineers. As she poured wine, Blanche turned to Brushy and said, "I'm bringing a secret celebrity guest and you'll never guess who."

When he responded by downing the entire glass of wine, she continued. "Hmmm, let me see," she said, "Are his initials JS?" But her attempt at light-heartedness failed, her voice was too high and Brushy refused to engage. He stared at a spot behind Blanche, and Elle stared back, noticing he had let his hair grow out into a thick gray and black mane that was surprisingly curly.

"Oh, let them gossip," Blanche said, desperately cheerful. Polite smiles from the engineers and Brushy's silence ruined the moment.

Elle wanted to flee, acutely aware of Brushy's discomfort. He was leaner, no longer the pompous man of the world she remembered. Something was shifting.

"Did you see the carpet? Or don't you care about that, either? Blanche said to Brushy.

That was the last thing Elle heard before gathering plates and exiting. Brushy found her in the kitchen. "Fantastic dinner," he said. "Are you testing out the party fare? Because if you are..." he began.

"If you are, you'll have to do better," Blanche spoke from behind. Then she moved and looked to Brushy for affirmation. But Brushy said, "It was perfect. Delicious." He smiled at Elle and placed a hand on Blanche's shoulder to move her out of the way, a touch that was not quite a shove.

Blanche turned to Elle, her back stiff. "Do the Waldorf tomorrow and a pitcher of cosmos. Seven o'clock sharp."

"She's off Sundays" Brushy responded, and it surprised Elle that he was on top of the situation. Not like the old Brushy, who took no interest in the workaday domestic schedules.

When Buster was co-opted to clean out the abandoned guest cottages, Elle said, "Don't toss out the iceboxes, bring them to me and I'll give you extra." Within a week, Elle had three more zinc iceboxes. Her stash of cash was growing, and she struck a deal with

Monty. Evenings she smoked ham or beef on her property, as she discovered men could not resist anything smoked. Elle found packets of neglected seeds and planted them: parsley, basil, and a few exotics she didn't recognize. Tendrils spiked out of the dirt, as if they recognized home turf, growing squat and thick within the week. The tiny plants gave her a measure of peace, something no one else had a hand in creating.

Time passed in a haze of activity. Invitations trickled back, sewing machines hummed, and the air was thick with the acrid stench of paint and kerosene to fuel everything. The men were exhausted, many with eyes like milk glass from working in full sun. Work was wrapping up, men sent away with a five or ten-dollar bill in an envelope, until Blanche ran out of envelopes and refused to use the good linen ones.

17

Two weeks before the party, Elle prepared for her early morning swim and someone opened her gate before she got to it. She hoped it was Rimer. Instead, Brushy strode in and she tried to hide her disappointment. He must assume she would welcome his visit.

"I don't know how long I can keep this up." He sniffed the air but was too polite to mention the putrid smell of mold. Instead, he lit a cigarette and turned to her as if she were a confidante.

"Well, good morning to you, too," Elle said. "And by the way, I don't know what you're talking about." Let him spell it out, she thought.

"I'm sorry, if I'm disturbing you," he said. "We all have our problems, and the last thing you need is to hear mine." He looked embarrassed, and she felt bad for him, despite his wealth, something she tried hard to suppress.

"I don't know what your wife sees in this place, if that's who you mean," Elle said, emboldened by his despair and the knowledge that she would no longer be working for him. When Brushy nodded in agreement, she continued. "She makes no sense to me, especially the way she dresses." She pretended to hold up a glass of wine or a martini, her back straight, an inane smile plastered on her face. "And if you want this place for storage or servants' quarters, I'm willing to sell you my cistern."

"You're leaving?"

"We all know how much I'll be missed, but yes, I'm going."

"But where?"

She shook her head. "I don't owe you my plans."

"Well, ok then, out you go."

It took Elle a minute to realize he was imitating his wife. He rose, tossed his head back, imitating Blanche's gestures perfectly. Elle gasped and when he sat back down and when he pulled at an imaginary tie under his chin, Elle could see it and knew they shared an intimate portrait of Blanche in an absurd hat, complicated dress and high-heeled shoes.

He took in a breath and looked like he wanted to tell her something important.

"My offer stands. Triple pay so long as you're willing to put up with things."

"Oh, for god's sake, I've already agreed."

Something shuffled outside her door. "I really can't take much more of her," he said.

"Listen," she said. The noise was coming closer. "It's a lizard. Maybe a rat - or maybe your shadow."

"Yes, I better go. This isn't finished." He reached for her hand and squeezed it, and when they both saw an opalescent fish-scale flake off, she tried to pull out of his grasp, but he held on and looked into her eyes with tenderness.

"Will you keep an eye on things for me?"

"I'm nobody's spy," she said, "And if I were, it would cost you more than a few dollars a week."

"What do you want?" He asked.

"Everything. I want everything." Where had that come from?

"Yes, Theda Bara," he said.

Elle smiled, though she had no idea who Theda Bara was. Brushy would revert to form but she'd be secure until the party, earning triple. Elle wanted him to leave before she was tempted to tell him she had other plans. She decided to find Rimer and tell him that yes, she'd leave with him. Together, they could carve out a life together.

Brushy gave a strange look that she didn't recognize, as if neither of them was actually who they appeared to be. His gaze dropped to Elle's hands. Her fingertips were red from making croquettes.

"How did you make your fortune?" Elle asked out of nowhere. She vaguely remembered something about steel, but couldn't remember the details.

"It's an old, tired story," he said. "I'll save it for the party."

"This one?"

"And the next, and the next after that."

Elle laughed. "How 'bout you tell me the real one? What really happened?"

Brushy took in a deep breath, waved his hand dismissively, and sat down. He looked exhausted, defeated. "Blanche never loved me," he said, then waited for her response.

"Come on, you knew what she was after." She fixed her eyes on him, tired of humoring his delusions.

"You're right, of course," he said. "I made a poor bargain."

Elle thought of Billy, and how she believed he would rescue her from a life of serfdom. "You're no different from the rest." She didn't like the sound of her own voice. And was she different? Didn't she just want some notion of a life that Rimer could offer?

Then she remembered she had left with Billy in a similar way, never asking if she loved him, never feeling she had a choice.

"But you're the mystery," Brushy said. "Who is Elle, formerly Elle Woodman? And what does *she* want?"

She was aware of a sudden reckless impulse to tell him everything that happened to Billy. And she was never tempted to confide in Rimer.

Would he understand she was the avenger? That she had done it for the world? Would anyone see the line of dogs unkicked, the women who wouldn't be hit, the bruises that would never form because she had absorbed it all for them? Because she did the dirty work.

Brushy's question helped her define a story she hadn't known existed. In the instant he asked, her history appeared whole and pulsing and painfully contained within herself. Like a swollen genie trapped inside a tiny lamp.

18

Ten days before the party, a worker pulled back the tarp covering the poured concrete foundation and there was no mistaking his shock. A spider web of cracks betrayed the incompetence of previous efforts to level the concrete base.

The head guy put a hand on Blanche's shoulder, squeezed it and made a comment Elle didn't catch, but she heard the strained sound of the men's off-key laughter, and an intense discussion followed.

Within the hour, a furious pace of work began, and Elle forced to prepare even greater quantities of food that left her limp and sleep deprived. More men arrived, co-opted from the highway project.

When Art requested a particular auger to get through caprock, Nathan said, "How about we just do it the old-fashioned way," and handed mattocks to the men. "Half an hour each, then the next group. Before you know it, the hole will be right." No one dared grumble, but shrouded looks told the story of talented men doing work usually reserved for chain gangs. "We're all in this together," Nathan repeatedly said, a hated phrase always recognized for the lie it was.

Progress was rapid, yet felt painfully slow. Mornings, ragged clothing hung on tree branches to dry. "Rinse it well before soaping," Elle told the group. "God's sakes, man."

Clothes dried stiffly in the sun, particles of cement baked into the fibers so within an hour of wearing, it was sweat-softened and remained that way until they removed it in the evening. Elle caught a couple of men looking much like statues, unrecognizable when the cement dust dried.

This new group of specialists brought in cement with an 'instant cure time' according to the head architect, whom Elle swore was wearing elevator shoes that made him unsteady and gave him a sinister and untrustworthy appearance.

A giant sun-shaped base formed the tower foundation, and within days scaffolding went up and a wooden skeleton erected at breakneck speed. Evenings, a gigantic spotlight illuminated men working long after Elle had taken breakfast orders and left for bed. Over the rest of the week, it seemed the ferries operated solely to convey construction supplies and workers to the lodge.

As quickly as they arrived, engineers and helpers departed, bitter words in the air between them on one side and Blanche and Nathan on the other. Money, plans, shortcuts all tossed into a hotpot of accusations, no one listening to the other. Monty's expression ranged between detachment and amiability, as he dispatched the casualties onto the ferry out, always helpful, a perfect sounding board for the journey back to Miami. Only when the wounded party reached their destination did they realize they had learned exactly nothing from Monty. His singular, true talent.

Within a week, new floors were installed and a giant water fountain teetered in front of the lodge with more cursing because no one could figure out how to make it work. A lone cherub rolled onto the ground, as if tossed from paradise, his chubby feet pointing to the heavens in despair.

Occasionally, Brushy sought refuge in Elle's kitchen, downing shots of whiskey in the pantry. "I better get that divorce quick before she tears down the entire place, and builds the goddamn Taj Mahal." Brushy said to Elle in a desperate need to blow off steam. He wiped his mouth with the back of his hand.

"I'll let you know when I hear…" What she wanted to say was *the swish of her broomstick.* Instead, she said, "her coming," then discreetly closed the door behind him. "Here she comes, the queen of No Name Key," Elle would say quietly to whoever was near, because by then, no one liked Blanche.

The place was a curiosity on the coconut telegraph circuit. Boats slowed and entire hulls filled with raised binoculars, and now the ferry landed so often it seemed to be part of a sightseeing excursion. Blanche bore the gawkers no resentment, not understanding they were making fun of her. "Elle, make the group a nice luncheon," she would say.

"I guess lunch is not fancy enough for her," Elle said to Ree. "She wants a *luncheon.*"

Blanche left invitations lying around, face down and labeled *Private Party,* making it irresistible for strangers to flip them over.

19

Rain fell steadily throughout the morning of the party. Occasionally, the sun teased through, making Blanche's mood even more bitter when the sky darkened, and a fresh deluge began. By late afternoon, the white capes Blanche insisted party staff wear were drying on porch railings. Dye from the streamers had ruined a few shirts and the fantastical paper flower bouquets and corsages destroyed. Between rain bursts, water drooled from window sills and railings. When the rain inevitably picked up, it soaked what little soil sat above the fossilized coral on No Name. Soon, the pathway became a maze of muddy pools that would take days to drain.

Elle watched the boats arrive, sporting tarps that served as communal rain-bonnets. Most guests gave up hiding their identities, clutching totes, suitcases and hat boxes with their costumes. A couple in bright green leotards wore rubber boots and carried sequined shoes and plumed hats. They were so careful of protecting them, their masks slipped, and heavy makeup ran down their faces, staining their costumes. Blanche looked annoyed because she'd requested everyone remain anonymous.

A small group of powdered, frilled and feathered women were the first to disembark, sprinting off the dock in between thunder cracks. Seconds later, a shock of lightning struck something remarkably close by, and a large man slipped on the pathway, his backside covered in muck as he struggled to rise. By the time Monty reached him, two more had joined him. "He pulled me down," one of them said. When Elle arrived to help, Monty was bent over, blocking a punch, barely able to remain upright. "He did it on purpose," the third guy said, and the smirk on the big guy's face proved his point.

Waves made docking complicated and tedious and Joe ran around with a large brass bell yelling "hear ye hear ye," getting his eras jumbled in an infuriating attempt to amuse. By then, all everyone wanted was safe shelter.

The orchestra had arrived the day before, and spent the morning setting up in Blanche's idea of Renaissance dress, all wearing white breeches, then powdered over to give the appearance of statues. Blanche's orders were "no movement," unless playing a carefully curated list of music.

"Play louder," she screamed at the orchestra, as if they could drown out the storm. They were already sweating in heavy white makeup while the hired help, dressed as jesters, somersaulted and cartwheeled their way to the wharf to help guests with their cases. Thunder and lightning drowned out the melody, as Monty headed out with a single pathetic umbrella, shrugging his shoulders, trying to make light of the disaster. "Mother Nature always ready to blow your wig," he laughed at the double entendre. He chose the oldest woman in the group, handed her the lone umbrella and carried her down the water-logged pathway while others looked on, unamused. "Wait here," he yelled over his shoulder, but they had already begun the trudge to the lodge, following close behind. "Like I said, follow me."

As lightning forked in the sky, Monty said, "Someone very important is ticked off they didn't get an invitation." Again, no one laughed. When he spied Elle, he whispered, "Get someone down here and hand everyone a drink the minute they dock. Hurry."

Once inside, Monty whispered to the musicians, and they switched from a ballad to some serious jazz until Blanche gave them a look, and it was back to a dull tune.

Rimer and Art emerged from nowhere and placed plywood planks over the worst of the flooded pathway. Both men were soaked through, Art's huge ears acting as a water reservoir, dripping a steady stream onto his shirt. Monty rounded up a few more umbrellas, but they were no match for the tempest. Guests with dripping feathers, melting makeup, blurred beauty marks looked like the morning after a night of unspeakable debauchery.

"What are children doing here?" Elle asked, and Monty told her a hardware magnate from New Orleans refused to come without them. A tall, thin man in a black suit and zebra mask pushed a young couple out of the way, almost causing them to slip on the wharf. Two large, terrified dogs and a parrot in a gilded cage arrived and all tried to cram through the lodge door, knocking over a hurricane lamp and shattering glass at the entryway. Buster spotted the scene and discretely swept up the mess, kneeling out of the way of the crowd and dumping the shards into the bin so expertly the line was never interrupted. Someone cursed, something about a shoe lost in the mud, a jeweled mask overboard and Elle tuned it all out, anxiously counting trays of pressed carnival glass plates crowding her long table. Plans to use the outdoor prep area fell apart. Now everything had to be made in the tiny kitchen, a room Blanche hadn't thought important enough to renovate, not understanding how to run a successful lodge.

Somehow Buster helped guests, yet remained dry and tidy. "Elle," he said, "give me those. We'll store them in the icehouse until it's time."

When he returned, he told Elle that water had pooled around the tower foundation. But that was outside and shouldn't affect the stability. Still, she checked the door was locked to the inner tower staircase that spiraled to the top and led to Blanche's showy Widow's Walk. The staff was threatened with instant dismissal if anyone entered the stairwell. Earlier in the week, Art and Rimer had leaned a tall ladder against the tower to board windows from the outside because the glass didn't fit. The inner spiral staircase had to be reinstalled because Blanche insisted on mahogany stairs. Time spent reinforcing supports to accommodate the extra weight ignited Brushy's rage and Elle remembered how angry Blanche was when the mahogany stairs arrived a day before the party. Too many workmen had crowded inside the narrow tower to replace the lightweight plywood with the heavier, oiled mahogany, constructing custom wall supports on the fly. Incredibly, they finished the job the morning of the party.

As the evening progressed, boats crowded the dock. Where would everyone stay? The cabins were small, many privately owned. They planned on sleeping fifty guests at most, the rest departing, but no one could leave in the storm and Elle stopped counting at 147 guests. "Either she didn't think anyone would come or she's an idiot," Elle whispered to Buster.

"Both, actually," and this time, Buster nodded.

Blanche stood in the doorway in her Harlequin gown, one of three outfits specially made for the party. She squeezed Brushy's shoulder, a shadow of triumph in her eyes, on her red lips. "They came. They all came," she said, misty eyed. But all Elle saw was a room of rich people, whispering angrily in wet clothing, drying their hair and enjoying the spectacle of a woman about to become a social ruin.

Brushy made a break for the ice shack where he had stashed a supply of good whisky and told Elle to hide it "from the teeming hordes," and when she placed it in the cupboard, she laughed to find a bottle of rum labeled "Buzz's Rum! Keep Your Grubby Hands Off!" behind a brass water pitcher.

Giant cornucopias of out-of-season fruits, cheese and grapes, an unheard-of luxury, were already on the long guest tables. Elle imagined they would have to eat in staggered groups, *get the ham, get the beef, get the eggs.* Sheila, the previous owner's niece, had returned to help.

Elle ordered the staff to serve drinks without pause. Monty changed into an innkeeper costume and mixed cocktails and highballs in the new teak and brass bar and Buster, designated runner, gathered a competent staff to bus tables and clean ashtrays. But even his finely attuned eyes couldn't keep up with the carnage. Defeated, he left bottles of wine and rum on the tables for guests to serve themselves.

Somehow the party began, the storm adding to the drama, darkness providing cover for stolen kisses and groping. The room vibrated like a broken tape in a majestic theater, reels of the grand movie houses, lightning flashes catching static movements, hands where they shouldn't be, each strike setting an image. Hurricane lamps lit small slices of the room, flickering flames illuminating gold and ruby lamp oil. White makeup and red lips took on an eerie horror movie look as night closed in.

When Elle left to survey the room, she caught Blanche unlocking the door to the tower, unable to resist showing off the custom-built staircase to the top. Elle spotted the New Orleans hardware king and his arthritic wife emerge from the tower, looking annoyed and shaken, but you would never know it by Blanche's smug expression. Before appetizers were served, Blanche ushered Rimer back into the tower, likely pointing out some flaw, as if he didn't have enough to do.

Had they climbed the staircase all the way to the Widow's Walk? Blanche loved spreading the rumor about the lodge having the tallest building on the Lower Keys, although Elle knew better.

"Quick. Gather up the bowls," Elle ordered the waiters, heading out with trays of consommé. Light from a ruby hurricane lamp illuminated Blanche shooing two workers away, her smile full and hard.

Elle summoned all the staff to the kitchen and put them in fresh aprons if they had time on their hands. She re-plated the Waldorf salad, cutting portions in half. "Bring these out with the soup as if we're offering a choice. Keep an eye out for cutlery, get it to the kitchen and wash it immediately. We don't have enough."

Blanche silenced the orchestra and moved onto the stage, her heavy tap shoes echoing, announcing her importance to the crowd. "And now, "she said. "I have a treat, Florida's very own visionary." Heavy brocade curtains parted to reveal a small, tidy man in a tight tux. "Meet the incredible Julius Stone, architect of the rebirth of Key West and soon- all the Florida Keys."

Elle made it out of the kitchen in time to hear Julius say something about the future of the Florida Keys as a mecca for tourism, ending with calling the crowd the "seers of America" to a round of tepid applause. He shushed the crowd. "We're well on our way to recreate Key West as The Bermuda of Florida." Blanche rose and clapped, hoping to stop the speech. Blanche hated any reference to Key West and must have warned Stone not to mention it. On cue, Stone nodded at her and continued, "So my advice to you all is… secure your spot right here at No Name Key Lodge while you still have time. And remember, you heard it here first. With the gracious Blanche Rowlands leading the charge, this beautiful spot, with the best sports fishing in the world and a state-of-the-art highway being built, will soon be known far and wide as the new frontier to paradise."

His small, balding head glowed red under the lights when he bowed, and this time the audience clapped. "And now I give you the world famous Fernando Orlandis, introducing his brand-new song, the Italian Tango for the first time ever. Here at the exclusive No Name Key Lodge!"

The lights dimmed, music stopped, and a sole violin let out a mournful lingering strain. A solitary spotlight illuminated Blanche Rowlands in a red bolero jacket and complicated bias-cut, checkerboard gown in red, white and black. Sequins glittered under a single spotlight when she tossed off the jacket. She turned from the audience to face Stone and the back of her gown was so low cut, her tailbone was clearly visible. On bended knee, Stone offered Blanche his hand, and the audience gasped as she pulled him up with exquisite brutality. They circled each other before beginning to tango. It annoyed Elle to watch Blanche execute moves with a certain measure of competence. This was to be Blanche's moment of triumph; a 'danse macabre' against a stormy backdrop. Sequins caught the light as she twisted and arched; the discs of her spine undulating like a poisonous snake. With hair piled high on her head and the violent color of her dress, she looked more like the Bride of Frankenstein movie poster Elle saw on the movie magazine cover from the lodge.

As she moved about the back of the dining room, lightning and thunder cracked so close by, something fell. The guests were now well-oiled and desperate to get out of their chairs and show off their costumes.

The big draw was coming, the contest for best costume and time to blow off steam. Center stage, Blanche announced changes to the lodge, praised Julius Stone and Nathan Foreman, who ran Pigeon Key. "I don't know what we would do without them," but the microphone whined, forcing her to wrap up her speech early.

Hidden in shadow near the kitchen, Elle spotted Nathan leaning into a petite, kiss-curled blonde in a flouncy pink dress with a sweetheart neckline. What a contrast to his wife in her dark green. Ruby Foreman had a face so bland that, despite their encounters, Elle wouldn't trust herself to pick Ruby out in a crowd. Finally, the orchestra played, but it was just another tango. Three couples tried, achieving an awkward version of the difficult dance, led by Julius and Blanche. Most retreated to their tables or gathered in small groups, looking around, alienated and unamused, and probably still hungry because Blanche hadn't stuck to the dinner plan.

In the kitchen, the roast was getting cold on the plates. Had Blanche drunk too much and forgotten the timing they had discussed? Or was it her natural disdain for food and fear they would be too stuffed to dance?

Elle motioned Buster into the mostly soundproof pantry, to discuss serving strategy. She spotted Brushy in the corner, backed against a wall, a bottle of expensive scotch between his legs, the nozzle jutting out at an obscene angle.

"The food will go out NOW. If Blanche gestures toward you, pretend you don't see her. They're not supposed to make announcements between courses. Jeez." A cloud of conflict shadowed Buster's sweet and even features. But he nodded, yes.

Finally, the orchestra added a little tempo to their playing. The bandleader stood and announced *Venice, American Style,* and played a jazzy tune completely foreign to Elle's ears; a tune that gained momentum, subtly gathering intensity. A young couple rose and led stragglers to the dance floor. Some stopped to nibble at food placed in front of them. Buster whispered something to the bandleader, and the jazz continued, but softer, forming a tinkling backdrop that oddly accompanied the rise and fall of forks and knives and lifted glasses. People sat or danced in syncopated rhythm as a lightness passed through the crowd. The hypnotic action of sound and feel and the heat of drinks and spiciness of the food, all senses activated through the unusual musical vibrations and the cozy sense of shelter from the storm. For that one, blessed moment, all were in synch and even Blanche smiled, genuinely grateful, mesmerized, and at one with the crowd.

In the kitchen, Brushy raised a half empty bottle to her, but Elle was in a frenzy, behind the illusion of ease, providing what they wanted before they knew what it was. She stopped a moment, feeling her sore shoulders and a fresh cut on her thumb from a sharp bread knife. Brushy motioned Elle toward him and she moved near, leaning on her haunches to take in his words. As the tempo of the music rose, she took the bottle from him and had a swig. Buster spotted her, laughed, and Elle waved him over with the bottle. He raised it theatrically before taking a hardy pull. The look of satisfaction on Buster's sweet face gave no opinion of anything beyond pleasure at doing his part to help the world spin smoothly and not a single complaint he hadn't handled. He quietly made his way back to the kitchen exit, giving Elle a thumbs up, then seized his chance to retrieve plates in an effortless economical ballet.

While guests danced, Elle took a moment to watch from the entryway. While they sized up each other's costumes, makeup, and noted who was dancing with whom, Elle noticed food ground into the carpet, spilled wine, and a broken wineglass under a chair. A plate teetered on the edge of the stage, vibrating to the music, bodies brushing against it as they danced. She pushed her way through the thickening dance floor, grabbing it in a fit of triumph, and spotted Blanche watching her, eyes wide in amused contempt.

Elle sighed, relieved that the worst was done. Everyone wanted dessert in front of them, but most wouldn't dream of actually eating it. She prepared for the irritation she always felt at seeing a contaminated piece of pie, three forkfuls desecrating the symmetry, sometimes a stubbed cigarette. Although protocol told her to toss it out, she cut out the ruined edge and saved the rest. From the corner of her eye, she saw Sheila desperately down some strange alcoholic concoction when she thought no one was looking. Elle made it easier by placing leftover drinks to one side of the sink where Sheila could find them.

While the evening ran smoothly, Elle exited the kitchen, heading past the tower toward the icehouse, unwilling to wait for Buster, who had enough on his hands. A dark triangle alerted her to the open tower door, the 'Keep Out' sign trampled on the floor. "Hello?"

she called in the dark. An awful rush of dread seized her. Had a child entered? The tower was too dark to see anything. She heard her own breathing, then the rasp of metal grating against metal from above. Lightheaded with fear, something was wrong. When she looked up, the staircase was gone- but that wasn't possible. She stepped into the congested space and kicked something flat. As her eyes adjusted, a dislodged mahogany tread came into view, and a low moan sounded from above. She looked up, straining her eyes, unable to take in what she saw. A desperate groan hit her, and she moved forward, almost tripping on a second pile of mahogany treads. The black staircase hovered midair like a demented corkscrew. Feet dangled above her head, out of reach. Crumpled in shadow, Rimer was half-hanging from the skeleton of stair, some ten feet above her. "I can't move my legs," he whispered, his voice low and hoarse.

"Rimer! What happened? Oh my god! Hang on! I'll get help. Hang on," she fought the impulse to scream.

A painted face peered in the doorway and let out a high-pitched scream and instantly a crowd stampeded toward the tower.

"Stay away. Keep back," Elle yelled at the tide of faces moving, straining against the doorway. Finally, the music stopped. "Get me a ladder." Art broke through the crowd and Elle repeated the order.

Brushy pushed through the crowd. "Back off." He shooed everyone away. The top of a ladder poked through the doorway, but the opening was too narrow to get it through.

Art yelled, "Get out," and entered with a smaller ladder amidst cries and screams.

"Any medics? Doctors?" Monty yelled, but no one came forward.

"He's alive," someone said, which made Elle aware of how injured he was. Rimer's uneven, choked breathing silenced the crowd. Did he have a chest injury?

"Are you bleeding?" Elle asked and Rimer tried, but couldn't answer, his breath coming in short, gurgling wheezes. A couple more mahogany slats shot down from the staircase.

A makeshift stretcher emerged from the stash of leftover plywood. Elle pushed her way through the circle surrounding him and leaned in. "You'll be okay. I promise you," she said, holding back panic.

Blanche turned to the piano player, "Get back in position and play when I give the signal."

Nathan shooed Art away, but he refused to budge from Rimer's side. Another workman broke through the circle and Nathan finally left. Tears flooded Art's face and Monty took charge of the scene.

"Get him on the... wood.... the stretcher... we're going to the hospital in Key West... Don't move him until he's tied in... immobilized." Women handed scarves and shawls to Monty, the room so silent Elle heard rain hit the roof, pinging delicately as Monty secured Rimer to the board. A few men removed their belts and offered them to Monty, leaning in to take in his directions.

"Everyone. Listen. Lift at the count of three. Ready... one... two... three." They rose as one, carrying a prostrate Rimer down the porch steps, over the muddy pathway, slow and careful not to slip. The posse of men moved like a giant centipede, the wounded Rimer silently carried to the wharf without a single false step.

"Monty," Brushy called, "Take the Big Wheel" but Monty already had Rimer on the ferry. He wasn't taking orders from anyone.

While the men were at the wharf, Elle returned to the lodge and made out the stark white of Nathan's white Shakespearean shirt as he entered the tower. She waited until he left and went inside. A couple of half empty rum bottles lay on the floor that hadn't been there before. Rimer was no drunk and Elle couldn't imagine him putting up with the mess. Farther inside, Rimer's blue duffel bag and a soiled bedroll Elle recognized from the shed lay face down, pinched between dislodged stair treads and the wall. None of these were there when Rimer fell. Nathan and Blanche disappeared onto the sheltered porch, motioned for the New Orleans hardware magnate and his wife and the four of them made a tight circle, talking and nodding. They were the only people Elle had seen enter the tower during the entire party. When they disbanded, Nathan nailed the tower door shut.

After the ferry departed in the roiling waves, Elle returned to the wharf and sat by a puddle of water on the landing, jazz notes pinging through the open door. A large tropical rat scuttled up the ghostly palm trunk and peered down with sad lemur eyes through a crack in the crown. The porch side lodge door remained open, the saturated air magnifying sound. Was Blanche running around, smiling, while the orchestra played jazz louder and faster, the piercing music notes hanging red in the sky? She sat still on the wharf at the water beyond.

Were they dancing? She imagined bodies colliding, flying by, braceleted hands, jeweled fingers dropping tickets into a fishbowl hoping for a prize.

When she returned, Elle took in the piles of dirty dishes, smiles on the faces of the dancers and the enormous bowl of tickets. The drawing for the car was next, and Elle watched Blanche's hand snatch at the tickets like Rimer's must've when he grabbed at the rail before he fell. Without a word, Elle exited the lodge, only realizing she had a dishcloth grasped tightly in her fist when she tried to open her chain-link gate.

She rolled a gigantic piece of coral against the gate and stood on the same flat-planed root Rimer rested against before she brought him inside her cottage to dress his leg. From nowhere, a cry snaked through her diaphragm, leaving her ribs sucked in and she began shaking. A wail of rage and sorrow for the men for Rimer - all of it. She was a woman without a dream, a woman who colluded for a few tiny gains, grabbing on to whatever came next. She was as likely to have fallen down the staircase as Rimer. Did anyone remember Rimer's voice? The color of his eyes? How tall was he? Did he like sweets? Not one of them mattered.

When she called Cat in, Charlie the rooster followed, with his hens and four tiny chicks, confused and agitated, hopping around the cistern and out of the storm.

20

The next morning, a different ferry arrived, and Elle joined the crowd departing for Key West. A newspaper reporter from Key West met Blanche at the ferry landing.

A momentary wave of terror crossed Blanche's face when she saw Elle. "He was always such a damn klutz in the name of God, there's no point in blaming him now... he was the best we had. But he'll be ok, I'm sure of it. I don't know how the Lodge will survive without him." The last Elle witnessed was the reporter consoling Blanche for her loss. Later, Elle discovered the reporter had lost a sister in a boating accident, and perhaps that was why she didn't press for details.

Everyone onboard the ferry was hungry for details of the tragedy, and Elle was grateful no one recognized her. She avoided all eye contact and didn't look up until the horn blew, announcing their arrival in Key West.

The Key West hospital had beds in passageways, makeshift rooms set up without privacy, and a single long shelf for common use. The only books available were Bibles, which had little chance of being stolen. Elle moved past the empty front desk, through corridors of half-naked men, down a hallway of echoing screams, of someone either giving birth or dying. In a far room, she spotted four children in beds. She was in the wrong section.

She followed a quick-paced and grim-looking woman with an untidy gray bun. "The man who fell from the tower, on No Name Key," she asked the retreating nurse. "Where is he?"

Elle saw the look of professional warmth followed by, "What's his name?"

And Elle realized she had forgotten his first name. How was it she had nearly lain with a man whose name she didn't remember?

"Mr. Rimer."

"James Rimer. Moved to Jackson Memorial Hospital in Miami yesterday."

"Can he walk?"

The nurse's expression turned matter-of-fact. "I'm sorry, but we cannot give out information unless you're family."

A man yelled to her from a bed against the wall, "He looked like rocks in a bag when they took him away."

"So, he's alive?" Elle asked. The nurse and the man in the bed made no move to answer.

"He's dead," a voice came from the doorway. Art leaned against a wall behind a bed with a man with a leg hoisted in the air on a contraption that resembled something from the funny pages.

A strong odor of camphor hit her, making her gag. They stared at each other; Art looked freshly shocked, as if she was the one who gave him the news.

"You again! I thought you left." The nurse said, turning to Art, determined to weed out this traitor who was telling everyone the truth.

"Are you his wife? Family?" The nurse repeated.

"No, I'm his friend."

Art moved slowly, as if emerging from underwater. His face was so mottled he looked in the early stage of some incurable disease. His eyelids were so puffy, he seemed almost sightless. Blond chin stubble formed a tattered beard, strictly forbidden to the men in Blanche Rowland's employ. All indications were he was in the early recovery stages from a monumental bender. If anyone deserves it, he does, Elle thought, although she'd never seen him drink more than a single beer.

"I brought him these," Elle said, stupidly, holding out a bag.

Screams from the hallway caused the nurse to sigh, then walk grimly out with a quick step, shoulders straight, holding some kinetic force in reserve for the next exhausting duty. A rush of orderlies moved past to another urgent situation.

"Here," Elle said, handing the bag of newspapers, sweets and sandwiches to an old man lying on a bed, abandoned in the hospital corridor.

A hysterical brawl broke out at the reception desk. A drunk said something unintelligible before a very large, round-faced orderly came at him.

Elle moved quickly toward the exit to avoid the scuffle, and Art followed her out.

"You're the only one who came," he said, brushing his hair back in a futile gesture at grooming, his face a mixture of hurt and pain.

"I'm so sorry," she repeated, hating the trite sentiment, but having nothing better to offer. The heft of his loss diminishing her own and she wanted to tell him she knew about him and James and she would mourn for that, too. Soon, she thought, the weight of everything we cannot say to each other will topple us both over.

"His mother. He sent her half of everything he made." And now Elle knew what her life would have been if she had accepted his proposal.

She longed to walk the streets of Key West, anonymous and alone, but Art followed her. A wall of hot pink bougainvillea pierced the cerulean sky, fluorescing the edges into purple. An emerald lizard watched from the wall; his movements arrested in the act of delicately plucking a vivid flower, petal by petal, into the fine tracery of his mouth.

"Thank you for coming to check on James." He spoke formally, signaling a promise not to break down, willing her to understand something important. His shoulders squared, his back straight, a posture she had never seen him in. A bead of sweat, or maybe a tear, swelled on the tip of his nose.

Elle had no desire to tell him what had happened between herself and Rimer, or more like what had nearly happened, somehow certain it would be treacherous to him.

"Coulda' been anyone. Shoulda' been me," he said. "I made him work at the lodge…"

"No," she said. "He loved you." As soon as she spoke, she knew it was true and his look of gratitude was so intense Elle feared he would cry.

"I didn't even remember his name. James," she said, with a sad little smile. It was a perfect, old-fashioned name for him. James, who wanted an impossible day to arrive. James, who longed for children of his own. He wanted to be a man in love with a woman and not another man.

She spoke quickly, "Where do you live, Art?"

Art looked at her strangely. "You know where I live. With four men in cabin eighteen at No Name. I have nowhere else to go."

Elle meant where would he go when he left No Name, but changed her mind about asking.

"When I got back, my girl married someone else."

"You had a girl?" Elle asked, too suddenly, but he laughed, and it seemed to lighten the mood. So, she said, "When you got back from where?"

"From the war," he answered.

"But that was fifteen years ago."

He had a spot of dirt on the side of his mouth that Elle wanted to tell him about. Or was it a bruise?

"After she left, I guess I just drifted till I sent James a letter and we met in Richmond, kicked around a few jobs for about a year, before everything dried up. So we heard about the Bonus army march in Washington. "

"I thought you met in Washington," Elle said.

"No. Richmond, Virginia. A year before." He looked at her, a shadow crossing his face.

"Sorry, I must have confused you with Petey or Al." His face went blank, so she said. "I've never heard of the march. What happened? Why was it called a bonus march?"

Rimer lied, she thought as he spoke. And Art thought she didn't have a clue.

"....and the Government still owes us a five-hundred dollars bonus for our services in the Great War." He warmed to the subject, so Elle asked, "Where did you meet him the first time?"

"James saved my life in Italy 1916... who'd think we'd get together again? I'll never forget it... we pooled our cash and got rooms in Richmond, then he told me about Florida and we both got in on the WPA road project." He smiled, a broad disarming smile that displayed his strong gray teeth.

"You and that famous backhoe," Elle said, picturing his long loose form climbing into the cab and the endless hacking into capstone, surrounded by men with pickaxes.

"I told 'em it wouldn't hold," he said, "then the stupid staircase with nothing to shore it up. Mahogany was too heavy, and James told 'em so. I should have..." He stared at her as if she had accused him.

"They gotta blame someone," Elle said.

He blinked at her as if checking to see if she was sincere. "That's nothing. Did you ever see his work? I mean, really see it?" He hesitated and Elle read his mind not to discuss the accident that weakened his leg, the way they used his body for joe jobs when they didn't need his talents. "Rimer could do anything with a piece of wood. He understood it like it was telling him things." Once he called him Rimer, Elle relaxed and Art laughed into his fist, which turned into a cough. He seemed embarrassed.

He stared at her as if not quite believing what he saw, and moved in closer. "You taking the ferry back?"

Elle contemplated telling him she was staying in Key West for a while, then wondered if she would. A gust of rotted meat puffed from an open trash can and Elle held her breath when she was well past it. A large family on a sagging porch turned to stare. On side streets, shacks were unpainted. A skinny dog snarled and yipped at them, tail low to his body. When Art bent down to pat him, he growled louder.

"Guess Stone hasn't given 'em the good word yet," Art said. Scraggy weeds lined the center of the street and everywhere the smell of mold and rot and skinny people with bloated bellies and peeling red skin. Garbage lay stashed in gutters, around trees and strewn throughout the streets. The entire town needed a good whitewash. She was sticky from heat and thirsty, weighted air heavy as a foul, smothering blanket.

"If you don't mind, I think I need a little time to myself." Elle said.

He scratched an eyebrow and looked at her blankly. "I'll stay out of your hair. But thank you anyhow."

Again, Elle was surprised at how polite he was. What did it really matter and weren't they in the same position? And wasn't she tired of the thoughts that rolled in her head repeating?

"Listen here, Art," she said. "How about I treat you to a dish of world famous El Anon ice cream?" Elle had always wanted to see how ice cream was made, thinking she could make a fortune if she could figure out how to keep it frozen in the tropics.

"One condition," he said, "No sob sister talk. And I pay my own way and treat you to boot. I'm no one's charity case."

21

Two days after Elle's return from Key West, Buster was waiting for her when she came in from early morning fishing. "Someone from the Sheriff's office is looking for you," he said. Down the pathway, a tidy man in sunglasses and a well-pressed safari suit walked toward them.

"Mrs. Woodman," He smiled blandly, his hand extended. "Kyle Thompson, representing the WPA here in the Florida Keys."

"WPA?"

"The Work Progress Administration. We employ war vets to build roads, bridges. Roosevelt began the..."

"I thought you were from the Sheriff's office," Elle said.

Well, we all work together. Please accompany me to headquarters. I have a few questions to ask.

"*Are* you from the Sheriff's office?"

"Well, Mr. Rimer's death is being investigated, and there's more than one interested party."

"Can't we talk here?"

He half circled her, drawing an imaginary barrier between wharf and land. Elle wondered if she was going to be arrested, but that was ridiculous.

"Will you please get rid of those?" He pointed to the bucket of frantic fish.

"They don't keep," she said. "I need to gut them. I spent the entire morning..."

"I said put the fish down and get in the boat." Then he softened his tone. "I left all my papers there–it'll just be a bit."

"Papers? Where?"

"We need your signature on a witness account. Don't worry, we'll ferry you back." He removed his sunglasses to rub his eye and, in that moment, Elle saw how strange the man's eyes were, like the eyes of a hungry bird. She looked at the fish in the bucket, then at him. Suddenly, she felt relieved that Buster had witnessed the encounter without really understanding why.

She pointed to her bike on the dock. "I'll take my bike and make my own way back." He sighed and allowed her to load it onto the boat as if granting some great concession.

'Coast Guard' was inscribed on the side of the large white cutter in heavy navy lettering, and Elle noticed someone at the helm. He was behind a partition, painted a bland shade of beige-gray that hid him from view. As they departed, bird-eyes reached behind himself and Elle heard the jangle of handcuffs.

But it was only a packet of cigarettes. He flicked the Ronson lighter in a gesture that reminded her of Nathan. She hadn't thought to ask where exactly headquarters was located, and now she was afraid of what he would answer.

"Make yourself comfortable." He motioned toward a padded leatherette bench and remained standing when she sat. Thompson's crotch was at eye level and she saw something she wouldn't forget: a swell there. He stared down at her with his sunglasses on.

"Where are we going, exactly?"

He took his time before replying. "We're almost there," And Elle asked nothing more, relieved when they arrived at Pigeon Key a long hour later.

The interview was in a quiet, old-fashioned room and, except for the oversized American flag on the wall, it could have been any officious study. Thompson motioned her to sit in a roomy green leather armchair beside a matching table. They want me to feel their presence; she thought.

The long blast of a ferry departing made the quiet seem vast and cut off from the world. Elle dreaded the coming interrogation; afraid she would implicate herself. An image of herself crouched and spellbound watching Billy drink the poison she gave him made her blink and sit upright, rigid.

"Accidents happen," he began, turning his head, nodding toward the outside. "Certainly, we know... They are not always preventable."

Elle froze. He wasn't finished.

"Not to worry, it has nothing to do with you. You're not the owner of the lodge. But you must've seen men come and go, building the tower... or what Mrs. Rowlands calls the dance pavilion." He smiled indulgently.

"I was the cook," she said.

"Yes, and by all accounts, you could teach my man Bernie a thing or two about flavor," he said, his tone false and flattering. His face took on a kindly look. "Bernie's the mess hall cook. At least that's what he says he is."

Elle understood how this worked. They wanted something from her.

"Talking doesn't mean you don't appreciate your boss or the job. It's not like that," he continued.

It wasn't lost on Elle that the majority of books on the shelves were law books, crime statistics, punishment suggestions by some famous lawyer, *Man and his Folly, Degrees of Guilt*. She reminded herself they knew nothing about Billy's death. This was about Rimer.

"Go on. Tell me a little about the party in your own words."

"I came in to prepare the food," Elle said simply. "My job ended after the party."

"One thing," he smiled when he spoke. "Not to interrupt, but by all accounts, the food was wonderful." He leaned back in his chair.

Compliments unnerved Elle, so she generally pretended she didn't hear them or spoke quickly, as if to obliterate them.

"Oh, I make these little wraps. They're simple, but…" she trailed off. Speaking about food and recipes calmed her. "Not everyone likes fish, so I always make sure we have chicken or a good ham." She prattled on, hiding in the provincial world of the kitchen worker.

Elle expected him to interrupt and move the narrative toward the tipping point of the tragedy, and his silence unnerved her. "I mean, people love fish when they do and won't tolerate anything but…"

"Okay, and then?"

"Well, we really couldn't hear anything from the kitchen, what with the music and…"

Behind him, the heavy draperies cast shadows upon themselves, an endless series of folds.

"Yes, Mr. Rimer. That was his name."

Again, he leaned forward, eyes fixated on her, "Oh come on. You knew him quite well, by all accounts. It's perfectly natural. Nothing to be ashamed of." He waved his hand in a failed attempt to seem casual. His bland smile returned. "Having lost a husband so recently. Billy, I think was his name?"

He tilted his head closer, looking for a reaction. His eyes reminded her of bird-eyes from the boat. She didn't want to let breath out, aware she had been holding it in. When he looked away, she turned the door that looked too tiny for a child to walk through.

"The men, they worked there in their spare time?" Her shoulders released tension.

Nine to six Monday to Saturday was not exactly spare time. "No, they worked full time for Blanche Rowlands." He looked dismal, unhappy with her response. His obvious discomfort worried her, but he had stopped asking about Billy.

"Yes," he said. "I've heard the Rowlandses took on some tough characters... helping men who'd been fired from the roadwork project."

Elle remembered the conversation she overheard between Nathan and Blanche. These men were not fired. They were paid by the Government, redirected to work for Blanche, who paid Nathan half what their labor was worth. Pure profit for Nathan and a bargain for Blanche.

But Elle said nothing. She knew what side he was on.

He shook his head in the tiniest back-and-forth motion. "Sad when doing a good turn ruins it for everyone," his voice trailed off, and he shifted his gaze to the window. When he turned back toward her, his flat and patronizing smile resurfaced.

"By the way," Elle said, "Blanche did all the hiring. The dance pavilion was her dream. Her husband had nothing to do with it."

"Yes," he said, leaning in so close she smelled the cloying sweetness of pipe tobacco on his breath. "And I wonder if Mrs. Rowlands is sorry she took those poor men on. But knowing her, I doubt it. Blanche Rowlands tried to do them a good turn and look where that got her."

His tone took on a sharp edge, warning her off. Then she remembered him. She was certain he had worn a zebra mask to the party. She had thought it odd at the time, wondering what a zebra had to do with Venice.

"I know nothing about it. I mind my business." Elle thought about the drunken men and the conversation she overheard between Blanche and Nathan. About Rimer, whose name he had only mentioned once.

"What are you thinking about?" he asked.

"Nothing."

"You can tell me."

She didn't know a thing about the man interrogating her. He wasn't in uniform, but the green and brown he wore blurred into a single muddy color and Elle imagined identical sets of clothes in his closet, an army of white shirts on the other side. His pale blue eyes were colorless and changeable, as if underwater. For someone so pale, he seemed unfazed by the oppressive tropical climate that steamed the sharpness out of everyone's clothing but his. The press in his brown pants was straight as a seam. Elle spotted a small, motionless lizard trapped between the double windows, his body the color of dying leaves.

"Did you see him fall?" The question shot out from him, returning Elle to the heart of the conversation.

She had been on her way to get ice when the heavy thump sounded, and she knew in an instant that it came from the inside and was more serious than a railing or roof shingle falling.

The lizard darted around the window, then stopped. Elle remembered Nathan kneeling over a crumpled figure on the ground. He'd said something to her, but the music was competing with the rainfall and she didn't hear a word.

"He doesn't have children," he said, in a dismissive tone, as if that explained it all, then picked up his pipe and a match flared. He gasped in quick pulls, coughed and allowed the smoke to waft about his face, obscuring his expression. "James Rimer was a good man, and we will, of course, do right by his family. He was the sole support of his mother and sister, who had some sort of trouble. We'll certainly help them out. Discreetly, you know... all the red tape... forms. You know." He shook his head dismissively and smiled. "I don't think it's important that anyone know they let him go, fired - no point to it now and it might interfere with the family getting his pension." He tapped his foot when he spoke, a nervous habit. The carpet was deep burgundy and expensive. Elle imagined the weight of carrying it and the journey required to bring it here, just so this man could tap his thick soled foot and feel the luxuriant padding that confirmed his own importance. He held one hand with the other, massaged his knuckles, and sat straighter.

He leaned toward her, elbows on his flattened thighs, entwined his hands into the shape of a pyramid, and spoke as if she were a sympathetic equal. "The papers will enjoy reporting this mess, looking for people to call on. Like that nosey writer in Key West after the Labor Day hurricane."

"Mr. Hemingway?"

"See? Even you know his name. Anyhow, I imagine you might need a little to tide you over until you can find more work. "

Here it comes. "No, I have savings," she said.

"Well, I imagine there will be an investigation and no more parties for a while. So, you might need a little insurance cash."

Insurance for whom? "Actually, I was doing this as a favor. I had no possibility of full-time work at No Name Key lodge."

"You know, Rimer had a history..."

Of course, Rimer had a past. "I'm not interested in his history."

"Well, it seems to me you have a generous nature, but others might not be so forgiving. You know many of the men building the road have real problems that have nothing to do with the war or the job. Government is working hard to combat this Great Depression."

A sound from behind the door told Elle someone was there. It was impossible to know with wall-to-wall carpeting, scatter rugs on top and flocked, striped wallpaper.

"I'm sorry I couldn't be more helpful," Elle said, a line she had plucked from some book or maybe a film.

"Wait," he said, pushing a paper toward her. "Sign this."

"But all it states is that I didn't see him fall. Did I really need to come all this way for that?"

The stamp is always what's important; he said, trying for irony and pointing to the official governmental seal.

After she signed, he hesitated as if unwilling to let her go, then stood and extended his hand, grasping hers and squeezing it a tad too hard and too long. When he finally let go, she had to control her impulse to sprint to the door. As she left, something caught her eye. Under the table flanking the door was Nathan Foreman's unmistakable oxblood briefcase, with the tortoiseshell handle.

When she stepped outside, away from the stuffiness, an old soldier she recognized tipped his hat to her. "Miss Elle," he said, and she recognized him as one of the men who bought food from her on the road. "You here for the job?" he asked. "Lord knows we'd all be grateful."

PART II

BIG PINE KEY

22

T he freshly paved road to Big Pine was bright black and periodically jutted with protruding railroad ties from the old Flagler tracks. The road crew had made much progress in a brief time. Ten miles outside of Big Pine Key, the spicy fragrance of cinnamon bark trees battled the sour smell of decay in the mangroves not twenty feet from the road.

Heaven and hell cohabit peacefully in the Lower Keys, one indistinguishable from the other. Life forms percolate in the stewing carcass of some downed beast. After the vultures have their fill, the delicate and precise pincers of flying scavengers make off with the remains. Whatever falls into water feeds the mangroves whose roots shelter small creatures whose remains in turn feed the trees. Finally, tender mangrove shoots feed the deer and renew the old cycle.

In the short time Elle lived on No Name, she understood how the tiniest uptick in drought or rainfall could take you out. Biting, flying, tunneling pests flourished in the relentless heat and humidity with no cold spell to cull the insect empire. Periodic outbreaks of dengue, malaria, and TB ran through small populations, but many swore mosquitos were the worst. The entire Florida Keys contained generations of thwarted schemes to hack through coral and capstone to farm fruit trees, burn charcoal, set up sponging operations. Remnants of enormous shark oil refineries jutted the landscape resembling hulls of abandoned ships on dry lakes in the Upper Keys. Lack of cheap and reliable transportation made setting up any kind of industry foolhardy. Yet warmth and open spaces still lured the desperate, the haters of order, the dreamers certain they possessed that one genius idea no one else ever imagined that would make their fortune. In the meantime, not freezing to death in a Northern winter would have to be enough.

Elle banked her bike by the turnoff to No Name to pee in a thick hedgerow. As she crouched, a Key deer fawn approached her, unafraid, like something from a fairy tale, and Elle didn't have the heart to scare him away. The tiny fawn's soft eyes and etched features had the dreamy sweetness of an illustration in a child's picture book.

When she was done, Elle remembered the empty building across the road where she almost made love with Rimer and wheeled her bike across the road to take in the building.

Why was Brushy here? He was standing, eating something, the other fist in the pocket of loose linen trousers. At least he had ditched the ridiculous "Bermuda" style shorts that Stone popularized amongst public officials. He broke into a welcoming open smile and waved her over. "Elle," he yelled. "Come, look."

He was eating an apple, of all things. Elle hadn't seen an apple for over a year.

"What's all this?" she asked. Trees around the building were gone, and a new series of roofs and windows added dimension. It looked like a hotel or store ready to be painted. A shock of anger washed over her. Building, building, building. More men to do their bidding. "And how many men's lives will this cost?"

"What? No, it's not like that."

"Aren't you people tired of this part of the world yet?"

Elle thought of Rimer broken and dead while the Rowlandses hired another architect, another crew of engineers. A winding procession of note takers, smilers, cranes and bulldozers trailing behind.

"Elle. Come here. Feast your eyes." He motioned with the half-eaten apple toward the building.

"I've just been interviewed about the accident," she said. "James Rimer's death at No Name." As she spoke, she became angrier. "Remember him? The man who died. James Rimer. You people. Getting away with everything. Using everyone to do your dirty work."

She turned away, and he placed his hand on her shoulder to angle her toward him. "Please Elle. I didn't know where the men came from that my wife hired. I need to talk to you."

"Liar. You knew. You should've known."

The fawn had followed her across the road, hoping for food, and Brushy's face softened when he saw him. When he held the apple out to the fawn, she batted it out of his hand.

"That's right. Enough to make him dependent, but not enough to survive. Just leave us all alone." She turned to the fawn. "Get out," she yelled, and it startled. She was probably the first person who had ever yelled at him. Elle dropped her bike and chased the fawn to the road toward No Name. "Get out. Get out. Get out." She walked past Brushy to retrieve her bike, walked it up the hill and pedaled across the road as fast as she could, not stopping until she reached No Name.

23

The pavilion was being dismantled at a frenzied pace, destroying evidence of the accident. A fresh group of builders arrived carrying their trademark cylinders or revised drawings. Elle caught snatches of Blanche's grating voice ordering Ree around. In the evening, Blanche mellowed after napping sporadically throughout the day, only to become loudest in the small hours, when Elle was in deepest sleep. But it wasn't Blanche who woke Elle that day, after the moon rose. Blanche never knocked lightly.

"Who's there?"

"I have your pay." It was Brushy.

Exhausted as she was, Elle was eager to get this last encounter over with. She wrapped a shirt around her shoulders and let him in the gate, then the house. The dank darkness was overwhelming, so Elle fetched a hurricane lamp and lit it. Instantly, the smell of kerosene filled her nostrils, a smell she found oddly pleasant.

Brushy looked around and shook his head. "You can't possibly live here any longer."

"Your pay doesn't come with the right to tell me how to live," she said. She remembered what Art had said to her in Key West when she offered to treat him to ice cream—that he was no one's charity case—and realized that's what she must seem to the Rowlandses.

"While you were counting your change and calculating profit, did you notice how many men were working?" Brushy said.

This sounded rehearsed, and she wanted him to stop pretending they weren't on opposite sides. Did he think she was stupid? "Yes, and make hay while the sun shines. They won't be here for long. Once the highway is built, they'll fold up camp and be off like the ones before them and the ones before that."

"True," he said, "to my point," and gazed at her, as if waiting for her to comprehend — an annoying habit of his when he used this technique on the workers. He bobbed his head and stared as if to bore a hole into her head and pour his vision into her brain. "Can you light another lamp? You must have one." She sighed and considered tossing him out. "Never mind," he said. "Listen to me, Elle. Think about it. What will remain once the workers leave?" He answered himself, "The blessed highway, for God's sake... like a great nervous system, a vein to ferry every luxury imaginable by land... just imagine..." He stood arms theatrically gesturing. "Pleasure seekers in need of thrills, men crazed with the fishing fever... you've seen them yourself... warm weather, exotic locales, a break from the wife and kids."

"Oh, sit down. Seems to me they have been building this thing forever."

"A private group is taking over, Elle, out of West Palm Beach who understand the terrain. Cleary. I spoke to him yesterday."

"I spoke to him yesterday," she mimicked his lofty tone. Trying to hold on to her anger about the men about to be tossed out.

"No Name is on the backside, cut off," he said. "Like a great carbuncle on the rear of the new highway."

But there, he lost her, for her love of this place was unreasoning and she was hoping the Rowlands would abandon it.

"Listen," he said, sensing he had lost her. "If you paid attention to more than the flies circling your wares, you might be interested in the great swath of cleared land we stood in yesterday and the building behind it." He pulled out a folded swath of documents from an inner pocket.

"So did you come here to tell me of your latest score? Don't you have anyone else to share your genius with?"

He shook his head. He looked hurt.

"You're building another lodge?"

"Not quite. It was... a good deal." He sounded almost embarrassed, so longer proud of tricking someone out of property.

"Well?" she said. His demeanor made her bold. "Blanche will never leave, No Name, if that's what you had in mind. She thinks it's her private harem."

"Did you guess?"

"Guess what?"

"That I plan on divorcing her."

"I didn't. But everyone would have more respect for you if you did."

His eyes flashed with anger, but Elle didn't feel bad for him. "Good to see you have some fight left. You can afford to be pissed at me."

"Alright," he tossed her the envelope with her final pay, stomped to the door and the sheaf of papers fell to the floor.

"Wait, I'm sorry. You deserve better, that's all I meant." She picked up the papers he dropped. "I'm crabby when I wake up," she said, handing him the plans. This might be the last time she spoke to him. "I'm listening. Tell me what you're up to."

"Don't know if you deserve to know," he said.

"That's more like it. A little spirit suits you." He made the smallest chuckle and she was surprised at how easy it was to treat him as an equal. He likes me, she thought. More important, he respects me.

"I'm waiting," she said, turning up the flame of the hurricane lamp. She motioned to the chair next to hers.

As he spoke deep shadows revealed the planes of his face. "A diner and motel to sleep and gas up and it will even have a couple of coin-operated telephones and a decent supply store and dining room. Tourists!" he said triumphantly.

Elle looked up into his feverish eyes and she saw it: the people's endless demands, the nagging needs for gas, toilets, for food, lodging and entertainment.

"Who will run it?"

"Don't know," he waved his hand dismissively, as if that were the least of his concerns. Then he saw it, her face. "You?"

"Why not? Who else can you trust?"

"But she..she hates you. It's impossible. So long as we're married, Blanche has access to everything I own."

"Well if Blanche doesn't approve…"

"I'm sorry. It was selfish of me to come showing off to you."

"Just because you're rich doesn't mean you have anyone to talk to. I have an idea. If I buy it from you before you divorce, it won't even belong to you. You said it yourself, she only wants the Lodge."

"But I want to keep it."

"Well, then forget it. It's a dumb idea. Impossible. I don't have any money anyhow." This conversation was exhausting. Wanting things, hope, plans saddened then angered her. She wanted him to go.

"Wait," he said. "I trust you." He sat back down and Elle moved between rage and hope and felt as if this had been her stance for her entire life.

"You might be onto something." He nodded toward the lodge. "She'd be happy to be rid of you and think you a sucker for buying the business. And it would be out of my portfolio."

"Yes. Blanche will never be able to get her hands on it?"

"If I sell it to you before the divorce. Will you give me your word?"

"I promise you." Elle held her hand out, and he shook it so vigorously, she thought he would wrench her shoulder.

See this?" He opened the papers and pointed to a large drawing. "This is where we were yesterday... when you drove that poor creature off."

The fawn and the apple and the building on the wide swath of cleared land that followed the Flagler's ruined train tracks. The building where she almost had sex with Rimer.

"A diner with a small, attached motel. The short, narrow shapes in front are for gas pumps in a vast parking area. Over top, that matching square could be your new home. Here, I'll prove it." He made a childish scrawl of curtains on either side of the topmost rectangle, destroying the pristine drawing.

"Listen. You," he stood over her and tapped his finger on her chest bone and repeated, "are investing in a diner with money you saved, money you received from an aunt that died or some... family. Anyhow, money no one knew about."

"And this time I pretended I was broke."

"In return for my generosity, I'll allow you to buy a fifty percent share after promising to work a year.

His voice rose, and the way he took her in unnerved her. She had spent most of her life on the edges, wasn't used to being seen. He gestured toward the lodge. "No Name Key Lodge will rot when the highway is built, and the ferries stop running. But my wife is not a woman with vision. Let her bankrupt someone else because I am done."

Elle recalled something buried. Before Elle murdered Billy, she had seen Brushy outside the cabin Blanche and Billy used for their trysts, his face under the kerosene lamp, flame low, his expression blank. He knew his wife cheated on him. That night, drawn to cabin 14 by light flickering in the window, she feared a fire or maybe vandals, because it was supposed to be empty. Blanche ordered it cleaned, new bed linen and pillows, and they always had trouble with kids and pranks and homeless men. So, she wandered down the pathway and snuck up under an orange lit window, thumb poised on the flip knife button and when she heard them, she peered in and saw Blanche bent over the bed rail and Billy choking her, thrusting. She knew those low growls, and dropped lower, crawling away, but stopped dead when she heard someone. Then she made out the unmistakable gait of Brushy, who turned away so abruptly she wondered if he had seen her.

Brushy continued, "Later you'll need a partner with vision to see what could become of the place."

"You mean you'll need a partner."

"Precisely." His eyes softened. "My own beginnings are not so different from your own..."

Flattery made her uncomfortable; had never done her any good. He was no enemy to her, almost seemed hurt by her lack of interest in his past and for a moment she looked beyond the embarrassed older man and saw what he might have been once, before he believed his wealth was the only interesting thing about him.

Later that day he returned with a new document and Elle, a woman of a thousand cautions, took the pen he held out without reading the papers, signing all five pages in silence as he pointed out spaces already signed by a witness.

"Good to be the first, Elle," he said, looking smug.

"Better to be the second," she answered. "Let the first guy make all the mistakes."

"And that would be whom?"

"Sometimes they're one and the same."

She stared at him hard, and he nodded. And at that moment, she thought she might be the only person he trusted. He seemed to want to say more.

"Wait. Sit. Please," Elle said, gesturing to the ridiculously gilded armchair she had rescued and pulled out a crate for him to rest his feet.

"That's more like it," he said, winking at her. "I haven't been in business forty years without being able to spot someone trustworthy. Until then...," he reached into another pocket and handed her a packet with cash. "$400 should pay for what's needed in provisions. Gas tanks are about to be installed and need to be filled. The extra $100 is a cushion for when you use that good eye of yours to find a bargain or two." He winked a second time, but it looked forced.

Elle couldn't look at the bulging envelope, afraid it would disappear and afraid of the responsibility at the same time. Later she had no memory of much of what he said, although he prattled on for another few long minutes. "Meantime work has begun on lodging above the store, so you won't have so far to travel to open or tend to night customers who need a room. "

Beyond her yard, she heard the dull thud of lumber being piled for work the following day.

"Why do you put up with it?" She nodded in the lodge's direction.

"It's gone too far. If it's not repaired, the place will be a total loss. No one in their right mind would buy it in this condition. I have to settle before the highway is done and Blanche realizes how worthless the property really is."

"Is she building another, bigger tower? Looks like just the beginning to me."

Brushy tilted his head back on the chair, let out a theatrical, agonized groan. He looked comfortable in her converted cistern. She found it wickedly satisfying to watch this rich industrialist arrange his spoiled self onto a discarded old chair with a milk crate for a stool. But something was different. His tanned face and ready smile made him more difficult to dislike.

"Do you have any idea how much I loathed working for Blanche?" She jerked her head toward the lodge.

"No. It doesn't show." He raised his eyebrows theatrically, imploring her to be in on the joke.

"Easy for you to say. You can hole up in a cabin, plan your moves. Leave. Go anywhere." But then she saw it again, his restless, coveting eye.

Elle sensed he valued her ability to escape into her work. She was a cook and exchanged her skills for money. She had something with a name and a routine and an order when little else meant anything. Mostly, she knew how to work and work some more. Nothing felt better than pulling her weight, making use of the day.

"What, and leave all this luxury?" Elle said, gesturing to the repaired armchair he sat in, sweeping her hand toward the walls of her crumbling cistern. Cat jumped onto his lap as if to seal the arrangement.

He wiped his hand on his vest and held it out, smiling faintly. "I know what's been going on with my wife and the rig man. I may be a fool, but I'm not blind. "He headed toward the door with a spring that surprised Elle.

"I can't imagine how anyone wouldn't know," Elle said, warming to the task. "They enjoy watching you squirm. Your wife has it in for you, and if anyone tells you different...." Elle glared at him. "Don't worry, I haven't said a word and I won't, but if we're going to be partners, I'd rather have it all out."

"It's my own fault. A woman like Blanche would never fall for a man like me without the money, and I knew it. I'm guilty as she is."

"You have a point," Elle said, realizing it had come out all wrong. She meant Blanche liked rough trade, and he was gentle, but Brushy's sudden loud intake of breath stopped her from elaborating.

"Take a good look at the new building, the cleared space. I don't have a name for it yet, but it follows the old railroad tracks."

"If it follows the tracks, call it the sidetrack diner."

"The sidetrack diner?" He squinted; his mouth pursed. "The Sidetrack Diner. I like it. Won't even matter if they tear those old tracks down. Sidetracked can mean lots of things." He looked into her face. "The Sidetrack Diner, Big Pine Key, Florida." She felt a world in the way he said the name. His face relaxed, his jawline strong and etched in shadow.

From outside: "*Brushy.*"

That voice.

Blanche called again, "Brushy, where the hell are you? Abbott is coming back tomorrow and..."

"Ugh. I have to go." He turned toward the door.

"For someone able to change fate with a signature, you sure look browbeaten." Elle instantly regretted saying it. She hadn't thanked him, but he was already moving and at the door before the voice got closer.

"Wait," Elle said. "Is the building open? Might be things that only a woman can see, like proper placement for a kitchen."

He pointed to the milk crate where a single key sat on top of one of Blanche's envelopes stuffed with cash.

24

$\mathcal{E}$ lle was neither fired nor asked back. She simply stopped going to the Lodge, and no one came to find her. They carried debris from the failed tower out on barges and dumped it into deep water. Old soldiers disappeared as if they had never worked on the property. The only evidence Elle spotted was a pay envelope torn into pieces on the pathway to the wharf.

Lately Brushy wore linen or canvas pants and short sleeves, and Elle never again saw him in Bermuda shorts or seersucker jackets. After he quit dying his hair, he gave up on his old pomades and oils and Elle overheard Abbott accuse him of 'going native,' with an edge that his laugh couldn't soften. "Good," Brushy replied, no longer afraid to crack a wide smile or laugh outright. The slightly uncomfortable, mildly embarrassed man was gone. Elle remembered him saying they were not so 'very different,' a comment that had struck her as ludicrous. Maybe, like herself, he could make himself over to survive a downturn in his fortunes, personal or otherwise. Once she found a newspaper folded into quarters on a page about the stock market, something so foreign to Elle that it might be an ancient language, making her feel stupid and unworldly. Maybe this was something else for her to study. For now, she was the keeper of secrets, operating on the margins, as if any who had dealings with her were too ashamed to admit it. That morning, at first light, Elle imagined what others saw: a tall, unkempt woman with hair like an osprey nest in patched and worn clothing. In the three months since Rimer's death, her grooming, what little there was, had completely fallen away.

Yet Brushy wanted her to work for him. "Treat this place like it belongs to you, because it will," he said. She was free to organize the store and diner as she saw fit. Maybe she would hire Buster to help inside and Art to work as a handyman. But Art was a waking reminder of Rimer and all she had wanted from Rimer was a sexual encounter. What kind of woman simply wants a roll in the hay? She knew to keep that secret. Clearly, Rimer would have put up with sex to have the children he longed for. Visions of the old recipes handed down to "hasten the menses," came to her... recipes as ancient as the mangroves hugging the shoreline. Pennyroyal, counting days between cycles — and the terror before her rich, precious blood spilled again, and she felt safe. Men had complicated relationships with their children, even Billy claimed to want a family. By far, the best defense against children had been telling Billy she wanted them, because she intuitively understood how much he would enjoy denying her.

Had Billy turned her into a liar, or didn't she know how she felt about anything? Would little white lies grow inch by inch so that one day she'd be married with children she didn't want? Eventually, Rimer would have tired of the novelty of fatherhood. Or would he? The tragedy was he had no opportunity to know how he really felt. Had he been relieved to conform to this one norm of his culture, this simple desire for a child? Eventually, he would not have been able to deny his true nature. When she realized he and Art were lovers, Elle was happy for them and the time spent with Art in Key West left her wondering how he would survive Rimer's death. Maybe if they had all been honest with each other, they could have had a life together, each with their own secret life. Would Art ever tell her? Did she want to hear it from him?

Temperatures reached the high eighties, although it was only mid-May. Conditions most would find unacceptable kept Elle tethered to the island. The population was sparse, skilled help only available in brief spurts and transportation unreliable. In between Miami and Key West lay the intractable 130 miles of misery, which is what she once heard Nathan say. But he must not be acquainted with the real thing because to her this was paradise, despite all its challenges.

The night after Brushy's visit, Elle set out for the diner. If she timed it correctly, she would arrive before sunrise. She rinsed her face, tossed grain to the chickens and walked her bike to the pathway. Last thing she saw was Cat give up the chase. The air had cooled, which made biking easy, and Elle felt an urgency to get to the property.

It annoyed her that the diner wasn't visible from the road. They'd need billboards, she thought, wondering what that would cost. When she looked at the property through Brushy's eyes, she marveled at his efficient genius. The building rose in the center of a large circle of chalk marked space. Gas tanks here, parking there, maybe a generous walkway.

She swooped down the slope and fished out the key, but the imposing padlock only appeared set in place, the chain slack and loose enough to slip under and open the door. Someone was sleeping on the thin cot when she arrived. At first, she thought it might be a tramp, but recognized Brushy's favorite jacket, bowed and worn, hanging on a lone wall hook in the middle of an empty sweep of wall. His face in repose was sweet, lids fluttering as if in the center of an intense dream. His cheekbones were generous, peering over top whiskers that looked rough and knotted as a lion's mane. Elle imagined anyone peering into the window would see their profiles through the glass, the two of them stranded in this place beside a road to nowhere.

Tanned skin showed the raised embroidery of veins on the back of his hands, finished with a scattering of fine bleached hair. His knuckles were large and sinewy, fingers curled into fists. His shoulders were square, more the product of good genetics than effort, she suspected. Then she remembered opening the door to the large supply cabinet at No Name lodge and catching him doing pull-ups, struggling to yank his weight up. Perhaps marrying the showy Blanche had turned him into a laughingstock and not the stud he had hoped to be.

Still, here he was, a large man lying on a narrow cot in a humid wasteland. How did men like him become visionaries? Elle searched his face, confused by her own rising anger. Would the one person who believed in her become the object of her rage? No, she thought with a dull stab. I am not like Billy.

She scanned the room, then circled the interior to stop at each window and survey each section of the lot, searching for some unseen danger, then back to Brushy. Had he moved? In the failing light, the outline of his face blurred, and she felt the years slip away and saw him as he had once been. She wiped her hands on her rough khakis and impulsively reached for his hand. A pronounced callus on his middle finger marked him as a document man, a paper flipper, and Elle felt a rush of pity, as if the ordering was more satisfying than the doing.

Elle kneeled beside him, listened to his deep breathing, feeling his slow pulse. He let loose a sudden snore, breaking the spell. When she moved to rise, he opened his eyes, and she understood he enjoyed her attention. In the pale light, he smiled at her and she smiled back. Like a magician's card trick, she felt his years slip away as easily as if she were flipping a deck of cards to shuffle back the years. He took in a breath and pulled her to him, and she allowed her body to loosen.

"I have begun to really see you," he said, and Elle felt a shock of sudden desire. As she had seen him, he was a man who put himself together a long time ago and lost some parts along the way.

She pushed off from his chest, stared at him but said nothing. They both let out thick breaths, then laughed at this sudden recklessness.

His eyes shone, then teared. They turned away, each from the other. Then she felt his chin bang into hers and knew with a sudden rush he came to a decision, followed by an awkward kiss.

Light crept into the unfinished dusky store and Elle heard machinery and distant shouts from the road and quickly rose. A rush of excitement as she smoothed her blouse against her body and stood. "When are you leaving?" she asked, her voice exaggeratedly loud.

"I think it can wait a week now."

She laughed. "No. Get it done. The sooner the better. Then come back." They both glanced at the newly installed window, almost expecting to see a face look back. "Why were you sleeping here?" Elle asked.

"Oh, I can't bear the pretense any longer. Blanche feigning a headache and the two of them off to the abandoned cabin they think I don't know about."

"Look, I'm grateful she found someone. Been a long time I couldn't lay hands on that woman." He stared at her with open admiration. Elle forgot where to place her hands and her feet suddenly seemed too big for her legs. Warmth suffused her neck, and she shook her head to make it disappear, then fussed with her bandana to give her hands something to do.

"Seems to me you wear that thing more to keep your thoughts from spilling out than against the heat," he said.

"My sister always said I had the hearing of a fruit bat." Why had she said something so ridiculous?

Something honked, then a scratch or brush, maybe from the window. Someone yelled in the distance. Elle sprinted to the doorway. "Meet you here tonight, around ten, when everyone's gone."

"Yes," he nodded, "of course." As if this had been in the works forever. "If anyone sees me, I'll say I was on my way to Pigeon Key, or needed a long walk. Or…. "

Did he wonder what happened to Billy? Elle puzzled. Where had that come from? She felt his eyes on her as she walked to the door and spun to look at him, surprised at how unafraid she was.

"Tell Buster I'm watching the store, so he doesn't come. He knows I cook."

Brushy tapped his temple as if to say, that's thinking. A sweet, impish smile appeared, as though he made it to the top of the heap in a game of cowboys and Indians, but wanted a friend to join him.

Back at No Name, Elle was unsure what to do with herself. She loitered in the house and Cat followed her around, unusually chatty. After feeding him and inspecting his body for fleas, she spoke to him as if confiding to a friend. "Look out for the chickens. You're not as tough as you think you are." He tilted his wide orange face at her, lifted his chin to be scratched before settling on her lap.

As the sun set, Elle realized she'd been sitting quietly, as if in a trance most of the day. She walked out of the stifling house to the side of the wharf hidden from lodge company and jumped into the tepid water, bobbing and swimming languidly. Then she headed back home to wash, scrubbing her body and inspecting it for bites, hiding her own purpose from herself. She mended her good blue blouse and dug up a skirt, but changed her mind. A small frisson shuddered through her groin and she knew what it meant. She dug out dirt from her finger and toenails with her flip knife and rubbed oil on them to bring out the pink and make them shine. Then she smoothed some into her hair while it was damp and could turn frizz into curls. Lord have mercy, she thought. I don't want to smell like a salad, and toweled out the excess.

Before leaving, Elle cut off the dry end of her ancient tube of 'Paris Storm' lipstick, took out her hand mirror, smudged some on, then wiped most of it away, hoping to look as natural as possible while adding a little color.

On her way to the store at a little past nine o'clock, Elle cut a wide berth around the lodge, avoiding the piles of building material. A loud whisper swathed through the silence. Harsh, like Nathan's voice, then nothing. The wood was almost too silent. Not a bird swooshed, not a rat scampered. As if all the world was fixed in place, waiting for a great event to unfold.

Elle crossed narrow pathways easily, walking her freshly oiled bike quickly through the wood, then riding on the bisecting path, finally pedaling across the wooden bridge to the little store that contained her destiny.

An elaborate brass cash register sat on the plywood counter, like a jewelled prince in a desert. Elle circled it then ran her fingers over the raised dot and feather images. Brass lettering on the bottom oak drawer spelled out "national," and Elle had seen this before, identical to the register at the lodge. She slid the 'no sale' button and the drawer opened with a satisfying ring. The cash slots were empty and one side seemed unusable. Elle pried at what looked like a block of wood, but it wouldn't budge and seemed a waste of precious space.

Brushy was late and she didn't want him to see her struggling with the register, so she moved away and tinkered with her papers, took out her measuring tape and concentrated on figures, but only the cash register made the store seem possible. Wherever she looked, she saw empty walls that needed specialized equipment, a host of connectors, an invisible working system to ferry gas, water, electricity. She rose and tapped on one, the sound hollow and lonely as an echo in a cave. All evening Elle waited, cursing herself for a fool, as the true motive for her visit revealed itself. Tomorrow she would find Monty, and get those papers mailed to secure ownership of the store before Brushy changed his mind.

With the back of her hand, she wiped off the ghost of her lipstick, but nothing remained. The front door creaked, and something told her to find a place to hide, but she did not have time to get behind the large sheets of plywood leaning against the far wall. When she heard him call out to her, she marveled at how stealthy he was, how steady his voice. Everything she had prepared to say disappeared.

He came to her in the middle of the empty room, and she pushed him down to the sawdust floor and used their clothes as a bed. Elle almost said foolish things like, 'this can never happen again'. They tumbled around in the sawdust and when it was over; he cupped her chin then placed his hand on her thigh, and she watched the tendons move on his forearm, his finger tracing the indent of her thick thigh muscle. Through this gesture, Elle's power swelled, and she felt vital and alive. His was a beautifully lined face, more so since he shaved his sideburns and mustache off. Elle knew he had done it to feel her face next to his. She knew many things without having to ask.

Brushy pointed to the back of the empty structure, "I ordered a good-sized propane stove, a Franklin," he said. "And I brought you these." He pointed at restaurant supply mail-order catalogs, something Elle had never dreamed of actually using. "Oh, and look. Every place I've ever built has one of these."

"One of what?" she asked. But he was already up, moving toward what would become the stockroom. He pulled at the braided rag rug and Elle made out the outlines of a trapdoor.

"A root cellar?" In Florida?"

"Yes, a massive, hidden safe. In a pinch, you can store cash here, cases of booze, anything valuable. We're a long way from a bank." He told her the story of dynamiting a small area and finding an old conch to mattock out the rest. Elle remembered her aunt's root cellar and thought it a great idea, because no one would ever think to look for one if she ever got robbed.

"And that," Elle said pointing at the cash register. "It's beautiful."

He took her hand and stood. "Come see. I'll show you how to use it."

"I already know," she said, but he kept moving toward it and she supposed he wanted her to admire it and give a few pointers.

He pressed the 'no sale' button, as she had done before he arrived. "Feel around the cash drawer and you'll find a lever."

She located a small latch attached to the block of wood. "I think I found it."

"Press it." The wood slid open and Elle jumped back when she saw the dark silhouette of a revolver burrowed in the cubicle.

"You're kidding," Elle said. "I have no use for a gun."

"Of course not." He raised an arm theatrically. "There once was a woman." He motioned toward her, then raised his other arm. "Alone on a lonely highway... as the night closed in..."

Elle laughed. He must have rehearsed this speech, anticipating her refusal.

"It's a military gun, an W1911. Good old Slabsides. There are thousands of them. Cheap, reliable and easy to use. I'll show you." He reached for the gun.

"No, that's enough for one evening. I'll keep it." She'd get rid of it later once he was gone. More than anything, she wanted to lie back down with him and stop speaking. In this perfect hideaway, his and hers alone that no one would ever imagine as their rendezvous.

She slammed the cash drawer shut and said "shhhh," but it came out sharply, making her sound bossy and authoritative.

"Yes ma'am," he said, emulating words often spoken to Blanche by the common workers at the lodge.

She didn't apologize for ordering him about. She sensed he enjoyed relinquishing his power to her, and she enjoyed taking it. "Kiss me," she said, straddling him. "Kiss me like we'll never meet again."

The moon barely lit the large, hollow room. And when they were through, he reached for the catalog and the two of them sat naked cross-legged on the floor and leafed through the images and descriptions of cooking tools, circling the ones she wanted.

"I see an orderly line of people waiting to be served." He looked toward the back of the store. "And you standing right there." He pointed toward the back, where the kitchen would be built, "There in your yellow blouse, pushing steam from your eyes, hair wild as a Florida sunset, ordering people about, your helper chopping vegetables for tomorrow's lunch."

But Elle missed the rest, envisioning only the yellow blouse, her one good top and the one in which she had massacred Billy. A rush of fear wrenched through her chest, making her stomach tighten, her nipples harden. And he seemed to know she had grown afraid. She reached under her to pull up clothing, but Brushy was sitting on it, so she tugged harder and something tore. He jumped up, "careful," he said, and the spell broke, the two of them aware of their nakedness.

"I changed my appointment... too much to arrange here.... so I don't have to leave for another week."

Elle knew he was lying. He had changed it to be with her, and it was the most incredible thing anyone had ever done for her. She helped him with his clothing, dressing him like a child, enjoying the fine batiste of his summer shirt, in awe over the inequities of their stations and feeling as if it meant absolutely nothing at the same time as defining her entire life.

25

The next morning, Elle wrapped the gun in a dish towel and stashed it in her bike basket. She'd never enjoy using the register without worrying about setting it off.

At No Name, she dug a shallow grave under the tallest palm tree in her yard and buried it. She'd engineer a meeting with Brushy and return it to him as soon as she could.

She was halfway through preparing sandwiches when the door flew open. Ruby stood in the doorway. "May I enter?" she asked. She wore an absurd skirt and long sleeves, like someone visiting from another century. When she crossed the room to extend her hand, Elle wondered why she hadn't heard her enter the gate.

"Ruby," Elle said. "I haven't seen you since the party."

"That's me, Ruby Foreman, the foreman's wife." Her laugh was thin and false, her little joke. "Buster asked me to get the sandwiches."

In the clear light by the open door, Ruby moved to the shelves Elle made from scrap lumber and picked up a jar of stewed tomatoes. "You've made a decent place for yourself here. For a woman... alone, I mean. It's a real accomplishment to survive here." Ruby ran her fingertips over a second row of jars with dark caramel flesh. "What are these?"

"Sapodilly fruit for pies."

Maybe Ruby would tell her what she really wanted.

"Do you miss him?"

"What? Who?"

"Billy."

"Billy. What about Billy?" The force of his name pushed Elle back to the prep table so quickly she nudged an unwrapped sandwich onto the floor, splattering bits of fish everywhere.

"I'm so sorry." Ruby reached for the cloth, but Elle snatched it away.

"Everyone knows the storm took him." Why did she say that? She bent down to sop up the mess. Fleshy bits clung to a table leg, traces on her shoe. A glob slopped back onto the floor and she mopped it up with sandwich bread, leaving a smear of fish that she would scrub once Ruby left. Grateful for the diversion, Elle wiped her hands on her apron and raised herself up to her full six-foot height. "He wasn't a lot of help. Worked on the road. Nothing steady." Last thing she wanted to talk about was that bastard.

"No help? Like Nathan. He's a big guy."

Who? Billy or Nathan? "Who are you talking about?"

"Nathan. My husband. Weighs 225. You don't want to mess with him." Ruby tried to smile.

"What does that mean?" Was she being threatened?

"No, I mean I don't want to or... um... anybody..."

"Please. Just take the bag and go. Some of us don't have time for idle chatter." A sandwich remained on the board, and in her eagerness to be rid of Ruby, Elle swept it aside to close the bag. When she handed it to Ruby, it slid off the table and splattered next to the spot she cleaned. "Oh, for God's sake..."

"I'm so, so sorry." Ruby's mouth was open, eyes pleading, and Elle hoped never to hear *I'm sorry* again as long as she lived. She softened her expression.

"There go the profits. All ten cents of them." Something in the woman's terrified face caused Elle to place a hand on her shoulder. "It's not life and death. Just a sandwich."

Ruby looked ready to cry. "No, it's more than that. It's yours, your livelihood."

"Yes, and I can make another. Like those." She motioned to the bag Ruby was holding. But Ruby seemed not to hear her.

"Billy left you with nothing, I guess. Like Nathan would. Not the kids, not the house, not the shoes on my feet if he had his way." Her face was mottled red and white.

Something scratched at the thatched roof overhead and Ruby shrieked. The woman was a wreck.

"Lizards, they sun themselves on the roof."

"I'll never get used to this creepy place. But he loves it here. Told me he wants to buy land, build a house. Move us off Pigeon Key, where there's even less to do."

"Then leave him. If you hate it so much. Just go."

"I got kids, and no schools out here, so I would be stuck at home teaching what I don't know myself, under his watch, with no neighbors anywhere to tell."

"Tell what?" Elle said, instantly sorry she had asked.

Ruby lifted her skirt and Elle saw purple bruises, old amber marks, a swollen knee.

Elle closed her eyes and looked away.

"I'm not asking for your sympathy."

Elle had taken in the red circles around her ankles and imagined ropes. She couldn't see Ruby's wrists, hidden under long sleeves.

Then the sound of the lizard's curved talons across the roof, tail slapping, feet scratching. They looked up at the ceiling.

Elle stared at Ruby. "Invasive species."

"But that's what *we* are. We don't belong here," she nodded at the ceiling. "Do you mind if I sit for a minute?" She looked up at the ceiling.

Earlier that morning, Elle had placed the radio on an outside chair to do yard chores and a bird made off with the foil she crimped to the tip of the antenna. Reception cut in and out, often correcting itself long enough for Elle to stop fiddling with it before it began again.

"Oh, never mind. I have to go. Thank you," she said, reaching for the bag of sandwiches, but Elle stopped her.

"You don't need an excuse to visit. We women should stick together." She said, though Ruby depressed her. Ruby was a reminder of a world run by men and what happened if you drew the short stick, and worse, had children that tethered you to one of them..

"Thank you," Ruby said, her smile compressed. She turned awkwardly and left the cistern.

Damn that woman, Elle thought, coming in here to pry me open. Ruby only stayed long enough for a few torch songs to play on the radio, but everything was different. Elle lost the will to feed the chickens. Her to-do list could've have been written by the rooster—meaningless indecipherable scratching. What the hell did Ruby know about Billy?

Elle bent over to scrub the greasy spot on the floor before ants found it. Bleach and iron hit her nostrils, a smell that came whenever she thought of Billy.

A neatly folded ten-dollar bill peeked from under the cutting board. What the hell? That was way more than her sandwiches were worth. Why had Ruby left it for her?

Her shoulders stiffened; her body moved as if in a brace. The weather-beaten RCA spewed static. Tucking the bill in her apron, she eyed her old crumbling one-room home as if it belonged to someone else, and walked out the front door, checking to see if anyone was watching.

Elle eyed her small front yard from the porch, then inspected the side and back yard. The tinfoil crown on the makeshift radio antenna peered out from a pile of coral rocks. A small gecko sat on top, his red dewlap swelling as songs drifted in and out. Volume low, then loud, then a dragging stutter came from the antenna, then something more from the roof this time. Dammit. That enormous lizard. Laying eggs out of reach. She grabbed her rake and banged against the side thatched edge. The pounding shook birds out of a nearby tree. They flew above her with a startle, moving in formation then breaking and shifting as if searching for some unattainable pattern.

Only eleven o'clock and she was exhausted, with an afternoon of cooking and planting ahead. Real planting. Trees, not seeds.

Her eyes settled on the ormolu chair with purple brocade embroidery, the oiled sideboard, the tree root table, discarded treasure dragged back in the middle of the night.

When 'Ain't Misbehavin'' came on, a sudden memory of Ruby formed. She had been present at the Labor Day party before the hurricane, back before Nathan became foreman. Nathan had danced with Blanche while Billy looked on, indifferent. Seemed to Elle, that was the way of men and women. Nathan wanted Blanche, who wanted Billy, who wanted Elle, who wanted to be free.

Like Ruby wants now, Elle thought. Ruby was the woman at the lodge window. Before the storm warnings, after everyone left on the ferry except Mrs. Dean, who lived miles away, closer to Big Pine. The evening before they departed, Ruby refused alcohol at the party, didn't dance and kept to herself, and Elle had wondered why she bothered to come at all.

Women like Ruby knew how to make themselves small. They could fit into the tiniest of spaces. It was her, sure it was. In the same lousy skirt. She remembered that navy skirt, too dark and heavy for the tropics.

Elle moved her hand over her thigh, her finger skimming the raised scar in the same place as Ruby's. Last scar he ever gave her. Ruby should've stopped for longer. She needed rest. That poor woman, Elle thought with a rush of horror. Why didn't I let her rest in the chair before leaving?

She headed to the hermit's grove. Perhaps she could recall an earlier vision of a fruited landscape, trees dripping with money. Cat followed, crying. Did he want to be fed? She picked up the one-eyed orange beast and hugged him, surprised by his sudden anxious purr. A thorn stuck in the thick of his paw pad and she held him tight, digging out the thorn that might be a lizard talon, happy to help something, someone — and shut him inside the cistern with a meaty chunk of snapper and bowl of fresh water.

Strange objects littered the pathway. A pull toy in the shape of a dog, with missing parts. Broken slats from a crab trap led to the hermit's grove. Elle fertilized the garden with rotted compost from lodge discards. Even decent garbage is scarce these days, she thought, thinking of all the tinned food the Dinkson's used. At the grove she checked the rows of young sapodilla trees the hermit planned to sell to the Coral Reef Nursery founded by Krome, the great nurseryman in South Dade. They stood upright, neat as headstones in a soldier's cemetery.

On the way out of the thicket, streamers of light bounced through the trees and a muffled noise grew in intensity as she approached the ferry landing. Young men leaped off the dock like a mindless stream of amphibians. More men come to build the highway? Their clothes were far too heavy for the climate, reminding Elle of Ruby. The image of a fragile woman beneath thick skirts had burrowed into her head. A guillotined coconut bounced off the narrow pathway and landed in front of her.

When Elle passed the lodge, she peered intently, as if she could make out the goings on behind window and wall. What did she expect? Blanche Rowlands holding up Billy's mummified torso with the anchor tattoo intact?

Less than twenty-four hours from Ruby's visit and Elle felt like a ghost, circling the remnants of her own life. Before evening fell, she lay on her narrow cot in the breezeless room. She had no appetite and imagined yellowtail, mutton snapper, emerging from the water already spoiled.

Cat limped to her side, and she hugged him close, afraid to sleep, afraid to leave the place she had rid herself of Billy, afraid to dream. Then Billy was suddenly back, her yellow dog dead at her feet and she knew Billy had killed it. A dog never seen in these parts; a friendly, robust boy, so happy to have someone to love. And that's what finally decided her. The owners would fire her because there would be no room for her dog, and maybe that's why Billy killed him, but even in her dream, she knew he killed the dog because she loved it. Dog gave her the courage to get rid of him. She felt Billy's beard on her face and, terrified; she woke to Cat licking her face with his sandpaper tongue.

26

Outside, a shard of light pierced through the perimeter of brush, illuminating a young tree. Volunteer saplings were common, but something made her look twice. The manchineel branch she buried had sprouted roots, and a shoot grew green and healthy to form a tender poisonous sapling. Once it matured and spilled its deadly apple harvest, it would be destroyed. Throughout the Florida Keys, manchineels were marked with red X's on the trunk, then chopped down. Elle felt mercy for the sister tree that felled Billy and wondered if she could use the sap as an astringent, something. Sharp serrated leaves flashed emerald in the sun, drawing her closer. Every part of the manchineel was poisonous, so Elle dug a circular trench around the young tree's delicate feeder roots, pulled her sleeves over her hands for protection, and lifted the small thing, wedging the root ball into a burlap sack. She dug up a few young palms and placed them around the tree for camouflage as clouds gathered overhead.

"Elle," Blanche's shrill voice. How often had she stopped, jarred by that squawk?

Having the poisonous tree in plain sight struck Elle as delicious, so she allowed Blanche to get closer. Blanche almost looked beautiful without her usual white face powder and eye makeup that created a startling resemblance to an egret in mating season.

"What did the Coast Guard want?"

Elle made her wait before answering. Impatiently, Blanche shifted her weight from one foot to the other, enhancing the impression of a shorebird. "Oh, this and that," Elle said casually. Blanche's eyes moved from Elle's face to the trees in her cart. But Elle wasn't worried; Blanche wouldn't know an eggplant from a cabbage. "They wanted to know what happened. I'm surprised they haven't come for you."

"Maybe they have." Blanche said, dismissing Elle with a wave.

"I told them to talk to you. I know nothing about lodge business."

Someone rose from a chair on the porch. Something in the way he moved made her certain it was Nathan.

Elle blocked his view of the manchineel, and when she turned to arrange a couple of palms in front of it, a sharp leaf scratched her hand. She jumped. But it was young, she reasoned. What harm could it do?

Nathan didn't quiz her about the trip to Pigeon Key as she expected. "Congratulations on the diner. I know how much work it takes to get a place up and running, especially here."

Her hand itched. His awkward attempt at charm was a dead giveaway. He must be worried about what she told the authorities. She remembered the overheard conversation between him and Blanche before the party. *The glazier was worth two bucks, the woodworker only one.* If anyone discovered the operation, Pigeon Key would be investigated, and Elle imagined it would be like turning over a rock. But after the trip, she realized they were in charge of investigating themselves. A perfect setup.

Elle enjoyed watching them squirm, trying to figure out the best way to approach her-Nathan the carrot, Blanche the stick. She would have stayed to see the show play out, but the sting from her scratch had ramped up and the trees pulsated, as if gasping for breath. Was the manchineel poison causing her to hallucinate?

"I'm late," she said. Blanche frowned, Nathan tried to smile and neither of them asked what she could possibly be late for.

On the road to Big Pine, Elle felt free and protected inside an enchanted wood. The little manchineel bobbed, peeking out from behind the palms, causing the sun to wink whenever she turned to check.

At the Sidetrack Diner, she treated the scratch with peroxide and Mercurochrome and wrapped her swelling hand in a bandage before wheeling the trees into the dark line of brush behind the property clearing. "I'll plant you tomorrow," she whispered. "I promise."

She would stay in the storage room, move upstairs later. After nailing both framed pictures of her mother and sister on the wall, her hand swelled, but she didn't care. Next, she moved the couch, and imagined the heavy ormolu chair she would drag from No Name to form an intimate spot for conversation or reading in a life she had not yet lived. It was the chair where Brushy sat in when he first took her into his confidence and she longed to pat it, brushing imaginary dust and debris from the worn seat. Inspired, with her good hand, Elle moved a wobbly table from the store to use as a desk, wedging a folded piece of butcher paper under a leg to stabilize it. She pulled in the old cot next to a box of tinned beans for a side table. Cocooned in the windowless room, she breathed easily and fell into a long and dreamless sleep, labels and lettering from all the goods in the pantry dancing in her head.

27

This new crew was more efficient under private management and Elle slept peacefully to the familiar strain of rocks and steel and engines revving down the road.

Cat trailed her back and forth from the cistern, but Charlie the rooster would only trek out a short distance, then double back. When she penned in a space out back, he escaped. Twice he made his way back to No Name with his troop of hens and chicks. What kind of rooster travels over three miles to find his way home? But again, she couldn't find him.

The pathway was silent after the last ferry left for Key West, and Elle carted her cache of jarred fruit along the deserted road to the diner. A smell of tar tailed her, and tree stumps on the borders of her cleared parking lot cast odd shadows. Elle unlocked the padlock and placed it on the inside. The oven here, the tables there, cash register by the door. But how would Brushy fit into this new world? They'd never spoken about the future beyond creating the diner, and Elle couldn't imagine him settling down anywhere in the swampy Keys. It made no sense.

Her heels echoed over the wooden subfloor until she reached the doorless opening to the large pantry. Even with her bed and desk in the center, the size seemed vast and thrilling. Room enough to stock everything she needed to finance a new life.

Elle imagined the diner alive with light, catchy radio tunes, patrons leaning over the bar listening to news on the radio. She imagined families in line for supplies and snacks, the low buzz of conversation, but most of all she heard the musical ring of the cash register in the background, like a psalm. As the sun descended, she turned the lamp flame up and walked around the space to better imagine the placement of chairs, tables and other apparatus necessary to a well-stocked, busy diner.

Beyond the kitchen, a hollow sound marked the trapdoor to the large root cellar. Under the fickle glow of a kerosene lamp, Elle spread a quilt over the trapdoor as the last light outside disappeared entirely. She moved the heavy trunk easily over the top to test the solidity. That old Conch knew his stuff.

Satisfied, Elle adjusted the flame and a low line of black smoke hung in the air, then disappeared. She settled against the trunk. This was home. "Everything is gonna work out," she said, stroking Cat.

After she spoke, Cat stiffened, then jumped straight up at the window. A faint noise halfway between a demand and a plea sounded, then the front door pushed open. Ruby hobbled in, hunched over.

Please, she mouthed, dark eyes staring out. "He's after me."

Instantly, Elle dragged the heavy trunk away, rolled the quilt up, and opened the trapdoor to the root cellar. "Go," she said, and Ruby moved, hunched and jerky, obviously injured. She descended the narrow staircase, and Elle closed it behind her. After pushing the trunk back into place, Elle moved to the window and looked out into the enormous and barren wood. Nathan would not be far behind.

A dim light shone from a place deep in the brush. A minute later, another closer. Someone was out there. She blew out her lamp. He would have seen the light by now, but not exactly where.

Workmen's pallets, crates and large glass tabletops covered in quilts leaned against the wall. Elle unrolled an old blanket on the floor near the kitchen and placed a pallet and crate over the top. She felt for her flip knife, but if it came to that, she would give Ruby up.

A loud rap sounded at the door. Then it flew open. "Where is she?"

"Who?"

"My wife. Ruby."

"I don't know what you're talking about."

He stood in the open doorway; legs slightly parted in that timeless stance of boss men. "Liar. Where else would she be?" He leaned his shiny silver bicycle against the outside wall. Had he come from behind the store? A land crab scurried away behind him. Only later would she remember the sign of the crab as if Billy were sending them to her.

"Come see for yourself." Elle motioned him in.

He jerked upward as if sniffing the air for Ruby. Elle recognized the gesture from somewhere. Billy used to do the same thing as a joke, sniffing the air then saying, *I know you're in there Elle. Can't hide.*

Did Nathan know about the root cellar? Maybe he was there when the old Conch begged a job from Blanche. *I'll take anything*, is what the old man said, the timeless giveaway of a desperate man. The old Conch with scarred, big-knuckled hands who claimed he'd excavated the tough coral with a mattock had returned earlier in the week, looking for more work. He said they wouldn't hire him at Pigeon Key. Too old. Could he have bragged about building it to Nathan when he asked for work?

Nathan made a show of banging around and moved toward the massive trunk. He circled slowly, slid the canvas runner off the top and rapped his fingertips on the brass edges. "Nice piece," he said, leering at Elle before he swung it open, his face alive with triumph before letting out a low blunt of air from his open mouth, as if he'd been deceived. Elle thought she heard Ruby take in breath, but it might have been air escaping when Nathan slammed the trunk shut.

"She's left the kids before. It's not the first time." He punched the trunk and looked directly at her. His eyes softened. "Something wrong with her," he began. He called Ruby fragile, self-destructive, unhappy, but Elle heard *lazy, worthless, bitch.*

"I saw someone on my way here."

Elle shrugged. "Lots of ghosts on the highway. Dead workers. Old soldiers. Maybe a deer." She stared straight into his eyes. This gesture unnerved most men; something she learned when she was young. Men never expected a steady gaze. "Maybe she's hurt... some strange critters out this way. "

"I might be worried about that if I were you. Your door wasn't locked."

"I've dealt with worse."

"So, I've heard. Maybe you've grown overconfident."

That thrilled Elle, the thought that he actually knew what she had done, and she hoped she read it right. She wanted to laugh.

"If you see her, tell one of my men. They know where to find me."

Elle walked past him to the door, giving him her back as if she had nothing to worry about, then turned and smiled grimly. "And let her know she's always welcome here, if she gets lost. Good luck to you."

He pushed back in and slammed the door behind him, and Elle had a fleeting vision of Ruby bounding up from the cellar, the two of them tackling Nathan, chopping him up and burying him in the yard or tossing him out to sea.

He hesitated long enough for Elle to know he imagined a similar scenario. He must've told someone he was coming here and couldn't summon the courage to get rid of her. Coward. They were at a detente. Neither could risk murdering the other, which struck Elle as funny.

"Well?" she said, and he scanned her body so hot and briskly Elle felt violated. Nothing in his history would explain her recklessness if she didn't have a gun. She moved her hand toward the back of her nightshirt.

He turned and exited, holding the door open. "What goes on between me and my wife is none of your business."

"Yes, and I'd appreciate you keeping it that way."

Her greatest asset was that whenever she was afraid, she became enraged. She stood in the open doorway and watched him pedal up the incline as effortlessly as if he were coasting down. When he disappeared, she hung a quilt over the exposed window, but it felt like locking the coop after a visit from the fox.

Before telling Ruby he was gone, Elle paced and planned. Cat shadowed her movements, tensing with each creak of the floorboards. The dark, shuttered space brought Elle back to the Labor Day hurricane, after she disposed of Billy in the crab traps. Another long night hunted by something.

Reflexively, she felt the outline of her flip knife in her pocket and the gesture brought Billy back. The lamp, the glass on the table, the jug of manchineel juice that poisoned him. Everything around her looked staged, like a theatrical replay of horror. Why hadn't she kept the gun?

Elle circled the barren diner to shake off the vision, anger subsiding, replaced by fear. Cat followed close behind, then stopped, his neck at a strange angle trying to make sense of her actions. Lost were the visions of happy families, the lazy curl of cigarette smoke, fresh coffee, the sweet refrain of the cash register. Now she saw the outline of mangled bodies, heard the shriek of the woman beaten and whimpering from below. She pulled on the quilt to drag the chest away from the opening, lifted the hatch and peered inside. "Ruby?"

"I'm okay."

"He's gone." If she could convince Ruby to stay underground all night, they would both be safe. Too late. Ruby was halfway up the ladder.

"Something horrible crawling around. Cockroaches? Crabs?"

"Palmetto bugs, but that's all," Elle lied. No idea what lurked below. Scorpions? Spiders?

Ruby shuddered. Black outlined her fingernails and Elle suspected dried blood, or maybe she clawed at the ground when Nathan was here.

"Shh. Sit a minute." Elle grabbed a couple of quilts and arranged them to make a lumpy seating area. Ruby folded her body tightly into her bent knees like a small child, then let out a quick scream when something outside thumped to the ground.

Elle felt for her knife, then relaxed. "Always something." She rose, tossed Ruby the broken mattock and Ruby nodded, forming a tight fist around the handle. A heavy coconut palm frond dangled over the window. "See?" she said triumphantly, giving Ruby a stiff little smile, her lips unable to complete the upward curl.

They leaned against the chest, silent, then Ruby raised her eyes to meet Elle's gaze. "His anger blows over quickly. So long as he thinks no one knows," Ruby nodded rapidly, grasping and loosening her hold on the mattock handle. And Elle felt ashamed for wanting to be rid of her.

"Stay the night. Tomorrow I'll get you out and to the church. Mrs. Dean will take you in."

"What about Betty and Perry?" Ruby shook her head and her gaze fell to the floor. "My children."

Elle reached for her wrist and squeezed it awkwardly. The gesture felt forced "Yes. Yes. I'm certain she'll take them as well. Children belong with their mother. She knows that."

Ruby let out a snort, which coursed through her body. "They're friends with Nathan. He and the pastor play cards." She pressed her thumb against a black cuticle.

"When they see you, they'll know what he did." What a sham. Nathan would come up with a justification, if he was questioned at all, and Mrs. Dean would hold Ruby in contempt for being unable to control her man.

Elle remembered sitting on Mrs. Dean's turquoise chair some days after the Labor Day hurricane. Earlier that day, she had gone out with Jim, a local fisherman, to search for survivors who had hunkered down in the storm. It had been Jim's idea for her to sit in the cushy armchair, and Elle could feel Mrs. Dean's resentment. Later on, Elle wondered if she had slept with Jim out of gratitude and the thought saddened her.

"It's hopeless," Ruby said.

Elle resented her pleading tone. Why was it her job to comfort Ruby? Elle earned everything from her own toil, not given by a man or a parent.

She wanted to tell Ruby to grow a backbone. "That's not true. Some women escape. Some men pay." The sound of her own voice filled her with pride. Never, not for one minute, had she regretted killing Billy. "Surely you know someone who escaped a brutal marriage and made something of her life?"

They stared at each other, and this time, Ruby didn't look away. "Maybe I do, maybe I don't. You tell me."

"What? What are you saying? Billy left me. Ask Monty. Ask anyone."

"But you got away before that. I mean, you came to No Name alone." Ruby stared at her in open admiration.

No one knew Billy destroyed her job at the lodge a few days before she killed him.

"You got him to leave you alone. The ferry guy told me how mean Billy was. You got the little shack by the water. Your own place. How did you do that? I can't do anything to handle Nathan."

Elle pretended to hear something and motioned for Ruby to get back down. Later, in the stark hours, Elle whispered, "you alright down there?" Ruby responded by climbing back up the stairs. Throughout the night, one slept, the other sat, a bucket of ammonia, the flip knife and mattock close by. Cat waited by the door as if sensing something on the other side.

When the first rays of sun softened the outline of the quilt in the window, Elle caught some sleep, head rolling, for a few minutes at a time. When she woke, they were curled foot to head in skewed quilts. Ruby's exposed shoulders and throat revealed a necklace of fingerprint bruises that passed over her jugular.

28

Elle awoke to Ruby in a dead sleep, snared in the linen sheet, a pair of Elle's canvas pants balled into a pillow beside her head. Light was coming in strong, so it must be late. The last thing she remembered was lying down herself, hoping this would help Ruby relax.

Carefully, Elle extricated her body from the twisted linen, tiptoed to the front door and closed it soundlessly behind her, alert for anything unusual. When had this feeling of being stalked become normal for her? When did everything take on a sinister cast, her gaze fixated on an out-of-place footprint, a ground out cigarette butt hidden in the bushes?

Nathan's bicycle tread formed two paths, one in and another out, she noted with relief.

When she returned, Ruby was fussing with the kerosene ring.

"Do you have coffee or Postum? I can't find it." She smiled and reached for her skirt. "Sorry," she said, embarrassed at exposing her bare legs.

"You need to get rid of that rag," Elle said, and Ruby smiled as if the previous evening had never occurred. Ruby looked happy, radiant almost, hair loose and barefoot in a long chemise. Nothing seemed wrong and Elle stared at her, finally understanding. Ruby returned

Elle's gaze with a sad little smile that said, oh well, there's nothing I can do. And with that, Elle knew she would return to Nathan. And Elle understood something deeper-she didn't have the courage to help her sister. She was as selfish and complicit as the men she loathed.

"You'll probably have a few good days. A week maybe." Elle knew the pattern, a brief reprieve after a fight. Elle turned to focus on the work ahead, the unfinished plywood, windows that needed to be fitted and caulked, but when she spied the open supply catalog, the pages of hammers, pliers and saws looked like tools to dismember a body. Turning away, she struggled to replace the vision with fresh chairs, bright countertops, striped blinds. A life.

"You can work here. You know, when you get away."

"Yah. Great. Thank you. And Nathan will come by to take the kids on bike rides. Sure. Then they'll all make sandcastles...."

"Um… Well, stay just until Sunday."

"No, I'll leave today. When the ferry returns. I'll tell him I missed it yesterday and tried to walk home, but it was too far."

"Then you came here, right after Nathan left. OK? Tell him to ask me and I'll back you up."

"Yes, that's perfect. Thank you," Ruby said.

He won't believe it, but so what? She motioned with her flattened palm to stop Ruby from thanking her.

"We live in the house furthest from the dining lodge."

Elle nodded. Of course they did.

"My boy, Perry, can't look after Betty for long. I won't do that to him. He hates me, but so long as that keeps her safe, I don't care."

"And how long will that be?"

29

Two days later, the knock came, and Elle half expected a repeat performance from Ruby. But when she flung the door open, Nathan jumped out at her like a jack-in-the-box.

"No one knows I'm here," he said, taking her in. "This is between us. I can help you with this place. No one has to know."

She thought he'd be subtler than that, and his quickness told her how desperate he was and how sure he was that she knew it.

"Why would you want to help me?"

The question caught him off guard and the look of confusion that passed through his face made her bold.

"I mean, thanks, but I have nothing to offer you in return and don't really need any help," Elle said.

"I'm talking about what happened at No Name Lodge. How we tried to help the men and how some have turned on us."

"Us?"

"Blanche, I mean. Blanche and Brushy Rowlands. And me... and what you did for my wife. We still want to help them... and you, too."

"Them?"

"The men." He stopped and stared at her suspiciously, suspecting she was mocking him. He moved toward her.

The flip knife, the jug of ammonia behind the cash-what was closest? Why hadn't she kept Brushy's gun?

She turned toward Nathan and the juvenile manchineel pinged her from the side window.

"I'm on your side," he said. "So long as you're on mine." He looked impatient, then unsure, then kindly.

The carrot and the stick, she thought.

Elle half expected him to tell her Ruby was sick or gone, or worse. "How's your wife?" she asked.

"She's fine."

"Like I said, I don't need any help. I mind my business."

"I think of us as the last great American pioneers," he said, and pushed his way farther inside, his eye on the door to the pantry. He moved quickly, flung the door open, and looked around.

"Nervous habit," he said. "Just want to keep this between us." Elle watched from the pantry doorway. "We're all in this together," he said, the usual lie.

Her hand throbbed. She clenched her fist to distract herself from the pain. Something occurred to Elle before the thought materialized in its entirety. A way to help Ruby.

Air escaped Nathan's lungs, as if he had been holding his breath.

"Look at the mess," Elle said, with a sweeping gesture. "And my hand is hurt."

She snatched it away before he could inspect it. "An old injury."

The place actually looked great, but Nathan would see what she wanted him to see.

"I have all the builders I need, but no customers until the road goes all the way to Key West."

"The workmen spend money here. You have that," Nathan said.

"Hardly enough to make it worthwhile," Elle answered.

"Bernie's looking for someone."

"Who's Bernie?"

"The cook at Pigeon Key. Unusual to hire a woman, although you're a different kettle of fish, as they say…"

"I'm not interested. But you could let your wife come here to help me. She helped with the table arrangements at No Name. And maybe it will give her something to do, make her feel better." Elle prattled on, "This place needs a woman's touch. An ability I lost long ago being husbandless… childless… And then there's the injury." She smiled and shrugged.

"You really think I'd let my wife come here? He looked at her in disgust. I came to tell you about the job, to do you a favor."

"I don't need anything from you." Elle said.

"I wouldn't be so sure. I know what you're up to with the old man."

"What are you talking about?" Had she been followed? "There are no old men here except the soldiers."

"What did the coast guard want?"

She wanted to laugh out loud. This was his true purpose. "Don't worry. Whatever they know, they found out somewhere else. I couldn't care less what you're up to."

"That's not what the men say." He advanced closer.

"I think we're about even in the guilt department." Which was ridiculous, and even he knew that. But so long as he thought she was afraid.

"We're just friends. What would that man want with me?"

His expression relaxed. It would be unimaginable for Nathan to think her an equal. "Of course you're just friends. And I'll be sure to spread the word. Just remember that next time they take you in for questioning."

He only wanted to know what she told the Coast Guard at Pigeon Key. What a fool.

30

Gone five days and Elle could barely remember what kept her occupied before Brushy. As she biked to her old cistern, Elle tried to focus on the menu she would create for the diner, something that should excite her. She imagined Buster filling gas tanks, tourists leaving the Sidetrack Diner with a bag of purchased snacks and soda. But today, even the image of herself at the cash register failed to excite Elle. All she imagined was her untidy apron, face red from work; a drudge counting change. Did Brushy really desire her?

A gigantic iguana sat on a stump, his gills as orange as they would have been at the height of mating season. His head angled sharply toward her as she passed, throat blotched and loose, eyes bulging and cold like a cunning old man.

One time, Elle was talking to one of the friendlier highway workers. She brought up Nathan and Ruby, trying to sound casual, but he had given her a strange look, as if he knew something. Did everyone know Nathan beat her? Did they know about Brushy? Had the entire Key been peering into the window that one night?

She reached the edge of the hermit's small grove and wondered how she ever thought this place contained magic. All she saw was endless toil, all to coax a few dozen stunted fruit out of stubborn soil.

As she reached for the tools, she noticed her hands and remembered that Brushy had commented on their gracefulness. He had found them beautiful. They seemed to defy the toil, temperature and rough work on No Name. She held them out at a distance to judge, dropping the trowel to better take them in. Posing this way and that, she imagined holding a martini glass, and took an imaginary sip, head back, loosening her hair. She put fingers up to her mouth in a wide-eyed gesture of feigned surprise, as she had seen Blanche do, imitating her idol, Clara Bow. She knew what was happening. Love turns you into a fool, a fawning coward, and all the signs were there. But so, what? There was little she could do about it and less she wanted to. She would weather the storm and when it ended as she knew it would, she'd be richer for the experience. That's all it was in the end. She nodded toward the abandoned stump. So long as she got the deed to the diner as promised, what harm? Hadn't she always bent in the tempest, emerging unscathed?

Sharp pain stabbed her heel and radiated up her shin. Leaning against a cocoplum, she removed her shoe to dislodge a shard of coral. She turned her foot this way and that, but no, her size twelve feet were not pretty.

The thought that Brushy was gone sent her in a rush to be home, out of the empty wood. She'd stay at the cistern and wait until Monty came in on the ferry. He would know something.

After a restless night, Elle took her skiff out for early morning snapper fishing. Cat pawed at imaginary prey on the prow. When Elle tossed a small fish at him, he glared at her as if affronted. "Yes, I know you prefer it cooked, spice and all." Talking to the cat again, jeez. She felt a flush of love for the bright orange guy who was becoming fat despite all the want on the island.

Lodge food will be terrible, Elle thought, finally realizing how jealous she was. Blanche's plans just might work. Maybe Brushy would regret his hasty decision. What about it? Guests from No Name Lodge would have to drive past the Sidetrack Diner to get to Key West, then again on the way back. They'd need gas and coffee on the way out. Yes, she thought, always the runoff, the remains.

No ferry this morning. What a waste of time.

A bright corner of dish towel stuck out from under the palm and a delicious surge of relief coursed through Elle's body. This was why she had come back. She brushed soil away from the bundle, carried it inside to her kitchen counter and unwrapped it as carefully as if it were a small, unpredictable animal. The flat contours of the black revolver presented an instantly familiar, bland lethality. Although she had never actually held a gun, it felt oddly natural. Once she became accustomed to its dark presence, she'd learn how to unload it. No one would have to know it had no bullets.

She cycled back to the Sidetrack Diner, relieved to be away from No Name. Again, she remembered the excitement at No Name Key Lodge, showing off her cooking skills, hearing the latest songs and seeing the newest outfits, reading the detective and science fiction magazines left behind. Now, she imagined Ruby everywhere, images of her bruised legs and what looked like a swollen patch near her temple came to Elle when she least expected. Pinging between Ruby and Brushy-one she couldn't have and the other she couldn't help.

The trapdoor called to her; the rug askew. Had she left it like that? Barely covering the opening. When she lifted the hatch, it creaked godawful long and loud.

Nothing. No one was there. What did she expect? Ruby? Bloody and scared? Worse?

At lunch, the road crew were subdued. Buster gave her a silent wave, his eyes barely skimming her face. When a few men made their way over, Nathan elbowed in. "Fish," he stated loudly, his face crinkled in disgust. He insinuated a large, booted foot into the small circle of men handling the food. She almost asked him, "How's your wife?" But the mood was tense, and he walked off, taking all but two customers with him. At the diner, she fixed a new lock into place and nailed the trapdoor shut and checked the gun was safe in its hidden compartment. Throughout the afternoon, she set to work sorting pantry items.

An out-of-work highway man came to paint the exterior for a small sum and meals. Elle agreed to allow his wife to join him as he promised no extra charge for her toil. The only paint they had was a violent, bright purple, purchased at a discount. At least they'll see it from the road. Paver trucks showed up mid-afternoon to finish the parking lot. Although Elle thought it a waste of space, Brushy had already paid for the job in full.

Amid all the toil, Elle paced about the place, and when she saw a footprint in the tar, she snapped at a boy on a smoke break.

Again, no sleep that night, up at every little sound. Then heading to the windows, wondering if this was the night someone would show. The painter couple slept upstairs after a supper of sandwiches that hadn't sold. "Best I can do for now," she said. Their work was perfect and when she told them, the wife asked her to please put it in writing if she would, "Appreciate any way to set ourselves apart, ma'am. Lots call themselves painters." Elle was happy to share food and talk about the lost art of craftsmanship into the evening. Only snippets of sleep.

Mid-morning, a truck stopped and the most extravagant yellow enamel eight-burner stove appeared, along with a tall matching icebox with shelves made to store ice lining the sides from top to bottom. She opened the card, and it read, "color of your blouse, B." Elle dropped it, angry that memories of that blouse kept turning up. Damn Billy. She paced around the outside of the building, then got back to work, inspecting the ice box and reading manuals.

Within a few hours, Mrs. Dean knocked at her door. "Just passing by and thought I'd stop in. Heard you carry the Miami Herald." She had probably caught wind of the stove delivery, big news in the Keys. Wouldn't take much to get her to talk.

"Looks like Blanche Rowlands won't be having the fishing tournaments," Elle said, as if they had these conversations regularly. "So much work. I won't miss cooking for all those people." Her laugh rang false to her own ears.

Mrs. Dean shook her head. "Too bad Nathan's missus in such a bad way after losing that child. What she did to herself. Unbelievable." Elle held her breath as the woman continued, "Heard she was in the hospital in Miami."

There it was. He had really hurt her this time. "Which hospital?"

"Why? Mr. Foreman said she's too weak to see anyone," Mrs. Dean responded, sensing she wanted more. She left quickly, the rubber from her dyed nurse shoes squeaked and a look of triumph flushed her face. For once, she had more news than Elle.

That evening Elle returned to No Name hoping to run into Brushy. She watched the ferry come in, relieved to see Monty at the helm. Three workers exited, a far cry from the earlier crowds of men and machinery swarming the wharf, whispering to one another in low, confused tones as they took in the terrain. They probably came to rebuild the tower, unprepared for the mess in front of them, the heat and coil of insects overhead.

"We're leaving right away for Key West," Monty said.

"Damn straight," responded a man who looked too well-dressed to speak so roughly. The Keys bring out the madman, Elle thought. Her look cut through the air.

"Ten-minute break," Monty yelled behind him. "Anyone not onboard gets left behind. No exceptions."

"And that goes for you, too." The same man yelled, obviously unaccustomed to taking orders.

"I'll put it plainly," Elle said, when they were alone. "I'm worried about Ruby Foreman. We've become friends, and I heard she's in the hospital."

"Oh boy, that coconut telegraph is better than the real deal." He smiled.

"It's not funny. You must have heard something? "

"I saw her. She's home. Why, what happened?"

"Oh, I guess I was wrong. Good. And don't bother to say hi if you see her. I don't think her husband would approve."

"Sure," he said. "Everything okay?"

"Yes, I had to get my things from the cistern, so thought I would ask." Elle sensed he didn't believe a word she said. "I guess the Rowlands are out together somewhere."

"I'll see you later," he said, shaking his head. "Take it easy, okay?"

What a fiasco, she thought. What a waste of half a day.

A couple more stray workmen appeared at the diner over the week, desperate characters, probably from the hobo camps in the mangroves. One drunk too many in Key West and the government would hand you a dollar and a ferry ticket to the mainland.

"We don't need anyone right now," she said three days in a row- placing an emphasis on 'us'. *We are the army of workers, the hidden men with guns and bats ready to lay waste to anyone with evil intent. Just behind the door... in the pantry... in the woods, so don't get any ideas...*

When the painting was complete, Elle found more work for the amiable couple, telling herself she needed the help but more the company at night when thoughts snuck up on her. Evenings cast long shadows, scaring, then angering her. Next thing you know, they set your place on fire, and you're on your way, the Keys washing their hands of you and back to the breadlines in Boston.

Nine days now and no word from him. Him. And she wanted to ask everyone she saw. *Is Mr. Rowlands back? Did you see him with his whore wife? Did he look happy? Does he know I'm here alone?*

Nothing more about Ruby. Waiting, always waiting for men, for money, for traffic and business, for love, for... She locked the diner tight, windows in place and the trapdoor so secure anyone would think she had a dead body below.

31

A lone family Ford found its way to the Sidetrack Diner in the wee hours. The young couple, a nanny dog and sleeping baby, roused Elle and seemed to catapult her into a new era. The courteous couple were relieved to find this stop along the way, and in that instant Elle realized she could be anyone. They would take her as they found her. This simple fact was a revelation. Along the wonky highway, the world was in motion and no one knew or cared who she was or where she was from. Unlike at the lodge, no one could boss her around.

Although the gas tanks were not yet connected, she had a large reservoir and filled the young couple's car with twenty-five gallons, charging the going rate of twenty-two cents a gallon. She asked if they wanted a cup of coffee on the house, but they refused, pointing to the sleeping baby in the back. There was something sweet and happy about the carload of strangers, the dog cautiously friendly, but never moving more than a half foot from the child. For a brief moment, Elle believed things would work out, however fragile they seemed from the outside. When she closed the door behind her, the couple on their way, Elle gazed at the yellow walls inside her shop and felt the muted glow of opulence, the beginnings. In her hands was $5.50, her first sale from strangers. She resisted the sentimental temptation to set it aside and simply placed it in the empty cash register.

Evenings Elle thought she heard work on the road, but must be mistaken. No one would work through the night. Finally, a week into hearing it grow fainter, she was certain the road was growing day and night, speeding up the schedule, assuming greater and greater urgency. Supplies were being trucked in from all over America, the abandoned rail lines, supply list and flurry of roadwork the sole topic of conversation. She hadn't seen Ruby or Brushy since April and June ushered in the truly hot weather. As the hot months began, sounds increased, until one evening, a sharp yell caused her to walk up to the road to investigate. The highway passed Big Pine now, and she knew a few of the men who stopped in regularly for a cold drink or a sandwich. It was a pleasure not to have to trudge lunch onto the road, but would again when construction moved farther toward Key West and doubling back became too difficult for the men.

A couple of workers corralled someone stumbling down the side of the road.

"Too far to walk," Elle recognized Art's voice and made her way up the incline, toward the group of four. She'd barely exchanged words with him since they met at the hospital after Rimer died over three months ago.

The man at the center held his arm at an awkward angle, his breathing shallow, eyes black.

"Where were you hit?" The men circled him.

"What happened?" Elle asked.

"Petey got hit with a rock kicked up by the backhoe. Then he was down."

"Art warned me to get out the way. My own damn fault."

Elle noticed the unnatural jut of his arm and the way he held it. Looked like a single break.

"Can we stop in? "

"You have anything that can help?" someone asked.

"Gimme a shirt," she said to the group of men, and when no one moved to strip down, she said, "You'll get it back."

"I told him it was time to quit," Art said, loosening his belt.

"I'll get you something at the diner. Come on back with me, the lot of you."

When Art removed his shirt, she made out a nude Hawaiian girl tattoo under his arm on his left side. Looked like a prison tattoo, crude. Everything about Art seemed a tunnel to his private life.

She fashioned the shirt into a sling of sorts, placed the sleeves across his back and chest, and tied them behind Petey's neck. "Loosen your shoulder. Let the sling do the work till we get inside."

"You know I'll get the boot if the boss finds out."

"We'll cover for you."

The four of them cautiously approached the decline. Art held on to Petey's good side and nodded thanks at Elle.

"He needs tending," Elle said.

The youngest guy said, "Has to go to the hospital."

Elle shook her head, no. "All they'll do is set the bone. Won't hurt to have a look."

She gave Art a sharp look, telling him not to speak. Elle suspected it was only a simple break that needed realignment to set properly. Her father had done that once in the basement in Boston and she remembered his screams.

"They'll fire him if they find out," the soldier with a kid's face said.

Elle winced and put a finger to her lips, silently shushing them.

The young guy turned away, "Glad you're here, Miss. But we all got to get back to camp and take it from there."

Art pointed at him. "We know you got six kids and a wife to feed. Just go."

"Yah," the third guy said, "If you can't stick by him, then get lost."

"I'll be getting out of your hair, Miss Elle," he said. "But thank you for..."

Elle ignored the departing man.

"Foreman doesn't like Petey as it is," Art said.

"Is that so?" Petey said, now inside and standing at the diner's unfinished lunch counter.

"Sit down," Elle said, drawing him to the barstool. "Hold your arm out so I can see."

Art and the big guy flanked Petey's sides, shoring him up. On the counter, Elle saw the unnatural jut of bone between wrist and elbow. "Looks good," she said. "You're lucky."

Both men looked at her hard, Art squinting as if trying to take her in as Elle stood there. "Think we could all use a good stiff drink." She thought about the case of liquor stashed in the back cupboard. "I have some quality scotch I save for special occasions such as this." She returned with a bottle in one hand and a large rubber mallet held out of sight behind her back.

"I got some bennies," Art said.

"Say what?"

"You get one shot at it," Petey said. He seemed to know what was about to happen.

Art removed a cylinder from somewhere, cracked it open, and rolled up the paper strip inside, handing it to

Petey. "When I say go, swallow this, then shoot back the booze."

"Here," he said to Elle. "One for you, too. This'll wake you up."

"I need nothing," she said, turning toward the arm, but he tossed it to her, and it rolled off the counter and hit the floor in the prep area.

Art held Petey's shoulder, and the tall man flattened his wrist firmly against the counter.

After he swallowed, Elle said, "Close your eyes."

A howl exploded through the room, but Elle expected it. "Pipe down. Yelling makes it worse." He swallowed hard, then again, before someone grabbed the bottle.

"Careful," she said. "And get some cups. We're not barbarians."

The look on Art's face was one of gratitude, as he nodded in agreement. Petey was breathing hard, and the big guy patted him on the shoulder. They poured him another drink and Art dropped something inside it.

"Something for every ailment," she said, "A walking apothecary shop."

Petey laughed. "Getting this from Art almost makes the accident worthwhile."

"Total waste," the big guy said. "One works against the other."

"Not true. I think they're complimentary. If you take one, then wait about a half an hour, then..."

"Regular chemists, the lot of you," Elle said, but Petey seemed strangely alright, as if the mere thought of the drug's effect calmed him. Art was up and clearing the counter, asking for a rag.

"Looks like you been busy." He said, taking in the diner.

The big guy's eyes were completely black. The iris disappeared. He stood, agitated, "If you ever need any help, Miss."

"C'mon, you know my name. If you guys need a place to rest up and a soda, you're welcome as guests of Sidetrack Diner-so long as you leave it the way you find it, you can have a tab and settle up on payday. Meantime, spread word that an eye is being kept on the place."

"Mighty generous of you," Art said. "Right boys?"

At that, they raised their glasses. "To the Sidetrack Diner," Petey said, the color completely drained from his face.

"But what if you're not here?" the big guy asked.

"Where else would I be?"

"We all wished you were the new hire at Camp."

Pigeon Key? They'd never hire a woman. Elle laughed when she saw Petey's guilty face. He just didn't think of her as a woman, and the thought pleased her more than it should have. She laughed, and all three joined her, except Petey, who looked appalled until Art slapped him on the back, hard.

When they left, Elle realized it was the first genuine laugh she enjoyed in a long time.

Next day she removed the spare key taped under the counter and wheeled her bicycle to the roadwork, drawn by the sound of cement mixers and the unmistakable thwack of Art's backhoe slamming into rock. She crooked her finger, motioning Art to step down from the cab and handed him the key.

"If it's locked, knock first, then enter… and no one is allowed unless you're with them. No fighting, booze paid in advance and only what's on the shelf behind the counter. Everything else on tabs."

He stared at the key she had placed in his palm.

"If you don't want it…." She began, but the look on his face stopped her. Someone trusted him.

As she turned to make her way back, he yelled after her, "Thank you. You won't regret it."

32

Elle locked the diner and pedaled through the lower Keys, over Flagler's old tracks and narrow outcrops of land that morphed into impossibly thin strips. A few stragglers passed; mostly men hungover from booze or too beaten up by the sun to look up when she pedaled past. In her cap and loose khakis, she could easily be mistaken for a thin man looking for work.

Mounds of fill shored up the sides of the recently paved road creating a mostly level grade until she reached the steep ascent to Pigeon Key where the tracks became too steep to pedal so she walked her bike to the topmost spot, high as a country carnival ride. Once the construction site for Flagler's Railway, this small Island served as the Southernmost base for rescue, relief and evacuation operations after the Labor Day hurricane. Taken over by Cleary Brothers Construction after the destruction of the tracks on the Upper Keys, the urgent need for a highway kept workers busy building the road from Miami to the storied bankrupt City of Key West, now being painted and washed, garbage finally hauled out, so the men said.

At the highest point, two old soldiers looked up, fishing from a lower section of the bridge. It would be natural enough for her to stop and look around. Another gawker after the storm. Not much going on in the Lower

Keys, and simple curiosity could easily account for her scrutiny, so she settled into surveying the small island from the bridge. Ruby said she lived farthest from the longhouse. Was that it? Was that her house? The one set off to the side behind a thick copse of tall trees, the sole walled-in, neighbor-less structure. Ruby and Nathan's house? What had she expected — the earth to swallow it whole?

Elle let out a breath when she spotted the swing set, Ruby's single victory for her daughter, Betty. She stared, now certain this was the house, and tried to remember the name of Ruby's son. But Elle had been eager to be rid of her and couldn't remember much about Betty's older brother.

From below, a watchman spotted her, and Elle froze, then waved, as if she had every right to be there. Two men were wheeling large bins to the end of the pier. Probably trash. Mattresses got disinfected once a week and debris tossed into the tide daily to wash out to sea. Cleanliness was strictly enforced to guard against pestilence and disease in this humid, moldy environment and patrols were a common sight. Ruby had told her about the cook being fired because he hadn't washed the produce carefully and a mass food poisoning broke out. After that, meals became blander still, which might account for the popularity of Elle's highly seasoned sandwiches.

Elle craned her neck to look closer, thinking she saw the colorful flower garden Ruby had mentioned. Yes, that must be it. She squinted, wondering if the sectioned squares of dirt flanking the swing set were an attempt at growing vegetables. The watchman motioned to stop her, then pointed his finger as if to say, "one moment," to the men pushing the heavy barrels.

"Can I help you, ma'am?" he yelled.

Elle nodded, no, "Beautiful morning. Lovely garden," she smiled, waved a second time and turned her bike back toward Big Pine, waited until they disappeared, then swooped down, riding a current of wind, enjoying the thrill of being suspended dangerously in midair. Elle calculated the easiest route to Ruby and Nathan's house from the tracks and planned to cut a broad swath around the work camp. On the off chance that someone would recognize her as the sandwich lady, she was ready with a story about seeking work as a cook.

Pigeon Key presented an entirely different vista when approached by land. But no matter how much fill they piled atop this tiny five-acre swell, nothing could arrest erosion by sea, salt and wind. The telltale rise of bone beneath man-made terrain revealed the true nature of the island. Formed from the skeletons of extinct sea creatures, the Spanish had named it Cayo Paloma, Americanized to 'Pigeon Key'.

Pigeon Key had two modes, buzzing and silent and not much in between and now it was almost deserted as she hoped it would be–the men off on one work detail or another. Hopefully, Nathan would also be absent, supervising the highway worksite.

Flanked by orderly rows of houses on one side and a gray ligament of road on the other, the tidy communal longhouse looked like the work camp kitchen that it was. Outside this ordered neighborhood, a fringe of fence blocked off rows of crowded tents the color of bleached skin. Nestled mere feet from water's edge, and reserved for unskilled workers. On the eastern end of the island, cranes, tractors and trucks with armored saws circled each other like prehistoric beasts at rest between battles. Behind them, two massive cement bridge piers formed the arched entryway to a watery nowhere.

Although she expected most of the men to be off working, the depth of silence unnerved her, like being in an enemy camp. Even using a circuitous route, she arrived at Ruby and Nathan's house quickly. Set back far from the road, a tall cement wall blocked the house from view. Randomly placed coral boulders softened the harsh gray geometry. Only an outsider would plant roses, Elle thought, eyeing a row of desiccated bushes. Trying to bend the tropics to a Northerner's will was futile. This was a house built for transient bosses, families on the move. Just then, a tiny, tiger-striped lizard chased a smaller one, slapped his miniature tail against a branch of dead rose leaves and darted away.

Enormous palm trees shadowed the structure and Elle imagined the house receiving little light despite being smack center of the tropics. The tall wooden gate was bolted shut, with the narrowest give when Elle pushed against it. Elle followed the wall to the back of the house and looked around. The only way in was to climb the spreading gumbo limbo tree, jump onto the top of the wall and hope something would present itself on the other side she could shimmy down. Nothing moved in the breezeless sky, no one on the streets, so she gained the barest foothold in the lowest crotch of the tree, then the second and took in the wide backyard, the swing-set. She was about to take the next step when she heard footfalls. A small posse of road workers walked through the center of the road. The acid smell of old hooch pitched up against her nostrils at the same time a dog barked. A trio of obvious drunks looped toward her, a small black dog nosing their feet, circling them before racing ahead. When she moved, the dog sensed her, raised his head and barked excitedly. The men ignored the creature, focused on holding up the middle soldier, baby-faced and heavy, who was clutching a bottle. The dog growled.

"Bonus, come here boy," one of them yelled at the dog. The middle guy stumbled and tried to focus, and the small black dog let loose and jumped at the tree, straining his snout to nip at the air, missing Elle's foot. The men stopped and stared at her, now halfway up the tree.

"What the…?" one of them said.

"He's just a pup," another said. "He won't hurt you." They dropped the drunk guy onto his unsteady feet, causing him to teeter like a bowling pin, then groan before vomit exploded from his mouth. Elle hopped down from the trunk.

"Yah, right in front of Foreman's house. Yer on yer own now." The sick guy held his stomach, groaned and let loose again, retching. The thin one spoke to the third man. "Foreman sees this. He's out on his arse. C'mon, for the luv 'o mercy, lend us a hand, missus." When Bonus sniffed at the pile of vomit, all three yelled at him and he took off down the street. They jerked the fat guy up. "Where's my dog?" he howled. "Only bonus we'll ever see." He winked at Elle, tried to laugh, then retched. One man looked at Elle apologetically, then grabbed his sick friend under the armpits from behind. The other grabbed his feet, and they wheelbarrow'd him away while he cried out "Bonus, come here. Bonus!"

Alone on the road with a pile of streaming vomit between herself and Ruby's yard, Elle made out a faint sound coming from the Foreman's house. Ruby's house.

"Dad?" A child's voice. Elle raced to the gate, crouching to find a sliver of space to look through.

"Betty?" Elle waited, then asked, "Is your mother in?"

"She's not well. She's in bed."

"Are you alone with her now?"

"I'm not supposed to talk to anyone."

"You know me. Don't you remember? I'm a friend of your mother's. Tell her the sandwich lady wants to see her."

"You gave me a mango."

"That's right, sweetheart. Now please let me in."

"I hate mangos. They're disgusting."

Elle heard the child run back inside and a few minutes later a click sounded, then another from the back of the house. Betty called, "My mom said I could let you in, but you can't stay long because my dad will be really, really mad if I open the door."

She looked smaller than Elle remembered, was a tiny thing in a loose shirt and green shorts with legs like two ropes knotted at the knees.

"Don't worry, I won't stay long. I promise. Where's your mom, sweetie?"

"Don't call me that," the little girl said.

The house was larger than it seemed from the outside, mushrooming into a wide hallway, a series of closed doors on either side. The walls were bare of pictures except for framed maps and a display of diplomas and awards Elle was accustomed to seeing in offices.

She smelled the roses before seeing Ruby. There must be three dozen of them, and Ruby dwarfed behind them. Her skin was yellow and gray. Her eyes fluttered. One opened halfway, giving her a bawdy, drunken look.

"Oh Ruby," Elle said stupidly, and moved to the side of her bed. Ruby's face was oddly shaped, her eyelid swollen. A second sweet wave from the roses hit her. Elle was seized with a fury greater than when she first saw Ruby's injuries. The soppy aftermath, the groveling for forgiveness. He must've gotten them from the mainland, ordered them in with the building supplies.

He probably had sex with her as soon as she returned from the hospital, like Billy always wanted, claiming her in the spot he hurt.

"What are you doing here?" Ruby asked.

"I was worried about you. What happened?"

She cradled her stomach. "I lost it."

"He did it to you, didn't he? Nathan." Elle turned to see the girl leaning against a wall, her hands over her ears, refusing to listen but refusing to leave.

"Here," Elle said. "I brought you something." She reached for the lilac drawstring pouch with the embroidered crown. "The ten you gave me and another thirty to boot. A very late Christmas present." The pouch had forty dollars and some change in it and Elle felt a pang letting it go. Betty looked up at her mother.

"Can we keep it?"

Elle watched Ruby's face as she weighed her options, finally nodding yes. "What do you say to the lady?"

"Thank you?"

"Sweetie. Betty. Go. Put it in your pillowcase." Ruby turned to Elle, exhausted, as the girl ran out of the room, gripping the pouch.

"He finds you here and I'll really catch it." She tried to sit up. "Thank you. I mean it, but you don't have to make any of this your business. You've done more than enough." Her hand was claw-like, bandages wrapped around her wrist, looking like a mummy when she moved.

"You made it my concern." Elle looked around the room at the framed sepia print of a grim couple, flanked by children with startled expressions. Bahama shutters blotted out light, turning the walls a non-color. The bed was narrow, too narrow to contain Ruby and Nathan, and Elle imagined Nathan kicking Ruby to the floor the way Billy used to do when he came home drunk.

Ruby nodded her head, as if resigned to her fate. As if to say, yes, it's all true. Everything you think is true. With effort, she sat straight up and asked, "Your diner? Is it ready?"

But Elle had forgotten about her own life for that brief instant and when Ruby smiled, it broke Elle's heart. The woman was pulling for her. Imagining a life she didn't think she would ever have. "You worked hard for it. I'm certain of that," Ruby said. She nodded and closed her eyes. "I'll come see you when I get a chance," Ruby turned away and Elle made out the bent, elongated shadow of her daughter outside the gray doorway.

"Nathan's coming back early. Cooks' helper quit, then a couple of men were too sick to work yesterday. Or maybe no one wants to work with Bernie, the cook. Got to be bad when they prefer roadwork."

"So, they need a cook?"

Ruby frowned "You? Sure, they'd hire you. If you want to work for nothin'. Put up with their crap."

"I didn't come here for a job. I came to help you." Until she said it, she wasn't certain that's what she was doing.

Ruby sat up. Her look of shock saddened Elle. She couldn't comprehend being important enough for that kind of effort. "You don't have to…"

"Do you want my help?" Elle said, uncertain of what she would do, but felt compelled to speak. There was so little she could do for Ruby because she had children. And then, of course, Ruby read her mind.

"But, my children," she said.

"Yes. We'll figure it out, but you can't stay like this. It's never going to end. You know that. Right?"

Ruby nodded.

"No, don't just nod. Say it. Say you know you can't stay."

"Yes, I know it won't stop. But what do I do?"

Should she tell her she didn't have a clue? She wanted to be strong for Ruby, but was tired of all the lies. "I don't know, Ruby. But both of us are smarter than Nathan. Right?" Her forced smile caused Ruby to force one of her own and then both of them smiled and this time it was real. "Can you get your hands on any money?"

"Yes. I have a stash."

"How much do you have?"

"About $200."

"That's incredible." Elle hadn't expected that. "You must have known someday you'd have to escape."

"I guess. Elle, Thank you."

It's going to be tough with two children, but we'll come up with something. Just give me a week to figure it out."

"No, not Perry."

"Ok. Betty, though?" And Ruby looked like she wanted to explain, but Elle waved her aside. She didn't want to know why not Perry. Men like Nathan value their sons more, or maybe Perry sided with his father. In many ways, boys are the greater victims. But this would be Ruby's choice. She was already too involved.

"When I tell you, you might have to be ready in minutes. You better be prepared. Can you do that?"

"Yes. I've thought about it. I even know where I can stay for a few days. My friend in Providence…."

"A bus is the best bet. Easy to get off and on."

"You better go. If Nathan finds you here…"

Before leaving, Elle twisted a couple of rose heads off the stem and shoved them in her pocket. Outside, she flipped them onto the pile of vomit and within seconds, Nathan turned the corner onto his street.

"Mr. Foreman. There you are," she said in a loud voice. "Word has it you're looking for a cook's helper. Just about to knock at your door, but the gate was locked. This is your house, right?"

The sun was high in the sky, bleaching out Nathan's expressions.

"Who told you where I lived?"

"Oh, I'm sorry. I guess I should've gone to the camp..." She tilted her head in what she supposed expressed cluelessness.

Nathan moved quickly and placed an arm across her back, trapping her shoulder in his palm. His voice took on an intimate tone. "Don't know if it's a good idea to work alongside the men, but seems you took care of yourself well enough at No Name Lodge."

His touch felt tight and oppressive, and Elle instinctively searched for an escape route through the street. Then she spied the seeping mound of vomit and walked him toward it.

"Watch out," she said, a second after he stepped in it.

"What the hell?" He dropped his grip on her shoulder and looked toward the house. He shook his foot, but the stink had gotten onto his trousers and a moist stain traveled up the leg.

Elle wanted to laugh, she wanted to smack him in the head and slam him into the pool of puke. "Word has it your wife took a nasty fall and ended up in hospital in Miami."

As soon as she spoke, Elle realized it was a mistake.

"Who told you that?" He glared at her, pushed her away and made his way through the gate. She followed, slipping into the yard behind him. He turned on a spigot set into the wall and carefully aimed the sole of his shoe at the stream of water.

"If I give you a chance and hear so much as one word of complaint." His voice was so low she barely heard him over the rush of water. He turned the faucet off and looked her in the eye. "But what about the diner?"

"Fixing it up, but ages before it opens," she lied. "So, I can only work a few days a week. Meantime, I sell sandwiches when I get the chance." He knew that, but seemed willing to play along.

A creak announced the front door scraping open. Ruby emerged, followed by Betty. When she saw her father, Betty moved directly in front of her mother as if trying to shield her.

Elle advanced and held out her hand in greeting, mouth set in a tight line, eyes wide and piercing. "Mrs. Foreman. My name is Elle. We met at the party on No Name Lodge."

"Oh yes, I remember you," Ruby said, a sad little smile on her face. "Just wondering what all the commotion was."

"Ruby," Nathan said, "Go back to bed. This woman's only one more person out of work looking for a job."

"Oh yes, you're the cook," Ruby said. "You made the most wonderful chicken soup before the party. I would love to have that soup again."

Elle spotted the second amputated rose head that must have fallen from her pocket. With Nathan's back toward her, she covered it with her heel.

"Soup? In this heat? I don't remember chicken soup," Nathan said.

"For the lodge, Mrs. Rowlands made a special request. Spicy."

The four of them stood in the yard until Nathan dismissed his wife, tilting his head toward the bedroom. "Go back to bed. I'll think about it."

Elle intuitively knew not to show desperation for the job, or he could not deny himself the pleasure of refusing her. But she also understood something deeper. Ruby was on the upswing of the abuse cycle, when he wanted to bring her favor, treats.

"Let me in that kitchen and I'll rustle you up some right now if you like. Make it like a little test. See if I get on with the head cook."

"Don't know if Bernie would appreciate that." Nathan wanted her to beg.

Ruby spoke from the doorway. "The cook's tired. No one knows what they're doing in that kitchen. And the men already spend their wages on her sandwiches."

"What do you know about it?"

Ruby was silent, caught in a lie, nothing Elle could do about it. Ruby tried to recover. "That worker, George, the one who walked off? Went on and on about the lady selling sandwiches on the side of the road. I just heard talk. Thought it strange at the time."

Nathan ignored his wife, turned to Elle. "Come back tomorrow. If you really want the job."

Which she did not. All that bicycling for a few dollars, but she needed to help the woman because Ruby's face did not look right and for the first time in forever, she hadn't thought about Brushy for an entire morning.

Ruby moved back into the house, but her stance seemed straighter than when she had come out that door.

"Just come alone," he said, waving her away. He waited for her to get out the gate, latched it, and Elle heard the door slam, and a series of locks click behind her.

33

The road back was deserted, the day spent and dusk setting in. Elle pedaled steadily, annoyed by the uneven tracks and unable to enjoy the burnished sky as the Florida sun began its histrionic decline.

The highway snaked past the diner like a living thing determined to reach Key West. Elle made out heavy yellow machinery and hills of gravel farther on.

Even in purple paint, the diner was invisible from the road. Perhaps she should copy the annoying Burma Shave people and place billboards on the road every 5 miles, *Sidetrack Diner, 10 miles*. Then *Gas, Food, Facilities, 5 miles* or maybe *Lodgings*. To hell with the cost. Somehow, the purple paint worked, adding a light-hearted touch. Finally, Elle could envision the gas tanks, the parking spaces, the outdoor latrine for customers. She saw tables with umbrellas and families eating ice cream sundaes or coffee in the cool season.

As she sprinted down the road, she spotted Brushy in a circle of men, as if she had conjured him. Why hadn't he given her a sign? Why hadn't he come to see her? "Elle," someone called out.

"Oh, it's you, Mrs. Woodman," Brushy said. "Congratulations on the new diner." He turned to the group. "I think many of you know Elle Woodman, the new owner of the Sidetrack Diner. She used to work for me at No Name and…" Elle recognized two builders and surveyors, and imagined they were planning more developments and she had nothing much to say to them.

"The purple one?"

Brushy smiled, which told her he'd seen the paint color. "May I come by later to see what you've done with the property?"

"Sure, anytime," Elle nodded and continued on her way to the diner. After being inside a few minutes, she turned back out to find Brushy. It would be natural to ask when he would be by, she thought. Anyone would want to know, but then- maybe he didn't want anyone else to know or maybe he had a reason to play it by ear. Could she trust herself to sound casual? "I thought I would ask when you plan on dropping by," she rehearsed out loud, "I'm not always home." But her voice sounded desperate and might crack. Terrified she would make a spectacle of herself, Elle changed her mind, relieved that no one was around to see her double back.

That evening she tidied, opened a jar of sapodilla preserves and made a pie in the kerosene heated stove. The large, salvaged ottoman struck her as shabby, so she covered it with a precious length of red canvas and imagined sitting on it, Brushy at her feet, talking, laughing before he pulled her onto the floor with him.

Two evenings later, he arrived at Sidetrack, sticking his smiling face through the unlocked door as if this casual visit was the most natural thing in the world.

"No, this isn't right," Elle said. "Buster is coming."

Brushy waved it off. "I'll come another time," he said, as if their meeting was of no importance. "This looks good, though," he said, taking in the work she had done, the refurbished old counter stools, the freshly painted yellow walls.

Elle's shoulders tensed; her palms felt wet. He looked ridiculous, hanging on to his briefcase in the open doorway so she pulled him inside, going along with the conversation. He had morphed back into the Brushy she knew before they began what Elle thought of as their affair; she enjoyed the glamor of the word, the sense of urgency and desire.

She took in his freshly shaved jawline, imagined his square shoulders through the pale blue shirt.

"Blanche doesn't know I'm filing for divorce."

Who cares, Elle thought? She moved toward him. "I'm glad you're here." She squeezed his hand, willing him to see her. If he would just shut up.

He moved inside a couple of yards from the open door. "She has the house and cottages in Rhode Island, and I've convinced her I've been hiding offers for No Name Lodge, the jewel in the crown. This way, she'll really want to hang on to it." He smiled, inviting her to be in on the plan, the only intimacy he offered. So, she took it and responded.

"Won't she contest you? Won't she demand to see the holdings?" She led him to the chair. "When are you leaving?" Why hadn't he reached for her? Did he want to pretend nothing had happened between them? She wanted to smash his officiousness, make him beg. She wished she had time to prepare, to wash and change clothes, at the very least. Worst of all, she had her monthlies and felt greasy and bloated.

"Elle, are you there?" Buster entered the open door and saw Brushy. "Oh sorry," he looked back and forth between them. "Not a word," Buster probably thought Brushy wanted to purchase the diner or maybe rehire Elle.

"I have an idea." She turned back to Buster, "Stay and look after the place. Meanwhile, Mr. Rowlands and I are going for a walk. We won't be long."

Buster nodded. "Sure."

"Oh, and you might need the gun... under the tray in the register. Just punch no sale then feel for the latch.

He looked shocked.

"Only kidding. I mean, it's there, but you won't need it."

Elle waved Buster away and shoved Brushy through the door.

"I'm taking you to my favorite place," she said, not waiting for a reply, and nudged him toward the road. "Quick, we're in the open," and turned to see what she had hoped for-his open smiling face, amused at her nerve. When the road morphed to bush on the downward slope, "serpentine," she said, "like a war zone," and laughed out loud this time, veering off as they approached the wooden bridge. Under the cover of the slender moon, Brushy joined her, and she felt more like a kid than a lover.

"I hear everyone comes to the diner now, even without the gas and all the rest of it." Brushy said.

"Nowhere else to go is the more reasonable explanation." Somehow, her language skills improved when he was around him, she thought.

"You're like a magnet. Always having something prepared, very welcoming."

"Is that so?"

"Yes," he said simply, smiling. He stopped walking to stare into the velvet wood ahead. "We can really talk when I get back. I prefer having things in order... until... "

"Is that why you came? To talk?" she heard the undercurrent of desperation. His eyes softened, but Elle didn't care. "Why haven't you been by?"

"I've been here twice. It was all I could manage. I felt I was being watched every minute."

Was it true? Could she have missed him? Why didn't he leave her a note? A sign? "And do you always do what people want you to do? What if I ordered you around?"

"I'm hoping I might find that out sometime soon," he said, and it seemed to ignite something in him.

"Like now?" she said. His face was almost the opposite of Rimer's, a face that didn't need to be handsome to be interesting. He squeezed her hand, and they moved toward No Name, quiet until reaching the wooden bridge. In the faintly moonlit night, Brushy followed Elle to a sheltered nook under a sprawling Gumbo Limbo tree, leafy branches providing camouflage from the bridge above.

"They must have saved this tree when they built the bridge," Elle said, taking in the shiny and gnarled branches jutting out in all directions. One low angled limb gave the appearance of a man on bended knee. "As if it was too important to kill."

"More like too costly," Brushy said. Elle was tired of the pragmatic that stifled the sense of wonder. Why had she thought this was a good idea? Yet there was something almost fated between them.

Someone walked directly above, on the bridge, moving leisurely, and Elle pressed tighter against the trunk, moonlight creating vague shadows, illuminating a section of lake close by. When the sound faded, she said. "Let's go in," peeled off her shirt and stared at him. "Well?" and his startled expression made her fear she had lost him, but she didn't care, peeled off her pants, ran to the inky water and waded in. A small eternity passed before he unbuttoned his shirt, removed his pants, folded both their clothes carefully. While she watched, he placed his hat on top of the pile and patted it.

"Oh, God," she said, noticing his shoes. He looked up at the bridge before breaking into a run and jumping in after her. They swam together, both more graceful in the water than on land. She didn't tell him she was having her monthlies, and when they made it back to shore, she secretly wiped some of her blood on the inside of his pants.

"I'm off to Nevada later this week," he said. "Nevada has a six-week no contest divorce. By the time I return, you should be open for business–gas tanks…"

"Does she know?"

"Not a clue. And I intend to keep it that way. She's way too busy spending what's left of my fortune," he laughed, too sharply, cupped her face with both hands and pressed the lightest kiss on her eyelids.

She pulled his hands away. "I hope you're taking the ferry out."

"Why?"

"The ferry's safe."

"And miss the luxury of the Big Wheel? It might be the last chance I have to sail in that rig, if Blanche has her way. That's something else I'm eager to discuss with the lawyers. Property laws in Florida are lenient to wives, but Blanche knows nothing of my plans. I bought most of what I own before marrying her."

"I don't trust her. Assume she knows everything."

He smiled. "She has nowhere near your powers of observation," he said, then rose and combed his fingers through his hair. Shards of moonlight outlined the ripples in the lake.

"I'm not kidding. That Popeye guy is a sneak, always lurking around."

"Elle," he said, lifting her chin and making her aware of how worried she sounded. "I didn't want to push you. I want you to take time to decide. That's why I haven't been by to see you."

She looked up to let him see the joy on her face.

"Things can change," he said, and Elle nodded yes, realizing this was the first man she slept with who didn't stake claims on her.

"What if I have a boyfriend when you return?"

"So long as he doesn't cut into the profits. It's your call. You're a free agent."

"Six weeks," she said simply. "I'll be here." Alone, she wanted to yell. Alone and waiting for you.

He kissed her again, soft and insistent, then began the trek from under the bridge, up the hill to the road toward No Name, and looked back at the spot where they made love, as if knowing she'd be watching. She imagined his expression, his voice as he left, felt the sting of his stubble on her face. He would return in the middle of August, she realized, at the height of hurricane season.

PART III

PIGEON KEY

34

At the work kitchen, Bernie took the job seriously. He had a habit of looking above Elle's head when he spoke to her. At first, she thought he had poor vision and wondered how a half-blind man could run a kitchen, but soon realized he simply refused to meet her eye, to let her know she was there on sufferance. He issued orders rather than actually engaging with anyone and took it as a personal affront whenever anything got dropped. The last cook had been careless about food storage and was blamed for a minor outbreak of food poisoning. Bernie ran an exacting operation. He knew to the last slice how many rashers of bacon remained at any given moment. Anything less than a dead, silent workplace was considered mutinous. Meals were bland and predictable and the last thing he wanted was to have the woman with the notorious foreign cookery tricks beside him on the hallowed kitchen tiles. His was an American kitchen.

He delighted in tossing hot pans into a large enamel basin when he was through with them, as if only he could make them clang and clamor.

No one likes you, Elle thought, watching him open up a can of beans the size of an oil drum. He tossed the sharp serrated top Frisbee-style into the pile, his nod to chaos, a clattering diminuendo to the sorry evening menu.

Bernie pointed at the metal trolley where two kitchen hands hoisted large pots of steaming beans and a bloated gray sausage in a metal tray dripping with grease. "Two per plate," he said. When she was poised to serve at the station, he strode over and wrenched the plate out of her hand, forked two sausages onto it and poured a ladleful of beans on the length of the sausages, shoved it at the worker, all without taking so much as a glance at Elle.

A rough man in a Cuban accent spoke. "Let the lady do her job." He nodded at Elle, who wished he'd shut up.

Most men looked old, although few were beyond forty. Years of disappointment, intense sun, and the terrors or "soldiers nerves," for any who had experienced the front lines or trenches. Whatever the ailment, few had enough teeth to tuck into the kind of beefsteak they dreamed about after a hard day's labor. Might as well be beans, she thought. Sops up at the booze as well.

The Cuban took it upon himself to welcome her. "My name is Pirro. It is a pleasure," he said. Elle could feel the prickly aversion many felt toward the flamboyant Pirro by the way they would willingly give up their place in line rather than suffer his presence.

Lots of workers don't like each other. Why would they be any different from any other family forced to live in close quarters? Everyone knows who slacks, who whines and who plays the patsy.

Before the first week was out, Elle had a decent handle on the pecking order and who kept tabs on who. Pirro made a daily show of lingering. "Hey, take off your hat," he said to a man who arrived for dinner. Then he would lean into Elle, whispering, "Like they never saw a lady before," and then wink. His friendly exterior hid a deliberate menace, claiming to be Elle's protector when no one had been anything but deferential. She wished they would all forget she was a woman, but Pirro was having none of it. Any chance he got, he would call her a lady, sometimes describing an hourglass figure in the air with his hands.

Few men showed up for dinner on Mondays, which made little sense until Elle discovered they often brought back food from weekends in Key West to avoid Bernie's cooking. They quickly learned it was never a good idea to ask if Elle would make lunch as it practically guaranteed Bernie wouldn't allow it. Although Elle had second cook status, Bernie did his best to undo all she knew about flavor, thinking black pepper was the devil's spice and could lead to more dangerous activities. Lord knows, next thing they might ask for bingo or demand to play baseball.

Nathan sent word to make chicken soup for Ruby after her first weekend at the job. Problem was, she had never actually made it before and no longer had access to the cookery books at the lodge–but how difficult could it be? All she needed was a chicken and some vegetables for flavoring. She had partly taken the job to check on Ruby, and this struck her as ludicrous now. How could she help Ruby? Elle's thoughts drifted, wondering if Nathan learned a lesson after he put her in the hospital. But Elle knew better. Sometimes when she pedaled back to Big Pine, she felt the trajectory of her life had some sort of strange undertow, dragging her back down whenever she broke surface. But she fought the idea, imagining Brushy in a lonely hotel in the middle of the desert, dreaming of when he would return to her.

High summer was upon them, and Elle felt the heaviness in the hot air. The superheated tracks she rode back and forth from Big Pine to Pigeon Key felt electrically charged. Flocks of seagulls were sparser than usual, and one day a lone bird simply dropped out of the sky, landing a few feet ahead. Elle placed the iridescent ring-necked pigeon in her bike basket, though she was sure it was dying. The bird's chest fluttered once or twice, but retained a faint heartbeat. A damp fluorescent wave of air announced rain, and Elle hoped it would revive the poor bird. At the Sidetrack Diner, she topped a wooden crate with chicken wire and scattered leaves on the bottom as a floor and brought it inside to monitor, away from Cat. Slowly he revived, but when Elle tried to release him, he looped back to settle in the box, his black eye focused on her. Just a few more days, she whispered to him as she tweezered a palmetto bug into his open mouth and closed the door to the storage room against Cat.

Activity over the summer months was so scant that even Mrs. Dean stopped coming around and Elle realized how lonely the next weeks would be with work on the roads slowing and the lodge under a cloud of suspicion after Rimer's death.

Newspaper articles in the Miami Herald appeared regularly hinting at the corruption in the Florida Keys without naming names. But it was clear Pigeon Key was the locus of the flow of money. Although the highway construction had been privatized, parts remained overseen by government men, and the locals knew who was on the take. At No Name Key Lodge, a few wealthier clients sold their trailers and Elle heard houses in Key West were getting dressed up, as if preparing for a suitor to come courting.

While Elle worked at Pigeon Key, Buster sold Elle's sandwiches to the crew when he wasn't working at No Name. Elle marked Brushy's absence on her wall calendar. If he had left immediately after she saw him, she had another month until his return.

Someone was at the door and again Elle imagined she had conjured Brushy. It wouldn't be the first time, she thought.

Elle slumped with disappointment. Art was like a distant and troubled family member that no one quite knew how to handle. She'd only seen him a few times since they set Petey's arm, although he had a key..

"Just wondering how you're getting on and thought I'd drop by. I brought you this." He handed her a paper about the latest scandal on Pigeon Key. 'A $10,000 liquor bill. What's going on at Pigeon Key?' ran the headlines.

"Come in," Elle said. Art looked around as if suspecting a trap. "I'll spot you a beer," Elle said, deciding she actually wanted company.

"One guy says it even made the Rhode Island paper. His mom clipped it out and wrote him a letter about it."

"Who's involved?" Elle handed him a frosty dark beer.

"Take a wild guess," he said, and Elle knew it must be Nathan, from the look of satisfaction on Art's face.

"Thanks for the news. But how come I never see you at the camp for dinner? Thought you didn't like my cooking."

"It's the crowds," he said. "I like to work when no one is around to mess up my plans."

"Ah, so that's what I hear in the wee hours."

"Yup. Just me and the lizards."

On her Sunday off, Elle carried her one large bag on the bike basket and made it to her old cistern, yanking open the gate, already overgrown with monster vines like some ancient jungle compound. She would swim before anyone woke, then decide if she was ready to sell to Blanche. Had Brushy left yet? After silently sliding off the wharf in her underwear, the warm water felt like coming home. The soapy water acted as a soothing astringent on her mosquito and no-see-um bites. She bobbed weightlessly on her back then turned, taking in the path to the lodge, imagining what it would be like to own this entire property. At that moment, she understood why the hermit loved his solitude. As the morning sun swelled in the sky, she padded barefoot through the gate, laid a towel on her bench outside, and fell into a dreamy sleep.

Brushy's soft voice in the distance woke her, but then she heard Blanche laughing, both of them far away, sounding as if they had never been at odds. Looking out through an open space in her fence, angled toward the setting sun, she saw them. His face was tilted upward, and she remembered the line of his chin and how it had felt on her face.

Blanche and Brushy walked to the lodge together, side-by-side, as if neither had a care in the world. A short while later, Elle exited her property and watched behind palms as Brushy struggled with his large leather trunk onto the wharf. Joe stepped up, and she heard Blanche speaking in the tone she used to issue commands, but couldn't make out the words. The boat engine sounded, and Elle spotted Joe carrying something vaguely familiar. It was large and awkward and when she angled her head; she saw metal teeth glinting in the sun.

As she turned back to her old shelter, the dried coconut fronds underfoot felt like broken glass. In the lot, an ice delivery truck and blue Ford waited for the ferry to arrive. And then she realized Joe was carrying the two-man chainsaw that Rimer and Art deemed was overkill for the spindly palms on No Name.

Not fifteen minutes after they departed, the Key Wester docked, and it thrilled Elle to see Monty's friendly face. Why hadn't Brushy waited for the ferry to take him out?

"I hope Brushy is safe," Elle said to Monty in a moment of unguarded fear.

"The Big Wheel is so tricked out, I wouldn't worry about it." He looked at her oddly. "Your problem is you got too much time on your hands," Monty said.

Elle was grateful for his light needling. Monty always brought her back to herself. He wanted nothing from her, or rather he was clear about what he wanted, and held no subterfuge.

"So, you're a moneybags now, Elle. Word has it. The whole lodge is talking about the Sidetrack Diner, the future of the Florida Keys, smack center of the highway."

Elle had no desire to tell him the story and suddenly wanted to be free of everyone. All roads led to Brushy and Brushy filled her with fear and longing.

"So, I guess you're not interested in making a few extra dollars."

"Doing what?"

"We've got to bring the Hermit's sapodilla saplings to Miami. There's four dozen of them and they need to be dug up and delivered. I got permission to use the ferry."

"That must have been quite a feat," Elle said, full of admiration for Monty's ability to squeeze money out of stone. He always had some scam going and never got called out on any of it.

"Nathan's plans to go off on some fancy fishing jag with a couple of bigwigs who endowed some university. You should see the boat, makes the Big Wheel look like a tin can. He's bringing his kid to meet them. Wants him to get Perry-I think is his name-in to some ivy league school. I forget which one."

"Is his wife going too?"

"Nope," Monty said. "Men only." He shrugged his shoulders as if the idea of a pleasure cruise without women was incomprehensible.

"When are they leaving?"

"Tuesday, back Friday. Why?"

They were standing where Ruby's daughter had discarded the mango and Elle had a flash memory of Ruby asking about her diner and the thrill she felt for Elle's success. She remembered Ruby hiding her bandaged hand, then showing her the scar on her thigh.

"You interested in the work? 'Cause I sure could use the help and always obliged for the company."

"Of course," Elle said. "When?"

"Next Monday."

"Can we leave on Wednesday instead?" Elle asked.

"I Wouldn't do this for anyone but you," Monty said. "But you gotta be sure because I have to arrange the ferry."

35

Parsley was her answer when Bernie sniffed the steaming air around the large soup pot. And when he ladled out a suspicious dark flecked piece of potato and looked at her, again, "Parsley," was all she said. They spoke in single or double syllable sentences. Stop or no or ok or parsley. So, when he looked like he was gearing up for an actual conversation, Elle pointed to the broth and said, "onion tops," and walked away.

"Those are no onion tops," he said. Bernie struggled with a large crate of lobsters. "And hurry with that pot."

"You gotta be kidding." Did he just want whatever she was using?

He poured the broth into a smaller pot, burning his hand in the process but refusing to cry out. Bernie was as tough as he was mean. The lobsters would spoil if he waited, so he tossed them into the boiling water one at a time. "Crab cakes are not good enough for him," he muttered. "Oh no, Florida spiny lobster not good enough–Oh no... gotta be from Maine." He mimicked Nathan perfectly, right down to Nathan's wide-legged stance.

In his kitchen, Bernie said what he liked and no one, not even the President himself, could stop him. "You're lucky I didn't pour that foul witch's potion down the sink." Then he pointed to the other worker. "Hey you, c'mere." He gestured toward Elle's soup. "I think I changed my mind."

"This is for Ruby Foreman. Mr. Foreman's orders." Elle placed her body in front of the pot.

"Well, how about we ask him?" Bernie said, heading toward Nathan, who was coming through the door.

"No one brings anything to my wife except Mrs. Woodman," Nathan said, moving away from Bernie after a few minutes. Nathan refused to call Elle by anything but her married name, and she was too overwhelmed at the prospect of seeing Ruby to be annoyed. When she headed out, Nathan's boy opened the door.

"I'll take it," Perry said, reaching for the bucket. But Elle was too fast.

"Your father asked me to bring it," she said, smelling cigarette smoke on him. He seemed to be barely in his teens. They walked together to the house. Perry took the bucket of soup he had allowed Elle to carry, called *Mom* and left Elle standing in the old-fashioned parlor dominated by a comfortless Victorian settee with two narrow gilt side chairs. Thin-legged fruitwood tables dotted the room, designed to support two china teacups. Elle disliked this small room, with its expensive bric-à-brac, convinced the slightest gesture would send everything flying. In the corner, a large shotgun leaned against the posy-papered wall that somehow seemed perfectly fitting.

"Elle, is that you?" Ruby called. Elle expected to see Perry trailing behind, but a gust of cigarette smoke let her know the direction of his exit.

Inside Ruby's room, Elle nodded toward the door to tell Ruby someone was nearby.

"Yes, close the door," Ruby said, as if they were in the middle of an ongoing conversation. Her manner was remote, as if she were somewhere else.

"I'm trying to help you," Elle said, annoyed at her passivity.

"Thank you, yes, of course."

An open drawer in Ruby's bedside table revealed a collection of make-up Elle had only seen in the movie magazines back at the lodge. Large powder puffs, black eyeliner, gold and jeweled tubes of lipstick, enough to make Blanche Rowlands envious. Ruby saw Elle's gaze and deftly closed the drawer.

"Is Nathan still leaving on Tuesday?"

"Yes," Ruby whispered, "Taking Perry with him. Who told you?" Her eyes turned down, matching her pouty mouth.

"Does it matter? All I need to know is, are you in?" Elle thought of the work ahead of her, getting the saplings out of the ground and onto the boat, calculating the time it would take, but when she looked up, Ruby looked guilty.

Elle felt a wave of numb anger. "Forget it. It's off—you're not going," Elle said. Something was wrong with her attitude. Did she want Ruby to beg? Yes, it should be important enough to beg.

"Please," the sound was indistinct, almost flirtatious, and Elle intuitively knew it was the voice Ruby used with Nathan.

"Fuck you," Elle said. This was the first time in her entire life she had ever uttered the word. But it was like pressing a button. Ruby gulped, tears instantly welled in her eyes and Elle realized this wasn't the first time Ruby was spoken to that way.

"Fuck you," Elle repeated. "You have to want this more than you tolerate him. You have to want this for yourself more than I want it for you."

Ruby's little fists formed. She looked like a dark Kewpie doll from the fair, and she squinted like a caricature of determination. "Fuck you, too. You promised, and I'm ready. Or isn't your word good?"

"That's more like it." She refused to smile or comfort Ruby.

Elle checked the doorway, but no one was there. Both windows in Ruby's room were empty, but the boy could be crouching outside. Perry had all the charm and grace of his father, Elle thought. She finally located him in the kitchen, and asked if wanted soup, hoping he'd refuse.

The boy moved the chair backwards and seated himself, facing her, legs spread, straddling the seat the way Nathan did. "What's that smell?" He made a face as the aroma rose from the pot Elle put on the hob.

"Called flavoring."

"You can't talk to me like that," he said. But Elle could tell he was unsure he'd been insulted.

"Bring this to your mother," she said. Ordering him would guarantee he wouldn't do it.

When he refused, Elle brought in the soup on a tray, leaned over Ruby and whispered. "Be ready with Betty before five pm on Tuesday. Bring nothing but cash. We get one shot." She left without looking back, her pointer finger sticking up behind her for Ruby to see. One shot.

36

"Leave it to me, I'll do the washing up," Bernie said Tuesday evening before the plan. Elle had worked all weekend at Pigeon Key to garner goodwill from Bernie and leave early.

"You got that big trip ahead of you," he said. "I know Pirro offered to give you a ride back to Big Pine, so I'll get someone to bring dinner to Mrs. Foreman.

"I don't know if the boss would appreciate anyone in with her, especially a man."

"Nathan's not here," Bernie said. "Besides, Pirro's harmless."

Elle's palms were sweating. Pirro was unpredictable and might try to make use of the backseat given half a chance. Elle had hoped Bernie would drive her, but then, Bernie was more difficult to distract.

She would stage a plumbing emergency to get Pirro inside Nathan's house while Ruby and Betty ran to the car. Elle would enter first and remove a washer so the water wouldn't stop running. They would open the back door when she shrieked, "Oh my God, Pirro," and race to the car when she yelled, "Oh no! Can you fix it?" Rushing water should be loud enough to muffle the car trunk opening and closing. If he was clueless, she knew how to make it stop running. But all the planning was for nothing. When they arrived at the house, he beat her to the front door. With a look of desperation, Pirro said, "Can I use the bathroom?" He grabbed a newspaper on the counter and ran to the bathroom.

Elle signaled to Ruby and Betty and motioned them into the car. The floor space in the back seat was narrower than she had hoped, but they would figure it out. The backseat footwell had barely enough room for Betty to hunker down and hide. Elle had expected the Phaeton and not the little Ford. First thing she did was tilt the rearview mirror away from the seat.

"You okay back there? He's coming."

Pirro leaned in to smile through the driver's side window before opening the car door. He had the kind of smile that let you know he had plans for you. When Elle turned to give him her usual *just try it* look, she was horrified to catch sight of knapsack straps on the backseat. She had warned them to bring nothing but cash.

"I didn't see anyone in the house. Did you?' Pirro asked.

"I think they're sleeping. I left the supper in the icebox."

He glanced behind him. "Hey, what's that?"

"It's mine." She thought she'd pushed the rucksack behind the seat, but the handles were sticking up.

"Looks like Foreman's duffel," Pirro said.

"No. It's mine. I left it at the house the last time I was here." Elle picked up the heavy bag and placed it by her feet. "Can we go? I'm tired."

"Hey, why you touch my cop-spotter?" Pirro frowned and frowned into the rear view mirror, adjusting it. "Whoa. Holy hell."

"What?" Elle panicked. Was an elbow sticking up in the backseat? A knee?

"That back seat is real dirty. Foreman will blame me." He sounded angry.

"I'm sorry. I'll clean it when we get to the Diner."

He sighed. "It's ok. Forget it." and winked at her. "I'm gonna say I had car trouble. After I drop you off, I'm heading to Miami for some real fun." He winked at her. "Nathan won't be back until Friday."

Elle laughed. "Your secret is safe with me." But he wouldn't have told her if he didn't trust her. Pirro was like everyone else on Pigeon Key. Trying to get by until something better comes along.

Pigeon Key disappeared behind them. The road narrowed, and Elle relaxed until someone coughed. Immediately Elle cleared her throat loudly to cover it until a stifled sneeze sounded.

Pirro braked hard.

"Wait, I can explain," Elle said.

"You trying to kill me?" The car screeched to a halt. Pirro flipped onto his knees and peered over the seat into the back. Betty's small, dark head bobbed up.

"What the hell...?"

"We just wanted to get out for the day," Ruby said. "She had nothing to do with this." She pointed at Elle.

"So, you don't trust me?" He said to Elle. A smile played across his face, eyes narrowed when he realized he had a carful of harmless women. "Hey, maybe you do something for me. Like a fair exchange."

Betty jumped out of the car and ran onto the road. "I hate you," she yelled. "I'm going to scream."

"No. Get back here." Ruby and Elle raced after her, but Betty was already across the road. Pirro made no move to help.

Ruby summoned a mother's energy and reached her daughter before Elle.

Pirro and Elle locked eyes through the passenger side window. The three of them watched him reverse and circle back toward Pigeon Key, cutting a wide arc that narrowly missed them. The Ford revved down the road, Elle's open door flapping in the wind. Abruptly he stopped, walked to the passenger side door, and bent over something. After a few minutes, he tossed the rucksack into the ditch and took off down the road.

"He won't say anything. He wants to go to Miami," Elle said. "We're close enough to walk either way. Your call." Elle said, surprised when Betty answered. "Mama. Let's go."

"Ok Betty," Ruby said, and turned back toward Pigeon Key.

"No, not there. Let's go away like you said."

Elle wanted to hug the little girl but was afraid of the tears threatening to well.

"What was in the bag that was so important?" Elle asked.

"Money and a few other things…"

"Jane. My sock monkey," Betty said. "Mom's old pictures and letters. And our boots."

"They were from my father." Ruby said, looking down. "I'm sorry. It's all my fault. If he hadn't seen the rucksack…"

"I saved my mother's pictures, too," Elle said. "It's not your fault. Look, it's only a few miles to Sidetrack. Stay here and I'll get the bag. Those boots you packed will come in handy now." Betty's mouth set in a determined horizontal line. Elle felt for her, and hoped the little girl wouldn't spend her entire life suppressing rage and fear, but for now, it was probably a great idea.

"I'm proud of you," she said to Betty. "Now get into the bushes and wait till I get back with the rucksack."

They arrived at the Sidetrack Diner at ten o'clock, where Elle had prepared a hearty meal in the icebox, but no one was hungry. "If we sleep now, we won't wake up in time. Let's get to No Name, where we can sleep before the ferry comes. I'll pack these." Elle took out the cold roast and sliced it. Betty was curled into the purple chair, her eyes already closed.

Ruby said, "We don't need to whisper. She sleeps like the dead. Oh, Bad choice of words. Do you really think Pirro won't say anything?"

"No, it would ruin his trip to Miami. Besides, everyone hates Nathan."

That seemed to calm Ruby, but when she was gone, Elle would have a lot to answer for. Pirro would speak in the end, but not yet. Even if he didn't, Nathan would suspect her.

Elle laid the flatbread on the counter.

"Your magic sandwiches, your salvation," Ruby had a sad little laugh, probably remembering when she first met Elle at the cistern.

Betty slept soundly for two hours and around midnight Ruby whispered in her ear and she woke instantly, and sprang into action like a cat. Elle signaled at the top of the incline and they raced across the road, into the dark, onto the wooden bridge and through the pathways Elle knew by heart. Spanish Moss hung like ragged lace from overhead branches. A rat-tailed possum skittered by with dozens of babies hanging on. They passed the giant strangler fig, which ushered in the entrance to the hermit's hidden fruit groves and his stash of trailers. Betty yelped and Elle remembered how she had mistook the strangler's tendrils for snakes when she first encountered this unlikely giant.

A faint rut in parts of the terrain bore the large wheel pattern of the hermit's wagon contraption.

Someone should have already piled the trees on the wharf. The hermit had done the hard part, but far preferred manual labor to painful human encounters. Betty stuck close to her mother and, halfway there, Elle turned to see terror in her face and heard her whisper, *this place is creepy*, which amused Elle, because she thought No Name the most perfect place in the world and night was her favorite time.

"Watch out for those," Elle pointed to an ordinary looking glossy-leafed tree. "It's called poisonwood." Ruby's eyes were enormous in the dark and once past the opening in the road, a collection of newly constructed shacks popped up and the overwhelming scent of bog honeysuckle suffused the surrounding air. "Smell that," Elle said to Betty. "It only grows in places like this. And look." She stopped to pat a tiny orchid in the crook of a small tree. "If you look carefully, you can see them grow."

When they arrived at the cistern, the smell of mold was too overwhelming to sleep inside, so Elle pulled a tarp from over the outside bench and a long lounge chair and all three slept in the yard and woke before sunrise. Betty ate three rolls as the sun peeked through the black silhouette of palms.

"You make up stories," Betty said to Elle. She had something on her mind and Elle imagined she needed reassurance.

"Like what?"

"Like I could see the plant grow. No one sees a plant grow."

"That's not true. They store light in the daytime and use it to grow in the dark and if you look close enough, you can watch it happen."

37

Four dozen saplings lined up inside Elle's yard in tidy piles when the smaller ferry docked without blowing the whistle. "Wait here. He's coming," Elle said, hustling Ruby and Betty outside and into the chicken coop.

Monty unlatched her gate as Elle walked to meet him. He raised his eyebrows and gestured toward the young sapodilla trees; root balls trussed in burlap sacks. "You said we'd have help loading."

"Oh yah, but you know how that song goes."

"Tell you what, mister," she said. "We get these in pronto and I got something special waiting for you in the house."

"Got no time for hanky panky," he said, winking at Elle.

On a small ring stove, Elle prepared poached eggs in stewed tomato, Monty's favorite breakfast, with a slice of precious tinned ham. While he ate, Elle moved the broom outside, the signal for Betty and Ruby to leave the property and wait inside a copse of trees. Once the trees were in the hold, Elle feigned a fall at the cistern, and when Monty raced to her aid, they ran out of the brush, checked that no one was on the wharf, and made a run for the boat.

It was a drizzly morning, unusual for the Keys, but perfect for executing Elle's plan. The four dozen saplings crowded the main body of the vessel.

"What's that for?" Monty asked, pointing to the large oilcloth tarp. "We're only gone a few hours."

"Can't I baby them if I choose?" Elle said. "Just stick to boats and girls," she said, but her laugh sounded false.

He stared at her. "For someone makin' good cabbage on an easy ride, you don't look so happy," he said. He didn't expect an answer, just wanted her to know he was concerned.

Elle sat well away from the hold but low enough that Ruby could lift the tarp high enough to breathe freely, out of Monty's range of vision. The trip was only three hours and docking planned at the Walcott Marina, where Elle had arranged dollies to wheel the trees to the road.

The Krome nursery workers wouldn't arrive until early afternoon. It was unfair to keep Monty waiting, but couldn't be helped. Lots of places to hide in the Hodge-Podge of shacks and boats at Walcott.

"Must be odd not being in charge of the kitchen," Monty said, interrupting her thoughts.

"Huh?"

"Pigeon Key. Working under Bernie. I heard how tough he is."

Elle sniffed the air. "I won't be there long enough to care or even notice," she said.

"Yah, after your mysterious rich uncle died, leaving you his fortune." The tarp moved suddenly, and Monty rose to check it out.

"No, I'll get it," Elle said.

"The hell you will. Might be some sort of animal got in with the trees," Monty said.

Elle almost pushed him back, "My lookout." She jumped into the hold, lifted the tarp, and made a face at Ruby before noticing Betty covered in dirt. A burlap bag must've come loose and dumped soil all over her. Elle turned back and Monty was still at the wheel, so she returned to the seat beside him.

"I'd be worried for you if you were the sort of woman who allowed it," he said. "Never seen you so jumpy."

"Got more than enough work and now this," she said.

The sky cleared to blue and pink, water clear enough to make out sea creatures trailing the ferry. A large porpoise sprinted backward, which made Elle laugh.

"More like it," Monty said, and Elle had a feeling of horror that he might make a play for her. As if reading her mind, Monty said, "No worries, Elle, you got too many prickly edges for the likes of me." He looked older and she was aging as well in the harsh, tropical climate. She smiled, and he smiled back, both of them embarrassed for reasons both chose not to discuss. He hauled rich clients around in a boat that belonged to someone else and she assisted them; an invisible force that swept up the mess in their wake. They both existed on the periphery, serving lives around them.

"Listen," he said, pointing to the radio. "I'll get this working so well, we'll get news out of Russia. We'll make a killing." He played with an antenna that moved in and out of waves, finally screeching so loudly that he stopped tinkering. "Work on something long enough and Voila. This is America!"

The Walcott Marina was small and in such disrepair that Monty shook his head and shrugged his shoulders as if to ask, *why here*? But Elle chose it because the bus station was two miles away. The ramp was ill-maintained; planks soft from mold, some jagged, others still missing from the Labor Day hurricane. Getting the trees off would be difficult, but Ruby and Betty would have a quick bus ride out.

"You get the dollies and wagons and I'll haul the saplings out," Monty said

"No…"

"Don't be a hero, Elle. If this rig gets hurt, I'm doing the wrecking."

"Alright, but you get the gear while I check on them. Then we'll both load 'em up."

"For god's sake…"

"Just go."

Monty threw his hands up in the air in a gesture of surrender and hustled out of the boat, walking backward with his Monty smile like he didn't have a care in the world.

When he left, Elle raised the tarp. They were tucked in on themselves in drab clothing, like anxious sparrows, ready to take flight. "Go. Go now."

Ruby's last look was one of intense disbelief, like she couldn't fathom why anyone would do this for her. Seconds after Monty disappeared from the wharf, they sprinted. Mother and daughter jumped from the boat heading to a decrepit boathouse mere yards from the wharf. Less than a minute passed before Monty returned, pulling a wagon behind him. He had a puzzled look on his face.

"I'll let you load," he said.

Elle felt the leaden weight descend as adrenaline left her body, her shoulders heavy with fatigue. "Who am I to refuse help? I'm just being careful about the trees," she said. "They are rare."

"You got that right, particularly the two that sprouted feet and ran off. Never saw that variety before."

Elle sat on the ferry side, unable to speak as Monty dragged the saplings onto the wagon, making repeated trips. He waved her away, perhaps knowing she wouldn't give him an explanation he'd believe, or worried she would tell him the truth. The trees were young and pliable and soon he had a system going while Elle returned to the hold with a mop and bucket, moving her mind to detail and chores as a barrier to thought.

"Where's the Krome people? You said eleven sharp, and I got to pick up those bags for the lodge, then make it to Matecumbe to pick up passengers. "

"If it gets late, I'll find my own way back."

He looked at her closed face and said, "Save it, Elle. But that's the last ride you're getting from me. All I gotta say."

And she was relieved. This was something she understood. Cause and effect. A world where you knew where you stood. She beamed an enormous smile at him. It was all worth it. "Thank you," she said, but he shook his head and turned away.

The Krome wagon arrived early, with two bored men stacking the trees so roughly they twined together in a maze of knotted branches.

"No," said Elle, "like this." She stacked them opposite each other; head to root, limbs embracing root ball. "Easier to separate," she said, thinking how stupid most people were at the simplest tasks.

Monty sat on his ferry; thick puffs of pipe smoke rose slowly in the windless air. At the Matecumbe landing, he barely spoke and didn't crack jokes for passengers on the way back, and Elle moved as far away from him as she could. They didn't exchange a word. Ruby and Betty were gone as far and as fast as she left Billy, and Nathan wasn't due to return for days.

At No Name, a handful of passengers disembarked and when new passengers saw the look on Monty's face, no one dared grumble about the lateness of the ferry's arrival. Elle planned to quietly slip away while Monty delivered his spiel on the wonders of No Name Key Lodge, but he unloaded the few bags and trunks in silence. Elle tidied up the ferry without exchanging the usual round of wisecracks with Monty.

I'll catch up with him later, she thought, feeling bad about the betrayal. Then she spotted it, peeking from under the jut of shelf by the hold; the small lilac pouch with a gold embroidered crown. Elle scooped it up and found forty-seven dollars inside and hoped this wasn't their total fortune. She said she had over $200, but was it all a story?

As she approached Sidetrack, she spotted Mrs. Dean pressed up against the diner window, and slowed her pace, stalking quietly while the woman alternately bobbed like a chicken to look in the window, then banged on the door. Frustrated, Mrs. Dean headed to the side of the building, and Elle seized the chance to sprint across the parking space, unnoticed.

When she was close, Elle yelled, "Hey, who goes there?" When Mrs. Dean shrieked in shock, Elle controlled the smile threatening to emerge. "Oh," she said, "it's you," reached for her keys and opened the lock.

An intense tang of citrus and jasmine wafted to her nose and Elle couldn't imagine where it was coming from until she spied an orange tree in an oversized urn with a large card done up in curled lime, orange and yellow ribbon, "Elle," on the envelope in heavy red ink.

Mrs. Dean patted the glossy leaves. "Someone's sweet on you."

"Don't be ridiculous, I ordered that myself," she said, impressed at how practiced a liar she had become.

"Then why is it addressed to Elle, with all these hearts?"

"Company policy - they don't know who ordered it," Elle said, rushing to the tree, tearing the card off and stashing it on the counter under the cash register.

"Well, I came for the Herald, is all," Mrs. Dean said, a sly smile curling her lips.

"Last one I received." She pushed a well-read Miami Herald at her. "Three days old. No charge."

"Must be grand to be independently wealthy," she said, intent on watching Elle's reaction.

"Yes, much better than bilking the public for donations. Anything else?" Elle asked, moving her heavy bag to the floor by the register, happy for the counter between them.

"Well, yes. I want to congratulate you. I was shocked to find out this belongs to you… and after losing the lodge job."

"Thank you." Elle turned from the small space, but Mrs. Dean leaned in so Elle would hit her with the hinged bar if she tried to exit.

"All this time, we thought you were down on your luck. Like you told us."

"From Billy," Elle said. "A gift from Billy." And she wanted to laugh because it was true. Everything she had was a gift that Billy's departure made possible.

"He was a good man," Mrs. Dean said, eyes softly unfocused, as if peering into the past.

And Elle thought of how she had betrayed her friend, Monty, and sucked up to her enemies.

"He made provisions for his wife," Mrs. Dean continued, nodding solemnly, face wrinkled with piety.

"His dutiful wife," Elle said, feeling rage at playing along, living her life in hiding. "His good wife, who said yes, sleep with whoever you like, spend your money on drink, move me from town to town when they catch on to your thievery and threaten the sheriff."

"Mrs. Woodman!" she was speechless, horrified.

An image of Ruby and the little girl hiding under tarps, terrified at being discovered while her husband turned their son against her to continue the tradition.

"His good wife, who lifted her skirts when people exited the rooms because the idea of getting caught excited him. Who never had a pet because his jealousy put it in danger. Who hated the same children he wished her to have so she would be more dependent. Yes, and is there anything more you wish to congratulate me for, or are we done?"

Cat jumped onto the counter and pawed at her arm, and Elle laughed. "You hungry?" she said, her voice low and sweet, to the brave little orange cat, who attempted to bite her finger.

"You're crazy," Mrs. Dean said, and Elle nodded her head, *yes yes, I am and best you know it now*. Elle thought of the highway and the strangers who would stop in, people with no history whose needs were honest, a place to sleep and a piss, a coffee for a dime and not a pound of flesh. "Yes, I'm crazy, and it's none of your goddamn business."

"You really are crazy," Mrs. Dean repeated, her mouth stuck open as she backed out the door.

Alone in the store, the orange tree sat in the center of the room. The emerald leaves didn't look real.

She reached under the register for the card. When she saw the date, her heart sank. Brushy must've planned to send this before he departed. Did he expect it to arrive after his return? A note on the reverse said, *July*

20,1936. Expect workers to install gas tank, finish up work -don't let them charge you–all paid for — B

Delicate clusters of pale blush flowers seemed so fragile that Elle moved her hand over them, tugging slightly to see if they were real. She raised a plucked blossom to her nose, and the fragrance was unlike anything she had ever smelled, sweeter than gardenia. Even a few flowers could fill a room to suffocation if you didn't like it.

Orange trees were fussy things, unreliable, and she didn't expect this one to last. Nothing like the leather leafed sapodilly with fruit that looks like it's carved from wood as a discouragement to the determined critters all about this State. Citrus was trouble. She remembered tales of the great blight which drove farmers across the Florida fruit belt straight to the poorhouse.

The store should have been soothing after the chaos and confusion and Elle set to arranging the cans, and slept unusually early, waking up to the sound of a car which seemed close-by. She ran to the door, but no one was there. Then onto the road, looking around, which made her aware of how lonely she felt.

Her workday at Pigeon Key began in two days and Elle tried to put it out of her mind and made up inventory sheets and a dream list of shelving and signs she wanted from the catalog. She missed Charlie the rooster. His crowing had a soothing effect on her, sending her off to sleep when she stayed on No Name. Cat was happy to have her to himself and slept on her throat whenever he got the chance.

The quiet in the evening unnerved her until the highway work began and disturbed her even more. This wasn't the critter haven of No Name with everything flocking to water. The rush of wings, the low grunts.

On one side of the diner, she imagined a few tables and umbrellas, but out back she would build a chicken coop and hammered in planks, sawing them into shape and trying to lay them into the hard coral rock. It was a shaky, ill-conceived affair, dilapidated, but it would do for now when no one was around to see it. She would ask for a deal on chicken wire from Pigeon Key when she arrived for her shift. They always had this and that lying around, much more than they needed.

38

Although she was exhausted, that evening Elle cycled back to her cistern to look for Charlie, bringing a can of peaches, a bag of dried corn and a jar of preserved tomatoes to entice him. The cement walls of the cistern sucked out sound and all she heard was her own breathing and whatever tapped on the ceiling and walls. The spreading mold crept onto the floor, holes in the cement now covered in green, but Elle wasn't certain if they were vines or a more exotic variety of fungus.

Out back, she spied Charlie's coop and the section she flattened to allow him to escape when he got into trouble. Mrs. Dean was afraid of Charlie, and refused to keep him, and Elle believed Blanche would kill him if she knew how much Elle valued him. Perhaps someone had throttled the crabby rooster. Chicks chirped beyond her gate, so she took her torch outside and saw a ragged hen and calligraphy of tiny chicks peeping from the folds of her wings and under her body. Elle fashioned a crate into a cage and moved jungle debris onto the bottom, positioning a large spatulate leaf toward the back after loading it with tomato and a peach half, trailing and tossing corn near the hen and chicks to get the smell. The chicks jumped from under the hen and Elle stopped counting at nine. They ran into the cage, starving. The hen followed far behind, but stopped when Elle approached too soon. Elle returned to the house, not wanting to spook them, hoping that they would stay near the food where Charlie could hear them. But the hen was wary and sensed a trap. These birds were not domesticated. Elle knew them to be gypsy chickens brought here as cockfighters from Cuba and she hoped Charlie hadn't met that fate, because he would make a prized fighter.

She felt exposed when she stepped outside her gate, so she waited until evening before tiptoeing to check on the trap. The little family was tucked into the cozy box, not budging when Elle approached until she sprung the top to trap them. The hen bellowed, the chicks followed rapidly, sounding in little panicked chirps, and Elle made out a ferocious screech behind her. Charlie bit her calf once, drawing blood and creating a painful bruise that grew in size, changed color and lasted weeks. But this was a more demonic sound, forcing Elle to back away.

"Charlieeee!" she yelled.

His ruff was up against his face like a feather duster on fire and he bobbed his prehistoric face, dancing around her yelping *bub bub bubbubbub*. He circled, and she followed, never letting his beak out of her sight. Charlie was measuring her, claiming her. They'd been through this before.

"Charlie," she said when he ran out of the gate that he had somehow straddled. She followed, calling his name. "Charlie. It's me. C'mere Charlie," as if he were a frightened child, or a cat. They were close to the lodge in the pitch black. Even Blanche would likely be asleep at three in the morning or out of sight in cabin 214 with her lover.

"Charlie, where are you?" She clucked, imitating his cries. *Cluck cluck cluck* . "C'mere Charlie... Charlieeee." But the bird had disappeared.

From nowhere, he flew at her, landing in her outstretched arms as a porch light came on. Whoever made it out to the porch saw a woman and a rooster embrace, his beak nuzzling her ears and Elle hugging him, tears in her eyes. She carried him through her gate, patting his head so he leaned against her shoulder, his powerful wings hanging limp by his side, yellow talons relaxed in her palm. "I missed you Charlie. I missed you so much."

39

When her shift at Pigeon Key finally arrived, she was so eager for news she arrived early. Her palms were sweaty, but she convinced herself she wasn't afraid of Nathan, that someone else had hid Ruby and Betty on the boat. The place was quiet, and Elle didn't see Pirro, who usually made his presence known. "What happened to Pirro?" she asked Bernie.

"Why?" Bernie said, his brows knitted.

Elle had never asked about anyone, but she was ready for him. "I never thanked him for his hospitality last week, for driving me back."

"Well, you're a little late for that," he said, snapping his work towel at a fly in the air.

"What happened?"

"Fired, Nathan drove him off himself," he said. "Big scene."

So, they blamed him for not monitoring Ruby. Maybe this was good news. But when she moved toward Bernie to ask more, he looked at her strangely, and she didn't want to risk him asking questions.

"Someone else took his place?"

"What do you think?" he said, staring at her as if she was a moron.

A kitchen inspection was due, everyone scrubbing out fridges and stoves, pots and pans, brief conversation and not a single sighting of Nathan. Then the tedious sorting of staples began, huge drums of rice, sugar and flour upended onto tarps, to check for bugs, the drums scrubbed, then everything poured back.

The long tables were empty except for smatterings of exhausted kitchen workers taking smoke breaks. An older soldier sat alone at a long table with a cup of coffee. He didn't look well.

"You can start the damn soup," Bernie said to Elle, banging his ladle on the tall pot. "

This time I'm watching, so don't be trying to sneak any of your strange smelling herbs into the pot."

It was difficult to make Bernie out. He wasn't called the ace of clubs for nothing. Bernie had the best poker face she'd ever encountered.

The helpers in the kitchen raised their heads, sensing a scene.

"You mean cilantro," Elle smiled. The only person who requested her soup was Ruby. "Has Mrs. Foreman made a special request?" There was no way Ruby could be here. Bernie had to be joking around.

"No idea. Just got a note, is all." Before Elle made her way to Bernie, he folded the paper and put it back in his apron pocket. "Especially not the one that smells like soap."

"Cilantro," Elle said. "Is she here? Mrs. Foreman?" Her voice rose, almost quivering.

"Who the hell knows? What I do know is cilantro is positively un-American. What the hell is wrong with basic old parsley?"

"You mean those funny looking Italian leaves?" the old soldier said, winking at her. Elle recognized him. He hated being in the bunkroom and spent whatever time he wasn't working in the kitchen, commenting on this and that. His hands shook constantly, so they gave him light duty out of respect for his bravery in the war. Rumor was he got shell-shock from putting pieces of his father into a paper bag when he was blown up in front of him.

Bernie replied, "I'm so good, I can make a chicken soup without a chicken, so don't be givin' me the gears."

"If they want my soup, I'll have to scare up some hot pepper to cut the usual blandness," Elle said, then repeated. "Who left the note? So, I can make it right."

"Don't get yer knickers in a knot, missy. This kitchen is my lookout," Bernie said, advancing toward her with the ladle in striking position.

Elle reached for the heavy stewpot lid, holding it out like a shield to defend herself.

"Two bits on the big gal," the old soldier said, banging his fist on the table and rising.

"I'll see your parsley and raise you two onions," a helper said. He picked up three onions and began juggling.

"So much talent in one kitchen," Elle said, reaching into a carton of carrots and tossing one into the air like a baton the way her cousin Maureen showed her when they were girls. Maureen was a twirler and Elle had thought being a twirler was the most glamorous thing ever, secretly envying her showy costumes and tasseled white boots. She picked up a second carrot and tried to envision the wrist and thumb do-si-do that set them in motion while the old soldier limped to the box of root vegetables, tossing a turnip from hand to hand playing catch, laughing and showing his gums, naked but for the canines that jutted out the sides of his mouth. Elle miscalculated, and her second carrot hit the ceiling with force and slammed to the floor as Nathan opened the door.

"What the livin' good jezuz?" Bernie said as carrots, onions, and turnips bounced and rolled on the floor. Elle and the helper scrambled to pick them up.

Nathan stood, his hands by his sides, the slightest narrowing of eyes while he breathed air out of pursed lips. He advanced toward Bernie and Elle. "Get out," Nathan said, and Elle reached behind her waist to untie her apron strings.

"Not you," he said, and pointed at Bernie. "You had two warnings, third's the charm. Now get out."

"I started it," Elle said.

Nathan advanced on Bernie. "This is your kitchen and you're responsible. Now get out. Now."

Bernie's hands twitched as if they wanted to form into fists. His was a sinewy scrapper's body. He had been in on the 1934 dockworker strike in San Francisco. Bernie was like the inflated clown who kept bouncing up, each time bloodier than the last. A man who would not back down.

"Take more than you to get me out."

"If he leaves, I leave," Elle said, moving between the two men.

"Me too," said the old soldier, sweeping turnips off the table for emphasis.

"Great! Get the hell out, everyone! Except you," he said to Elle.

"My wife says she wants your soup and wants you to deliver it to her. Says she's more comfortable with a woman, if you don't mind."

Ruby? Three days after Elle dropped her off at the wharf. Elle tried to look at him, but couldn't. "I'm out," Elle said. Nothing worked, nothing changed.

Nathan lifted her chin with his fingers. He wanted to tell her something.

"Make your own fucking soup," the old soldier said, cornering Nathan twirling his fists like a scrapper from the funny papers.

Elle fiddled with the ties around the back of her neck but couldn't get the knot out, so it hung off her like a shapeless sack as she turned to leave, gaining in confidence as she strode to the door.

"Wait," Nathan said as she placed her hand on the doorknob. And let out a deep sigh.

"What?"

"Can't you guys take a little fun from the boss?" he said, turning to face the kitchen. "You're not the only ones who need a chuckle. It was a joke. No one's fired, not even you," he pointed at the old soldier, who was nodding and mumbling something inarticulate.

Bernie didn't respond, just turned away in disgust.

Elle stood still in the center of the room, an apron hanging from her neck. Nathan motioned her toward the porch. They made their way through the door to a pair of chairs underneath an umbrella covered table.

"My wife," he said, looking contrite, at his hands. "She gets herself into trouble. She always had problems, trusts the wrong people."

Elle could not form a sentence, felt her chest tighten. She could only sit there, forcing her mouth to close.

"I think you know what I mean."

He knows, she thought. Elle stared at the back of his chair, afraid to meet his eyes. Nathan reached across the table, squeezed her shoulder and then nodded his eyes kindly. "The Cuban guy. Pirro. Did something to her.

Couple people told me about the comments he made to you. "

"Pirro? But you sent him with the car."

"Who told you that?"

"He did. He drove me to Big Pine after I dropped off a meal for your wife."

"Sonafabitch."

"You didn't let him have the car?"

"The key was under the sink. Lots of people had access to it for errands. Not him though." He was building up into a rage. "Sonofabitch," he said again, and looked like he stopped himself from rising.

"He did nothing. He was all hot air," Elle said. An overwhelming desire to see Ruby battled with total exhaustion.

He stood, mashed his lips together and stared at her with eyes like gouges in coral targeting hers.

"Look Elle. If you want to leave, I won't stop you, but you and I need to have a little talk in private," he said, for the first time not calling her Mrs. Woodman. "It's in your best interest. Name the day, or maybe I'll just pop in sometime. You let me know when, ok?"

Elle heard the blunt tap of his footfalls and wondered what happened to Pirro. If Ruby had come back, so be it, but she would hear it from her lips one last time. Coward. Bernie peered out the door like nothing in the world had just happened. Bernie was always more peaceful after a conflict.

"You coming back?"

"Yes. I just need a minute."

Elle took a short walk around the compound and something hissed near her feet and she spotted a tiny white kitten with a limp. When she bent to pick it up, it scratched her and bolted into the brush.

Bernie said nothing when she re-entered the kitchen. The youngest worker, a teen-aged boy, brought over a tray of vegetables and Elle felt him sneak peeks at her while he peeled. When she went out back to grab and butcher a chicken, Bernie followed. He had one ready and Elle felt relieved and pushed back tears. The hypocrisy of it all. Someone else doing her dirty work. Elle felt a stab of the old self-hatred. Was this nothing but a dance between the two of them, Nathan and Ruby?

The soup cooked slowly, Elle made a bouquet garni, adding the neck and sweetbreads for flavor, skimming as it simmered gently, imagining Ruby's bruises as the potatoes bobbed, her swollen eye socket, adding the carrots last so they didn't get mushy.

"Something smells divine," Al, the old soldier said, and it surprised Elle to hear him speak so eloquently. Instantly, she understood he had played to the crowd as well. Was she always the only one not in on the joke?

When the soup was done, Elle removed the carcass and plucked meat off the bones, separating it until the broth cooled and doing a sink full of dishes to pass the time, despite it not being her job. Bernie eyed her, allowing her to do whatever she liked, and Elle suspected that he actually enjoyed having a competent and silent helper despite earlier reservations. When the soup was reasonably cool, Elle replaced the meat, added cilantro and parsley, crushing peppercorns and salt, buying time. She was almost afraid of seeing Ruby.

Before she tidied up, she brought a bowl to Al. He patted her retreating hand and a second impulse to tears took her by surprise.

She ladled a good amount into the large picnic bucket with the lid, turned to Bernie, and spoke. "If you see Nathan, tell him I'm off to bring soup to his wife."

Elle made her way out of the mess hall, unsurprised when Nathan came up from behind.

"You can take this yourself," Elle turned to face him, offering the heavy bucket, tired of playing this game. If Nathan wanted to go, he would go alone.

"My poor, poor wife," he said, taunting her. "Like I said, it's your call." His haircut was choppy, unevenly cut and as he reached for the pot, she noticed fresh cuts and scrapes on his hand.

"I'll go, if you let me speak to your wife alone."

He blinked, his long blond eyelashes casting shadows, but he straightened his posture, stared down at her and nodded, "Sure," he said. "Go say goodbye. We're leaving soon. Oh, and I'll carry this for you." He smiled sympathetically.

"No, I'll take it." She moved it from his outstretched hands. "Sunday night. Meet me Sunday night."

He laughed a thin wheeze and put up his hands in a mock gesture of surrender. "What a coincidence. I'm leaving on just that date. Another fishing trip because you know how much I love to fish. So no one will expect me to be anywhere near Big Pine. I think it's time we negotiate a truce. Just you and I."

A trio of men passed her, moving like the soldiers they once were, stinking of Hercules disinfectant, a common smell after a spate of TB passed through the tents. Stiff clothing from handwashed clothes that dried in the sun marked the men who slept in tents. They sped up after spotting Nathan, and sensing prey, he hurried after them. "Who goes there?" he asked in a loud voice, as if joking. But Nathan's jokes always had an edge.

Elle tightened grip on the handle, slipping around a corner as the men recited their names, as if they were prisoners of war.

All four shadows followed her, bending like carnival clowns on stilts until she put a building between them.

40

Scrub grass replaced the ill-conceived rose bushes around Nathan and Ruby's house. Disgust welled up in Elle for the newcomer's contempt for the natural landscape of the Keys. The great walls around the house seemed impenetrable, and Elle cursed until she remembered to pull the odd medallion on a wire that sprung the gate open. Hoses lay around the yard, coiled like snakes. Freshly planted squares of grass were already dying. A stack of Bahama shutters sat by the faucet. Although they were modern and practical, Elle disliked them for casting rooms in permanent gloom, rivaling the dead of winter in the middle of the tropics. Revulsion passed through her at the thought of entering the house. Ruby Foreman might as well be an invalid, locked away.

"It's me. Bringing more goddamned soup," she yelled. *Bang, bang, bang,* but nothing. Elle was tempted to leave it on the stoop, but the longer she waited, the angrier she became. What right did this cowardly woman have to involve Elle in her pathetic schemes? She moved to the back, banged on the window and saw Betty's tiny figure scurry away.

"I see you," Elle shouted. "Open up."

Elle held the soup bucket so tightly the wire handle cut into her hand and it was threatening to bleed. She switched hands, pulled her sleeve over the injury, and walked through the dark hallway to Ruby's bedroom.

Ruby wore an airy knitted bed jacket tied at the neck with a pale satin bow. She was wearing a cap which struck Elle as strange, something from another era. She looked absurd and Elle felt tired, no longer wanting to talk to this stupid, stupid woman wrapped up like a box of wedding pastries. Nobody dresses like this. Just looking at her was exhausting.

"I'm sorry," Ruby said, and her little girl voice enraged Elle. The pathetic utterance she was certain Ruby used with Nathan.

"Who are you talking to... me or Nathan?"

"I just..."

"I risked everything for you." She turned away to contain her rage. "Long as you're ok," Elle said. "I'll bring the soup to the kitchen and let myself out."

"Ok, thank you," Ruby said.

Elle turned back. "Ok thank you," she said, mimicking Ruby's voice. Something caught Elle's eye. Ruby's mouth didn't look right; the jawline was off.

Fine shell-pink powder had scattered into the pillow. One of Ruby's eyes looked slightly bigger than the other, misaligned. Elle took out a handkerchief and wiped Ruby's cheek.

"Ahhhh ow," Ruby cringed. When she brought her fingers to her face; the pale skin of her hand contrasted with her makeup. Elle leaned over and wiped her cheek, revealing swollen red skin under the powder.

"That's enough," Ruby said. "We tried. You tried; I mean."

"Does he know? About my part?" Elle felt a sharp pain sear through her temple. Her own hand throbbed in sympathy.

Betty stood in the doorway, looking angry. "Leave my mom alone or I'll tell," she said.

"Come here, Betty," Ruby comforted the child, who was on the verge of screaming.

"I'm leaving now, I promise."

"Shhh, Betty. She tried to help us. Go get mommy a glass of water and drink a whole one before coming back and count to two hundred and by then she'll be gone."

"Promise?"

"Yes, yes, now go." Ruby sat straight up, looking more animated, the ghostliness and shadow-like quality of her previous movements absent. "No one's ever... please don't be mad. Thank you for trying."

"He'll never, ever stop." Elle wanted to run, to cry, to hug her, to hit her. She turned away.

"Nathan thinks Betty and I hid in an empty cabin in No Name overnight, then snuck onto the ferry."

Elle imagined a dark wood and Red Riding Hood running from the huntsman and the wolf.

"I took advantage of you and Monty, hiding under a tarp in the hold."

'But the kid...'

"Betty knows he'd kill me," Ruby said. "So, she repeated what we rehearsed over and over. He found us by chance, by dumb luck, when the bus wouldn't let us on. We stopped at a house and they took us to the police. We tried to get out but..."

Elle tossed the pouch with the money on the bed. Was it that simple? Forty-seven dollars between her and freedom? "You said you saved two hundred dollars, but there was forty-seven dollars in the pouch."

"What? I had two-hundred and forty-seven dollars."

"Pirro must've taken the two-hundred. I'm surprised he left you anything."

"Even that would have been enough. We could have made it to Providence....I could work."

Elle imagined the panic when they felt for the pouch and it was gone. She wanted to flee that fetid, dark room. Nathan knows I'm here, she thought.

Ruby sat up and leaned toward Elle. "You did it, didn't you?"

"Did what?"

"You killed Billy. I heard Blanche and Nathan."

No one but Blanche had ever accused her of murder.

"They said what?"

"I'm glad you did. Because he must've deserved it. Tell me... just tell me how you did it. I'm ready. Please. I know it's the only way." Betty appeared in the doorway and Elle felt trapped with this woman, who would be dead within a year, the same way Elle would've been.

"Tell her to go," Elle said.

After a hug and a promise of some sort, Betty left with a picture book, her face solid and unreadable.

Elle turned toward Ruby, a look of triumph on her face. "I put him in the crab traps."

Ruby's head jerked back, but she said nothing

"He would never have left me alone. I had something. I had a job and even found a place to love. I mean to live."

"Yes, your cistern."

"It belonged to the hermit, but he never used it. In exchange for giving him storage for his saplings and selling his trees and fruits when they came into season... I had a dog," Elle said, everything coming out disjointed, tumbling one image over the other, popping randomly after being so long under pressure. She felt the sheer relief of letting it all out.

"I met him when I was seventeen. Seventeen!... and living with my uncle and I knew he wanted me and so I married him. But he could never settle down, and then... he hit me and.... nothing I did made him happy. It's the same story you have, maybe a different age." She took a breath and Ruby nodded manically.

"Please, please go ahead." Ruby's makeup was uneven, and Elle pulled the handkerchief from Ruby's hand to wipe her face until Ruby took it from her and finished the job.

"Why are you dressed like that?" Elle pointed to the jacket with the bow.

"Sometimes he comes home."

"Say it out loud–say that he doesn't like to see evidence of what he did and you collude with him. Say it."

"Yes. I'm afraid of him."

"Ok, that's enough. Where's your son?"

"Perry's at the schoolhouse."

"Nathan's gone to the road," Elle said, and Ruby's shoulders relaxed.

"How long have you been married?"

"Nine years," Ruby answered.

"Yes, but you have children," which would explain why she stayed.

Ruby nodded. "And then what happened?"

"I tried to leave but he wouldn't let me, so when he got the job in Miami on the WPA project, I told him I had a rich uncle and would get him work as a chauffeur and couldn't believe he fell for it. I thought Billy was my destiny and, in some way, I was right. So, I took off, left the work camp, jumped on the first ferry out, but it was going the wrong way. I planned to go north, but I was so scared he would change his mind and come after me, I stayed on it. It was called the Key Wester, and I got off at No Name when I heard they needed a cook." She closed her eyes, then went to Ruby, and grasped her hands. "I had no idea life could be so good, cooking and then getting a small place to fix up and then this beautiful dog came to me and my life was complete. Until Billy found me."

Ruby closed her eyes, as if she didn't want Elle to finish.

"Do you remember those trees I was carting out when I left the cistern?" Elle asked.

Ruby shook her head, no.

"One of them was a manchineel tree, one of the most poisonous trees in the world–every part can kill you. The bark, the leaves, but most of all the apples it produces in September. Well, my dog found the apples and Billy kicked him over and over and the kick finished him off and that's when I knew he wouldn't stop until I was dead. The lodge owners were sick of him hanging around, getting drunk and causing trouble and screwing whoever he could. Even Blanche."

"Blanche Rowlands? You're kidding!" Ruby's mouth opened so wide, the cut on her lip split open and bled down her chin and onto her jacket.

"She's a moron. She was in love with him."

"I think Nathan is sleeping with her, too," Ruby said

"I know," Elle said, "Jeez," and both women found this funny and laughed.

Elle warmed to the story. "Well, I considered myself lucky, but he still wouldn't leave me alone," she said, and Ruby nodded. Elle knew the same thing was happening to Ruby.

"So, then, what happened?"

"Well, the owners wanted him gone and Dog was dead, and they wanted me out. I always thought Dog helped me by finding the poison apples, so I made a concoction with them. There was a fishing tournament at the lodge… everyone was drunk…. and the hurricane was closing in, so everyone had to evacuate on the morning ferry. That night Billy got drunk, and I made a concoction with the manchineel's apple juice, rum and sugar water and I couldn't believe my luck when he downed it, like the hillbilly he was. The jug might as well have been marked XXX." Elle smiled widely, remembering the scene. Ruby's mouth opened, but not from terror. Her eyes were shining, filled with awe.

"Wait, what's that?" Ruby said, then Elle heard it and put a finger to her mouth, although she was doing all the talking. Ruby stood and moved the curtains to look out, but no one was there.

Elle motioned her over and whispered, "Give me a minute." She walked silently down the hallway, then outside and around the house. Nothing was out of place except for a large palm frond, which would account for the sound.

Ruby crouched behind the bedroom door, ready to clock anyone who came through, and Elle, returning to the room, gasped, which made them both laugh. Elle imagined a childhood friend's slumber party, with everyone telling scary stories.

"You don't have to tell me the rest," Ruby said, settling back into her position on the bed.

"But I want to," Elle replied, realizing this was true and how much she had kept to herself and how important it was to tell Ruby exactly what happened.

"So, you poisoned him," Ruby said, sitting back onto the bed and leaning against the headboard, settling a pillow under her head for comfort.

Elle let out a breath. "Not exactly. The juice took too long, and he knew, he just knew I had done it, so he pulled me down and what they say about the strength of a dying man. Well, it's true. He gashed my leg," Elle said.

"Like yours. That's what brought it all back. When I saw yours."

Ruby pulled her nightgown up and Elle pulled down her pants to compare the almost identical scars. "Real blood sisters," Ruby said, and Elle nodded, her face set and determined, and they both heard the noise again.

Betty burst in; her mouth open in shock before Elle could pull up her pants.

Ruby said, "Please, sweetheart. Count to two hundred again," and before the girl could protest, she jumped out of bed, shoved her out and shut the door behind her.

Elle leaned in closer to Ruby and whispered, upping the tempo, speaking rapidly. She'd been at the house too long. "Billy knocked over the kerosene lamp, trying to set the place on fire, and I hit him on the head with a heavy pitcher until he was dead."

"Oh my God! Dead!"

"The storm came, and everyone left, or I would have been discovered, so I cut up the body and I put him in the crab traps." She had never said this to anyone except Ruby, not even herself. She was suddenly aware of how ghoulish it was. When she dared to look up, Ruby was nodding gravely.

"You put him in the crab traps! That must have been so hard to do. All that bone…." she said.

And Elle thought, I won't tell her about dumping Billy's head. Enough is enough.

"Yes, the storm did the rest. He was just another man lost in the Great Labor Day hurricane."

"Like God Almighty was on your side," Ruby said, tears streaming down her face.

"Um, right," Elle said.

Betty busted into the room again, ran to the bed and folded herself into her mother's body, her intelligent eyes meeting Elle's with accusation.

"I'm leaving now, but it's not over," Elle said. Ruby looked like a doomed and elegant Gloria Swanson, head bowed, comforting a child on the cover of a detective magazine.

41

Elle retrieved her bicycle, hyper aware of the men she passed, each a montage of bad luck or disadvantage. She strode quickly, head down, through this makeshift town of heavy booted, disappointed men. A couple of miles on the road out, she hit something and felt her tire flatten. She was out of patches and too wrung out to return to the camp, so she walked her bike the remaining twelve miles. The Keys were in full bloom. Bushes on the margins of the road released their sweet odor, holding it in until concealed in the safety of darkness. Birds rode invisible currents, flying languidly overhead. What a pleasant life they have, she thought. To live in the woods in a sheltered den or nest high in the sky that no one could reach.

Until recently, the Florida Keys had escaped detection from the larger world. Now everyone around her schemed ways to squeeze a nickel out of it. Elle thought of the vast parking space Brushy had cleared. He understood people would flock to an altered landscape made familiar.

The moon hid behind night clouds as Elle walked close to the fringe of wood. Brushy should be back by now. The note on the orange tree said he would return mid-August at the latest, and that was almost two weeks ago. Maybe he was there, waiting for her at the diner.

The last leg of the trip was her favorite, and she listened for the blunt sound of hooves, hoping to spot a tiny deer or spot a velvet nose peek out of the curtain of pine. The road swept up and the nascent smell of tar hit her, and then the long sweep down to her little building, exposed inside the sacred circle of flattened land.

A note on her door read, "Gas installation scheduled for Tuesday, August 27. Thank you." Oddly shaped red bulbs and clockfaces leaned against the side of her store, the gas pumps resembling a recent movie advertisement about flying saucers.

Tomorrow she might have her gas-powered stove if the digging went well. But she could no longer ask Monty to bring her ham or beef for smoking after using him so badly. Until the highway spanned Miami to Key West, supplies would continue to come in via boats docking at No Name.

Early morning, the first squeal and groan of a gigantic backhoe sent Cat out the window and into the wood. A line of trucks followed, men jumping from running boards like trained circus artists, bent on getting the job done. Their clothes matched in dark denim, some with metal name tags, and most of the men had buzz-cuts. A decade younger than the men on the WPA projects, they moved with sprightly ease, enjoying the challenge of the job, seeing who could out tough the other.

"Bud," someone yelled, "stand watch while I work this jackhammer."

"More like rescue you from fainting," Bud responded, gaining a laugh as he pried open a wooden crate.

Giant hoes dug into the coral, the men helping with jackhammers, some with industrial sized mattocks to finesse holes that never seemed deep enough. Would they ever replace the damn mattock, Elle wondered, amused at how everyone spoke about progress, but the work remained primitive as ever. Welders arrived in the afternoon to assemble the gas containers on site.

Another welder lowered himself into the trench to work on a drainage pipe. His blowtorch hissed and spit, sealing the pipe that resembled a bloated snake before the crew moved in to bury it underground.

Elle looked up from an instruction manual. "You boys gonna tell me how to operate these things?" Elle asked, pointing at the pumps, silently thanking her mother for teaching her to read.

"In due course. Dry as a bone 'til they pass inspection," the younger one said.

"Even my stove?" she asked.

"Yes Ma'am."

Noise from the highwaymen competed with the backhoes, grinders; oily particles coated nostril hairs and eyebrows, impossible to scrub out.

A large dump truck came perilously close to falling on its side when the newly installed fill crumbled.

The men installing the tanks and plumbing were the elites, worth their weight in gold in the new oil wealth. They were unafraid of the inevitable explosions that occurred from time to time. A worker smiled at Elle, reminding her of a curly-haired boy she had been sweet on back in Boston.

"You might want to steer clear until we're done. It's a heckova smell."

"I've smelled worse, Chester King," she said. He shrugged as if to say, not a lady like you. And she wandered off, confused and annoyed. Flatterers.

Elle cleaned, but the place was already spotless, so she considered painting the back room, but when she walked by with a paint can, the same man stopped her. "Oh no," he said, "that might be flammable and will have to wait. Purple paint's the worst," he said and winked at her.

She knew she should find Monty, but didn't want to answer his questions with more lies. So, she stayed and watched the shade canopy rise over the pumps for weather protection. Chester handed her a long box, and she knew from his smile that these were the two neon signs Brushy ordered for the Sidetrack Diner. One would run the length of the store under the roofline and a second smaller one would hang over the front door.

"What?" she said. "This is all wrong." The eight-foot-long neon sign read *Sidetrack Key Diner* in foot-high neon tubing. "There's no such place as Sidetrack Key," Elle said, cornering Chester King.

"What?"

"I ordered Sidetrack Diner. Sidetrack Key doesn't exist."

"Well, I guess it does now." He ran his fingers over the neon glass. "We're only here one more day. Do you want it or don't you?"

The flowing cursive of the large sign was modern, lending a sense of welcoming musicality. He pulled the smaller sign from the box and held it up above the front door.

"Your own private Key." He smiled.

And she liked it, liked the sheer bluster of claiming territory. "Put it up, dammit." She said.

"Yes, of course," he said, and patted her on the back in an oddly intimate gesture.

She moved from the window to the door, rearranging cans of fruit in syrup and running her fingers over the raised metal of the cash register, opening and closing the drawer, checking the gun remained hidden. Even if someone opened the cash, they wouldn't have a clue.

"It's a bit much to take in all at once. Come, I'll show you the stove hook up," he said. "I'll return next week to set it up after you pass inspection."

When Elle discovered they were bedding down at No Name lodge at company expense, she asked, "Are both owners there?" He shrugged as if he neither knew nor cared. When Chester King was about to leave, Elle said, "Tomorrow, then…. nice place, the lodge." And he looked at her curiously, sensing her discomfort. Elle couldn't trust herself to sound casual, convinced that speaking Brushy's name exposed her. "Oh, I just forgot to feed the chickens," she said, which was ridiculous because he had seen her wheel chicken feed out back an hour earlier.

Elle smoked the ham she had in storage and made flatbread for tomorrow's lunch break, annoyed at having to use the small propane burner. After a long talk with Charlie, she lay in bed with the kitchen supply catalog and fell asleep. Blanche and Brushy played in her dreams and she waited for dawn when the workers returned. She rehearsed out loud. *Is Mr. Rowlands back? Did you see him with his whore wife? Did he look happy? Does he know I'm here all alone?*

On Labor Day 1936, all work stopped, but the mood lacked cheer. Each man seemed to harbor a story about a friend or workmate who died a horrible death in the hurricane.

Elle walked the nascent highway to check on progress. The omnipresent smell of tar mingled with dust from coral stone disturbed from its millennium-long slumber, felled vegetation covered the roadside, filling ditches that stretched out for miles. Beyond the road, iridescent light pinged a tiny flower stalk clinging to a dying tree branch. Elle almost snapped the branch, charmed by the strange beauty that only appeared delicate, but was actually leathery and tough. She wanted to take the tiny plant, aerial roots, and all to the diner, but it reminded her of the orchid she pointed out to Betty during that long failed escape, so she left it where it was.

Elle positioned the "State Beverage Department" certificate near the cash register. She displayed tailor-made cigarettes and loose tobacco in a cool, glass case beyond the customer's reach above the cash register. Booze and tobacco would pay her way until she could fill the rooms with travelers and their cars with gas to drive the highway between Miami and Key West.

The coterie of sociable drunks and jokesters trusted her after word got out about Petey's arm. Sometimes when they saw her on the road, they drove by holding up an arm and laughing.

Art rarely joined in on the banter, and had taken on a depressive tone when he stopped in. "Sometimes I think I'll die building this highway. They might as well bury me under it," he said, and Petey punched him in the shoulder to silence him. "Wouldn't take that much," Art said. "All those rocks, then the cement, then the tar. No one would even know I was gone."

"Nathan would miss you, that's for sure," Petey said.

"Bastard. He likes me about as much as he likes her," Art nodded at Elle.

"Not so sure about that. I hear he wants a date with you," Petey said to Elle. "I heard you and him on the road to his place with a bucket of soup for the missus."

"Jesus H. He's off fishing this weekend."

Petey stared at her. "Sorry, Elle, I was just joking. Didn't mean nothing by it."

"Bastards, all of them,' Art said. "I'm sick of struggling. I think of James all the time… trying to help his mom." He opened a second bottle of beer. "Still don't have the bonus pay," he said.

"I'd offer you that beer on the house, but you might be too proud to accept," Elle said.

"Try me." His sudden grin warmed up his face and Elle saw a trace of dimples and imagined the big-eared prankster he might once have been. "I see the way they look at you," Art said, "Like you're nothing. That you'll be out of here by the end of the summer and someone else running this sweet spot."

Can't these men just have a drink and a smoke, enjoy the money they made, and make plans to better themselves? The ones who stopped here had no short list of grievances.

The shopkeeper bells rang and a government man stood in the doorway. He eyed the permit on the wall and said, "Soon, these will need a license." He pointed to the cigarettes and tobacco and shrugged, taking obvious pleasure in delivering bad news. "You got the ownership papers handy?"

Elle pressed 'No Sale' to pull them out from under the cash tray and imagined old Slabsides cozy in the slot, perfectly at home in his little cushioned cell. She smiled, grateful she was never tempted to follow rules.

Outside, the bean counter took out a ruler and compass and ostentatiously measured the space between gas tanks. "Half a foot short, I'm afraid they have to be rebuilt."

"For six inches?"

"Might as well be a mile. Dangerous is what it is, Miss. Can we see the owner or the manager?"

"You're looking at her." Art said from behind. Everyone knew she owned it. It was common knowledge.

"You know you need that fixed, "he said to Elle, ignoring Art.

Art moved next to her. "We got all the tools." Petey motioned to him from the door.

"I'll see you back inside," she said to Art, and he walked back slowly.

"Yes, I was planning on doing it myself."

He laughed out loud. "That's capstone. Worse here than Pigeon Key. I'll send the chief in from Pigeon Key. He'll tell you what to do. In the meantime..."

"Who's the head guy?" Elle had a sinking feeling she knew what was coming.

"Mr. Foreman. Nathan Foreman. Chief of Operations." He opened his briefcase and removed a pack of bright red 'Closed/Danger' stickers and placed one on each tank. "He said to make sure you know he's leaving tomorrow night."

"He wanted me to know that?"

"Yes - Tomorrow night... he'll be off on a well-earned fishing vacation all week. I'm just the messenger, ma'am."

So that's why he sent this guy. To remind her of their meeting tomorrow night. Nathan hated fishing.

Elle missed Monty. She would take a couple of bottles of beer and a pack of high-end Parliament cigs to him with her stewed tomatoes, which he was in the habit of spooning straight from the jar. She couldn't afford to lose Monty.

42

He would come at her slowly, she was certain. She was ready, and grateful for the two bennies Art gave her. No wonder he was able to work all night in this heat. It wasn't right. The stink wafting up all hours, the endless biting insects worse when the sun went down. Rats falling from the felled palm trees. Before the darkness thickened, she broke open the second cylinder as she had seen Art do so many times, rolled up the strip of paper, and swallowed.

It was a mistake. She knew it when the edges of the shelves blurred, and her heart raced. She punched the the register and grabbed the gun. The small, perfectly formed pistol, a gift from Brushy.

A rubbing sounded on the back door and Elle sprung up, raced to the back to see enormous black eyes stare into the window, but upon second look, it was a deer trying to nose in. She had told the men not to feed the damn deer. Elle relaxed her hand on the pistol, stuck it in her waistband, and opened the door.

Go! Go! she said in a strained snarl, half expecting someone to leap out. The deer turned away, but when she closed the door, he returned, snout on the window, fogging up the glass, leaving a spot resembling a giant fingerprint. Elle rapped on the glass again, hard, opened and closed the front door in a series of slams, the chimes screeching.

Nathan wanted her alone because he wanted to kill her; she finally understood there would be no negotiating. And just as they got away with Rimer's death, hers would be a footnote in the county records, if that. She moved to the back of the store and headed to the cooler. The ice had melted and although she didn't like the taste of beer; she hoped it would help with the jitters. The release of gas made her stomach lurch, but she downed some of the warm yeasty liquid. A dull thud close by startled her, and she felt the bottle loose from her hand. She placed it carefully on the counter and turned, but a nudge from her elbow sent it smashing into pieces on the hard floor, the operatic sound reverberating through the diner. A glass shard nicked her hand when she gathered the pieces. Unclench, unclench, she told herself, breathing loud, and dizzy from moving fast. The deer watched from the side window with his beautiful, stupid face. Was something behind him? No, he had lined up exactly next to the tree, whose branches looked animated as hands on hips. She smelled her own flesh.

The gun in her waistband slipped so she moved it into her pocket, then back to the waistband. The hell I didn't figure this out before, she thought. The rubbing of her clothing chafed against hypersensitive flesh.

The diner seemed to tilt a few degrees, and she twisted to see a smaller deer, their matching coats the color of the wood the color of Nathan. And Elle could barely see in the dark. The gun fell through her loose trouser leg and thudded to the ground. She picked it up and aimed at the sky, almost shooting it off in the compressed landscape to blow off steam, but stopped herself in time. A hot, seeping resentment formed in

Elle's chest as she skulked around her own property. The leaden stench of the heated gash of highway percolated in the dark. As the deer galloped easily up the slight incline and slid across the highway, she patted the gun to seat it securely; the vista calming her. *I hope you come Nathan I pray you come I will you to finally come.* She was ready. She was looking forward to meeting him. Until that moment, she hadn't known that all along she planned to kill him.

Amped up and exhausted, she could neither sit nor stand. She paced around the outside of the diner, Charlie following close behind, clucking low. Cat joined but tired of the game and perched near the manchineel tree, watching. Charlie grew suspicious and nipped her ankle, which brought her around. She stood outside the coop until a shard of moon rose, turning the purple diner fluorescent, like some deep-sea creature.

Back inside, Elle realized what must've happened and slowly she moved, looking at the chest she used to cover the root cellar. It seemed slightly angled. Metal braces secured the lid and sides and covered with an unlikely red linen cloth. Inside, Elle kept booze and cigarettes, food packages stuffed with cash.

A toxic sweat broke through her clothing. No wonder the highwaymen got so addled on this stuff. Elle had a hard time remembering how she got here. Simple calculations eluded her. She imagined Nathan trapped in the root cellar. He would suffocate down there, so she sat on the trunk and yelled, "Suffocate you bastard," her words calming her.

A second beer had no effect, so she opened the trunk, then remembered she moved the booze to the cellar when customers became more frequent. She'd have to climb down the ladder into the hole for the rum she wanted.

Once the idea took hold, she imagined the liquid burn, coating the raw surface of her throat, cutting through mold and black tar from the road. Calming the nerve endings. Maybe if she took her gun with her into the hole....

Then she saw Nathan peering down at her, sliding the trunk over the hole where she would take her last breath. Back to the window to peek through the blinds. Then outside to the still and untrustworthy evening that hadn't relinquished a single degree of heat. Behind the diner, the moon's shadow lengthened her into a lone spectral figure. Charlie's eerie trill sent Elle out front again, her freshly bitten calf pulsating. A slight breeze shook a low clatter from the shopkeeper bells.

Elle pulled out a few strands of hair, wedged them into the doorframe, and closed the door carefully. They would be invisible to anyone who didn't look closely. Up the hill, bush and highway merged without dimension or detail in the low light until night clouds obliterated the scrap of moon. Elle moved on to the highway in silence, steps deliberate and cautious on the dark velvet road.

Where was he?

Along the highway's ditches, great canisters of concrete dust waited for the men to return. She skillfully avoided the scattered pebbles from the huge piles that had stopped her dead many times on bike rides back and forth on the road.

She headed toward Pigeon Key, to waylay him away from her diner. She kept low in the ditch where she could easily hide. Little moved in the underbrush. A colony of ibis rustled on the upper branches of a few tall, ragged pines. And in the background, with her preternatural hearing, the comforting whine of machinery; men cradled in armor, the bobcat and the backhoe far enough away that Nathan wouldn't worry about being spotted. Light caught something on the road before Elle hit her shin on a piece of dark metal jutting out from a bush. It was a bike placed on its side. A new black bike that Elle didn't recognize. Like a cue to move back. Could this belong to Nathan?

Her mouth was dry, eyelids scratching her eyeballs as if she hadn't blinked the entire trip. Again, that smell, that disgusting trickle down her spine. She unclenched her fists and turned back after rising with a curve in the road, risking a last paranoid long view in both directions.

Her heart outpaced her steps and she willed it to slow, but it would not obey. And she became consumed by the idea of that golden flush of scotch or rum, anything to numb her nerves. The sky took on a bloom of amethyst and she walked like the dumb beast she was, deliberate and void of thought save thirst. He should be here by now and fears of being ambushed at the diner rushed through her.

A heavy thud sounded close by, gears grinding and the groans of metal. A strange exhilaration moved her toward the noise, keeping low to the bush, running, slowing, then running again toward a louder thud. The gun, feeling for the gun. Clatter sounded then settled like a piece of heavy machinery coming to rest. A distinctive whine marked it as Art's backhoe, and she headed toward the disturbance, stealthy, head low, paranoid. A massive ringed palm lay across the road, fronds sticking straight up in a lunatic haircut, and she heard grunts before she saw them, rolling down the incline under the upended roots of the palm. Two men rolled, one on top of the other like a struggling downed beast. The man on top looked like a shadow all in black, and as she moved closer, she prayed they hadn't seen her.

Art's legs were pinned under tree roots, or were they both pinned? His face angled toward hers, their eyes connecting in a *what the hell* moment. Nathan turned his head long enough for Art to twist and Elle caught the quick motion of Nathan's hand moving behind him - was he reaching for a gun?

She gripped her gun, knowing nothing about how to operate it beyond pulling the trigger. She'd have to get closer or might shoot Art by mistake. The thought terrified her and whenever she was afraid; she became furious, and rage shot through her.

"No," Nathan yelled when he saw the gun.

Elle closed in and shot in the air, hoping Art would seize the chance to gain advantage. For a split second, the hollow clunk of the empty chamber echoed, and all three jerked in shock. Nathan pushed away and Elle swore she saw the glint of metal, but it was only fear. Seconds later, Nathan had Art in a chokehold, Art's free arm flailing, unable to pry free from Nathan's grip.

"Drop it," Nathan yelled, his mouth twisted, and Elle aimed again, hoping it would stop him long enough for Art to do something. She aimed at his head, knowing the gun was empty but hoping he didn't know it. He wrenched Art's head harder, at an angle so unnatural, she thought she heard a snap of bone and then she shot, and a deafening echo knifed through her eardrums, like twin hearts exploding, slamming through her skull. Nathan's black python eyes met hers as he crumpled to the ground.

Where his head had been was the bright yellow of the backhoe.

Elle dropped to her knees and pulled Art away from the body. His face was coated in Nathan's blood, clothing spattered.

Art felt his face with both hands, spit in disgust, and pulled a rag from his pocket. When he wiped his face, Nathan's blood striped in an odd pattern, like demonic war paint.

"Check the road," he whispered and got on his knees, then stood and walked over to his backhoe on the side of the road, shovel level with the ground.

"Can you drive it?"

"Not much choice," he said, limping slightly, but what disturbed Elle was the angle of his arm. She turned to look at Nathan and vomit rose in her throat.

"We have to get him out of here."

The screech in her ears prevented her from hearing what he said. He pointed at the backhoe shovel and she nodded.

"No, both of us," Elle said.

Art struggled to remove his shirt, placed it over what remained of Nathan's head and Elle heard him retch.

"Try not to puke... attracts vultures," he yelled, pointing upwards in a circling motion.

He dragged the body by the ankles and Elle held Nathan's wrists and together they swung the headless body onto the backhoe, as if they had been doing this forever. Nathan landed smack center on top of a bed of palm fronds and other road debris. Elle gathered felled branches and placed them over the body.

"How did you know he was coming?"

"Government guy who checked the pumps. Remember? Petey was there...so I wanted to meet him before he got to you. I saw him on the road, and he had to stop. He came over, smiling like it was the most natural thing in the world to be dressed in black riding down the side on a black bike."

"You knew it was him?"

"Yah. Who else?

He looked at her like she was stupid. "Government guy said Nathan was going fishing. Nathan hates fishing..And here it is… Sunday night."

What else did Art know? "Was he scared when he saw you?"

"Me? Hah! I'm a nobody. A hole digger….something about the way he smiled ….I thought….maybe he has a gun and then it all came to me and I saw my dead body out on the road or in the water. They'd think some hobo knifed me. Nathan wouldn't have to say a word. I never thought he'd come to kill you. That's how dumb I am."

"So, you didn't plan it?"

"Hell, not very well. All I had was this". He pointed to a machete, a saw and a pair of ratcheting heavy duty pruners. "For the brush."

"Better that you didn't use a gun."

"Better because I don't have one," he said.

"No one knows about this one," Elle said.

She thought about how perfect it would have been for Nathan. He could murder her and blame it on Art, maybe move the bodies and make it a double murder.

"Hah." He said again. "Nathan's big surprise–I caught the Fucker pants down on the crapper." He moved to the backhoe and slid in, angled it toward the road and for a second Elle feared it would tip over, but he steadied it.

"She's purring," he yelled over his shoulder. And he was right, the beast purred.

"Walk home," he yelled from the cab

"What about the bike?"

"I'll get it tomorrow," he said. "No one knows he's gone."

"We don't know that for sure," Elle said. "And you know there's no reasoning with me."

Art lifted the scoop with Nathan inside, and the machine screeched like an enormous yellow elephant trumpeting victory. He's crazy. Someone will hear him. And yes, someone would, but they heard him the night before and the night before that.

Elle turned her shirt inside out and stayed long enough to change her clothes and dump the rest into the fire barrel but wouldn't light it until she returned. Over the wooden bridge and into the wood, she raced the bike with its superior tires, which negotiated every bit of terrain on No Name until she reached the pathway to the lodge. His seat was the perfect height, and she thought what a waste it would be to destroy the bike, but no, she wouldn't take the tires, her mind preoccupied with minutiae to distract herself from what was actually happening. It was close to 4AM and light feathered the sky when she arrived at her crabbing place. She'd planned to take the bike out to deeper water, but a light was on in one cabin, so she wheeled it past the strangler fig, stepped out onto thick mangrove roots and pushed it into water close to where she'd sunk Billy's remains.

When she returned to the diner, a flock of vultures had already gathered in the distance, but the double strand of knotted hair on the front door handle was undisturbed. Hand on gun, she stepped inside and found a wretched half-finished bottle of beer abandoned behind the counter. She guzzled the remains and got deluged with black sludge from cigarette butts and ash someone discarded in the bottle. So, she opened another and by sunrise had demolished a half dozen and still had the jitters.

When the first stream of supply trucks drove by, Elle lay down, but couldn't sleep and decided the place needed a good whitewash. No wonder the men went crazy, she thought. These benzos are pure poison.

43

$\mathcal{E}$lle looked for a familiar face in the first truckload of men that drove by. Someone tipped his cap and yelled out to her, "Open for lunch today, Miss Elle?"

"Yes," she yelled back. "Coffee and American cheese sandwiches. Is the boss with you?" Noise drowned her out.

After the procession moved past, Elle walked down the shallow incline back to the diner, exhausted. The saturated buzzing in her ears subsided as the drug loosed its grip.

A procession of workers on a flatbed traveled back the other way toward Pigeon Key. Petey yelled out, "Getting more gravel! Back in an hour. Sorry."

They returned later with a heavy load of gravel and by two o'clock they still hadn't stopped for lunch, so Elle wrapped the sandwiches and placed them in a basket. So far, it was like any other day. Trucks blurred past, with men hanging off the sides. The noise and dust and sound of men singing stupid songs made her crazy.

When she arrived at the worksite three miles down the road, they greeted her like a homecoming queen, or better yet, one of the boys. Art was almost unrecognizable, his face and hands blackened by tar and covered in a thick layer of coral dust. White eyeballs peered out from under his hat.

He was speaking to George, Nathan's henchman.

"I am a hole digger," he said. "Cement ain't nothin' without a proper bed to lie on. It's the rocks that do the work, the setup. If that ain't right, the whole mess will crumble, no matter what magic you think your cement will do. Don't want entire families dumped into the drink on their way to vacation paradise."

After George left, angry and defeated, Elle closed in.

"So that was you last night, tearing up the rock?" She said loud enough for anyone listening.

He nodded his head yes.

"Art figures our sole purpose in life is to slow him down," someone said, and someone else snorted in agreement.

"Don't wanna mess with Art."

"Hand me that water jug." Art pointed to it. "You know, Miss Elle, every job required barrels of fresh water standing by, in case needed.

"Art, when was the last time you ate?" Elle asked, desperate to get him alone. The pupils in his pale eyes were black. He was still whacked on bennies. His clothes hung loose on his gawky frame.

Conscious of being watched, Elle settled her basket of sandwiches on the flatbed of a pickup. "Honor system. Help yourself." She turned back to Art. She needed to get him alone, but there was little entertainment and Elle knew she was all they had.

"Looks like that shovel got the better of you," Elle said.

He stared at her blankly, took a rollie from a cargo pocket on his pants and flicked his Ronson lighter, a smell she associated with Nathan. He flicked it twice more before it flamed. The smell of naphtha burning nauseated her, the click click click like cocking a gun.

Art's hand was covered in black dust, but she made out the usual gashes from the job.

"You know, Art," Elle said, once the men moved off. "You gotta quit those bennies."

"Yes, and now I can. It was high time," he smiled at her. "Waddya say you spot me one of those cheese sammis."

"Not unless you wash those hands first." The men moved farther away, losing interest. Most had just returned from a day off in Key West. Their hangovers, the bad patch of limestone and the higher temps of September seemed to blunt their curiosity.

"Have it your own way," he said, his voice light and generous. He massaged his right hand with the left, heel over his thumb. One of his fingers seemed screwed on the wrong way.

He let go of the injured hand and walked back to the idle group. Art was the true leader, no matter who was called boss. Art's authority came from his innate mastery of machinery and a willingness to work harder than anyone else. "C'mon boys, let's finish up-don't want to be slacking when the big boss gets here."

He headed toward his cab and took out his mottled rawhide gloves, and Elle followed him. They were alone when he handed her a paper bag of clothing. "Right as rain and worth the pain." He winked at Elle and she thought again how crazy the Keys made all of them. Or maybe it had been the war.

"I need to keep my eye on this spot for a bit," he said, stomping the section of road next to his backhoe. "Seems it needed a bigger hole than I first guessed."

"So how big did it need to be?" she asked, stuffing the bag of bloody clothes into her duffel.

"Oh, about six feet deep and a maybe a little longer. The whole thing needs to be done perfectly. Don't want the tourists to have any accidents."

He had led her to this exact spot intentionally. She was standing on top of Nathan's body, buried under the highway.

He adjusted his eyes downward, and she felt her mouth fall open, quickly closing it when someone said something she didn't hear.

"One last thing," Art said. "If I were you, I might take one of your usual walks along the other side of the road and clean up whatever you might find. We all need to do our part."

44

In the three days Since Nathan's death, she slept long and hard after cleaning up debris around her property, searching pathways and ditches for anything that might have belonged to Nathan. Work gloves, ragged clothing and a pair of broken glasses that looked too old to worry about. Nothing stood out, but Elle was surprised at all the debris she found. Wrappers of all sorts and lots of broken bottles, shoes. When she returned from scoping out the area, she noticed she'd forgotten to lock the back door, and wondered if she felt safe for the first time since moving to Big Pine. Unless Nathan had confided to someone about their planned meeting, no one would have a clue. Evenings, heavy machinery in the distance sounded like the full-bellied groan of some contented predator, and she slept an easy dreamless sleep.

On the third afternoon, Elle made it to the cistern, hoping to see Monty. She would take his ferry to Pigeon Key and officially quit her job. Then she'd find someone to give her the green light on the gas tanks.

Buster must have heard her approach and shaded his eyes with his palm, squinting in the sun. He was happy to see her.

"I'm leaving in a week," he said, "I have a job in Miami." Elle remembered saying the same thing to Brushy, but then it was a lie.

"Are you telling me the truth?" she asked, and he looked confused.

"Why would I lie?"

"I'm sorry. I wish I had a job for you... leave me your address... you never know..."

"Yes, I'll write when I have something permanent," he said, and the sadness in his face almost moved her to make an offer she couldn't afford. She almost answered, *who has anything permanent,* but it would have been the exact patronizing platitude she hated most. She smiled and held her hand out, and he pulled her toward him and hugged her close, squeezing out a tear that almost broke surface.

Soon enough, Ruby would know she was free. She could move wherever she wanted. Elle was almost afraid she wouldn't be able to resist confiding in Ruby again. Maybe she should bust into the house and swirl around the room like Isadora Duncan. *You're free... free... free.*

Someone had to have some information about Brushy, but Elle couldn't come up with a story to justify asking his whereabouts. Anything to do with the diner might put her ownership into question, but she would take the chance when she saw an opening.

When the ferry horn sounded, Elle was certain it was Monty by his stance, one ankle in front of the other, knee bent, hand on his hip, the other loosely holding the wheel, his cap tight and low on his head the way he said Babe Ruth wore it. It thrilled her to see him–might as well get this apology over with–what's one more? He flashed a smile when he recognized her, followed quickly by hurt, hardened his features and turned away. But it was too late. She knew what she saw.

The Big Wheel was gone. Only a few fishing boats remained at the dock. Her skiff and a pair of canoes floated next to the pier in rougher condition than she remembered, but everything aged quickly on No Name. Except the new tower, in a strange shade of rust that didn't match the lodge, and its odd, squat roof, like a poisonous mushroom, a hacked lighthouse or a much less impressive penis. She wasn't thrilled at how ugly the place looked. She still had fantasies of someday owning the lodge, something she hadn't allowed herself to imagine until now. How long until Blanche moved on? Maybe she already had plans to leave, Elle thought. *Or maybe Brushy will return to her.* The thought always threatening to break surface.

"Fifteen minutes," Monty yelled. "We leave in fifteen minutes. Next stop, Pigeon Key, with or without you, so make it quick."

Most stayed close to the pier, ready to hop back on for the rest of the journey to Pigeon Key or Matecumbe. No Name Lodge was nowhere near full, judging from the absence of parked cars, and no one to help with luggage.

When Monty was alone, Elle said, "I brought you something." She offered him a bag containing two jars of her stewed tomatoes.

He shook his head. "You serious?"

"Well, I'm not going to sleep with you, if that's what you mean." This would have gotten a laugh, or at least a smile, out of him a few months ago.

"You've played me for a fool one time too many."

"You need a friend as much as I do," she said.

"Friend being the operative word," he said.

"Okay, but if I had told you Ruby was onboard, you could've gotten into trouble and..."

"Just stop. You didn't trust me. It's that simple."

She stopped. "Could I? Would you have...?"

"I don't know..." his honesty always floored her. "You frighten me a little. I have no idea who you are sometimes," he said.

They hadn't noticed Buster waiting nearby with a wagon, come to pick up a few boxes. "Anyone would think the two of you were married," he said.

"ew," they responded at almost the same time, then all three laughed. Elle pushed the bag of stewed tomatoes at him. "Here," she said, and he smiled the tiniest smile and took the bag. Later Monty said that's what he liked best about her–the way she left stuff alone, didn't prod and poke and dissect every little look or comment to death. It would take time, Elle thought, but he was too good natured to hold a grudge and too practical.

Later, she wondered what kind of woman she was. Arguing with a man one moment, and appreciating the odd jade color of the water and how lucky she was to live in a place where the sky turned a different color every day. All the while knowing a murdered man's body was secretly buried on the same road that brought her here.

Yes, she thought. Maybe Monty was right about her.

"Hey, Elle. You coming or what?" Monty asked.

Elle joined the group of men and a couple of families trickling back onto the ferry. The horn sounded, and they were off.

45

At Pigeon Key, when Bernie saw her come toward him, he rose from his cigarette break and said, "Well, I got something to tell you."

"I quit," she said, not letting him finish.

"Have it your own way." He wiped his right hand on his blood-stained apron, held it out, and they shook.

"Is Nathan here? I need to talk to him."

"You haven't heard? No one's seen him. Left a week ago and was supposed to be back... going on... what... five days now?"

"Well, I need to get my gas tanks turned on. Is George, his um... right-hand man here?"

"He's around, but who knows for how long? Everything's changed since Cleary took over. Much more efficient," he said with a sneer. "Old vets mostly let go onto some other project. Who the hell knows anything?"

"Did Nathan leave with the family?" Elle asked, looking for a word about Ruby. Damn, she thought, I promised myself I wouldn't get involved again.

"You friends with Ruby Foreman?" Bernie asked.

"No. Why do you ask?"

"I think she mentioned you to someone." Elle's stomach lurched. Bernie looked at her strangely. He knows something, she thought. He's not stupid.

A group of men watched them speaking outside the kitchen. One of them smiled when he saw Elle. "Are you back to cook for us?" he asked. Bernie stubbed his cigarette out on the ground and put the butt in a tin can under his own hand-written sign: *Clean Up After Yourself. Butts HERE! This Means You!*

"The lady quit," he said, edging away from the group as they mumbled their disappointment. "Good luck, Miss," someone said. Then another, "hope you change your mind."

"Thank you," Elle said.

Bernie motioned her away from the door and made deliberate eye contact.

"You might say your goodbyes to Ruby Foreman if you got the time. She looks like she could use a friend."

They parted, and Elle wondered which direction to take before she saw George.

"I need to talk to you about my gas tanks. I have these papers that say I can turn them on, but…" He dressed exactly like Nathan and looked as absurd. Someone should tell him orange and blue plaid Bermudas look ridiculous with a green leather briefcase.

"Nathan knows where everything is. If I were you, I wouldn't touch anything without his say so," he said, eager to be off.

"Fine," Elle said, and headed to Ruby. The hell with him. She'd turn it on when she returned to Sidetrack. She had this one last thing to do, before finding Brushy. A last goodbye. One last very short goodbye and tell Ruby to get out and do something for herself. If it was a mistake, at least it would be her own.

The door to the gate was unlocked, which spooked Elle, but maybe it was a good omen. The gate open to allow the world in. Maybe Ruby somehow knew that Nathan would never return.

"It's you," Ruby said. She looked shocked, almost scared.

"I came to say goodbye," Elle said, "And I came to say something else. Hallelujah!" She raised her hands in celebration, but something in Ruby's face startled her. "I mean... I quit the job. Now that the highway is almost finished, I'm concentrating on that." Ruby looked toward the door, deliberately enlarging her eyes, probably warning Elle that Betty or Perry could be listening.

"Yes, a good idea." Ruby said, formally. "Well, I wish you the best."

"Ruby, where are your children?"

"They're back at school."

"So, you don't expect them?" Ruby made a face, another warning, and Elle said, "thank your husband for everything when he returns."

Ruby's face had a wild and panicked expression. Something wasn't right.

"I'll walk you out," Ruby said, and then Elle saw her, Blanche, which sent a shockwave up her spine.

"It's okay, Mrs. Foreman. I'll walk her out." Blanche said.

"I know the way," Elle said, turning toward her. "And I don't have to put up with your bullshit ever again."

"Or anyone else's," Blanche said.

What the hell did that mean? Elle wanted to run. The ferry wouldn't return for hours, but she had walked to Big Pine before. Blanche must have used the private dock on Pigeon Key, or Monty would have mentioned it. Before Elle could go over the conversation with Ruby, Blanche said, "Hallelujah?"

"What?"

Blanche reached out and smacked Elle's arm.

"What..." Blood spattered over her bare arm.

"A mosquito," Blanche said. "I was trying to help."

The incident struck Elle as hilarious. "You look like you spend your life in a cave," she said, taking in Blanche's thin body and white skin.

"What do you know about my life?"

"Quit with the theatrics." Elle was more comfortable now inside her old, familiar role.

"Maybe Brushy was right all along. He said you told him once we were–what did he say - sisters under the skin?"

"Where is he?" Elle wanted to ask. *Is he back?* But she couldn't utter a word.

"Who knows why someone falls for any particular man," Blanche continued, keeping pace with Elle, whose speed had increased. Blanche wore tennis shoes; the first time Elle had seen her wear something so practical.

Elle saw a chance to sprint away when the old soldier appeared, hunched over, with a cane. Elle remembered him juggling vegetables in the kitchen. He yelled at her. "If I was young like you, I'd get the hell away from here as fast as I could."

The houses had disappeared, and tents lined the streets as they moved closer to water's edge. Tents? More like sheets of canvas held up by poles and a few pegs in coral. The sun shone too bright. Blanche smiled widely, showing teeth. Elle knew what was coming.

"Remember when you said," she mimicked Elle's voice in an exaggerated hillbilly lilt, *"all the choice in the world and you go for Billy?"*

Elle stopped. "Shut up, just shut up."

"I chose your husband like you chose mine. *Exactly* the way you chose mine. In every way." Blanche stopped and Elle ran toward the road out until Blanche became a tiny dot, the last words on Blanche's lips: *Hallelujah.*

EPILOGUE

Don't leave Miami for Key West after the sun goes down or you'll face a thin strip of bumpy road dogged by water on either side. It will tail you the entire trip, scrub palm sniffing right under your armpit. If you roll down the window, it might seem like a couple rocks or old tree roots are all that separate you and a great inky emptiness. A sudden sideways tilt could decant you and yours into the widening drink.

If you decide to go anyhow, my advice is to hold on tight to that steering wheel and move your eyes quickly, as if scanning for a guerilla force, all the while looking forward. But drive slowly, keep it slow.

At around the four-hour mark you will be greatly relieved to see a spot of comfort on the horizon: The Sidetrack Diner. dead center of Big Pine Key and an hour and some out of Key West. You will sense that this is the sole trustworthy stop for gas, coffee, maybe even a rest. There, in the middle of the mildewed, sketchy terrain, you'll see warm yellow lights and a generous swath where you can park the family Buick. Clean painted parking lines defy the encroaching swampland.

No matter how late, someone will answer when you ring the bell. For a modest fee, one of five rooms might be available to rent for the night. "She had a friendly smile," you'd say if someone asked to describe me, which no one would. Clean. Efficient. Color of eyes, don't remember. Nor hair. It's a trick, that. Bright red is not the easiest to dull down, but no, you wouldn't have the first inkling. I'm just about the same tone as the Sidetrack Diner's appliances, in the dim evening light. You'll do the talking, I'll nod agreement, smiling, happy for the business, and the price will be right, no extra charge for the kids' beds. You'll remember a sturdy lock, crisp sheets on a soft bed, a sink and tub so clean you'll check for dirt before you go.

If you stay for the breakfast special, the smell of bacon and coffee will obliterate any memories of the tall, aproned woman who served you. You'll be eager to hit the road and grateful for what I put in front of you. Go ahead, dig in. It's delicious and it won't kill you. That's a promise. Only one I poisoned is long gone now. And so far, none have been so evil that they begged to be dispatched - well, at least not in that particular fashion. But if I had to, I'd do it again in a heartbeat, so don't be thinking that what follows is an apology or even an explanation. Because it surely is not. Oh, I almost forgot… there is a slight bump in the road just outside of Sidetrack, but you'll barely notice as you make your way to fun city, Key West. But never mind, the tale itself does all the talking.

I am a way station between Miami and Key West. In my diner you will gather energy for your destination wherever that might be. Anywhere but here. But this is my destiny, my South Star, my kismet and my last stop. I am not in Boston cleaning for my uncle. I am not moving from town to town with Billy Woodman, waiting for him to get fired again and taking it out on me with his fists. And I am no longer trapped in the cistern, plotting ways to finally be free.

ACKNOWLEDGEMENTS

Special thank you to the Anne McKee Artists Fund for believing in me even when I had nothing to offer but promises four years after receiving the grant. You issued the second half of the award with a note that you believed in my project and I will never forget that gracious gesture.

Thank you to the incredible Allyssa Matesic who dissected the early manuscript with a sharp discriminating eye. Your suggestions and ultimately your championing of the manuscript convinced me to dig in and do the work. Your optimism pushed me forward to do a better job than I thought I could do. I am lucky to have you.

To Brendon Goodmurphy, for the wonderful line edit and detailed notes on continuity, setting and character.

To the Guillotine Gals, for making me think more than I wanted to.

To Sean MacGuire and Bill Keogh, who each came up with variations on the same murder site. Two diabolically clever minds who pose as ordinary humans.

To Rosalind Brackenbury, my gifted and prolific studio mate. We exchanged bits of our stories over time, reading aloud to each other to spot a glitch but mostly for the sheer enjoyment of sharing our work.

To Rebecca Bennett A wonderful Key West painter whose work deserves a wider audience.

Thank you KK for my own private cistern by the cemetery where I go to dream.

Most of all, I thank Sean MacGuire, my brilliant husband who has always believed in me. I don't know what I did to get so lucky–ok maybe a little…

Goodbye to my beautiful black cats–Binky who was really an aye-aye. I really didn't believe you would ever die and I don't think I'll ever get over it. To Puss-Puss, the most beautiful cat in the world with the mournful big-eyed beauty of a silent film star. She was Sean's constant companion. We hope we did right by you both.

Thank you to first readers Rosalind Brackenbury, Dawn Kyle Davis, Lauren Dean and Harriet Garfinkle.

ABOUT THE AUTHOR

Jessica Argyle writes Historical Fiction featuring powerful women living and surviving in a male dominated culture. She promises at least one murder per novel and many secret tales of lust, greed and corruption, and always shares historical tidbits lost to time and dug up in her research.

She holds an MA, specialty Creative Writing from Concordia University in Montréal, Quebec. This book began life as an Anne McKee Artist's Fund grant winner in 2018.

If you enjoyed this book, and want more of Elle's triumphs and struggles in the haunted, offbeat Florida Keys of yesteryear, please leave a review on Goodreads and/or Amazon. It would mean the world to me and is the best thanks you could give to an Indie author.

Made in the USA
Columbia, SC
10 January 2023

75897678R00193